MW01195078

STEEL JUNGLE

GLENN STARKEY

Steel Jungle

Copyright 2017 by Glenn Starkey

Cover design by Jake Starkey, www.JakeStarkey.com

All rights reserved. No part of this book may be reproduced or transmitted in any form by any means, electrical or mechanical, including photography, recording, or by any information or retrieval system without written permission of the author, except for the inclusion of brief quotations in reviews.

This is a work of fiction. All of the characters, places, organizations, and events portrayed in this novel are either products of the author's imagination or are used fictitiously.

ISBN (Print) 978-1-54390-221-1

ISBN (E-book) 978-1-54390-222-8

Books by Glenn Starkey

BLACK SUN

"Gold Medal 2016 Historical Fiction Award" —
Military Writers Society of America

"…It was Glenn Starkey's ability to capture humanity at its worst and at its very best that touched me so deeply… Where some authors write a great story you can't put down, Glenn Starkey weaves a richly coloured tapestry and breathes life into every thread of the story. Every sentence, every paragraph, every description, and every character matters..."

"2016 Readers Favorite 5 Star Review" —*Readers Favorite.Com*

SOLOMON'S MEN

"… genuinely suspenseful… a cascade of power struggles… Exciting and unpredictable, Solomon's Men is highly recommended as an original action/adventure thriller."

—*The Midwest Book Review*

"Silver Medal 2012 Mystery/Thriller Award" —
Military Writers Society of America

AMAZON MOON

"Notable Indie Book of 2013 Award" —*Shelf Unbound Magazine*

"Bronze Medal 2014 Thriller/Mystery Award" —
Military Writers Society of America

"… This would be one incredible action movie for sure! 'Amazon Moon' is deeply layered in emotions and themes of both revenge and redemption. The human elements of his characters are sharply focused but layered as well…"

—*W. H. McDonald Jr., American Authors Association*

"Amazon Moon is the sort of novel that grabs you by the throat on the first page and doesn't let go until the last. It is an exciting story and, at the same time, something more. It is a fable about one man's redemption, his rediscovery of innocence."

—*Nicholas Guild – New York Times Best Selling Author*

The Spartan Dagger, The Ironsmith, Blood Ties,
The Assyrian, Blood Star…and more.

MR. CHARON

"…One of the evident appeals of Mr. Charon is Starkey's descriptive prose. It gives vivid pictures of the surroundings and moves the story flawlessly, which also contributes to the plot's deft execution. The classic good versus evil theme mixed with love, hate, and redemption makes Mr. Charon a great read."

"2016 Readers Favorite 5 Star Review" —*Readers Favorite.Com*

YEAR OF THE RAM

"… it felt as if a hand had made its way out of the novel, gently grabbed me around the neck and pulled me into its story until such time as what was being told had come to an end. After accomplishing what it set out to do, the hand would then draw me out of the world I was in, pat my cheek, and disappear leaving me sitting there in wonder…"

—*Sandra Valente, Novel Review Café*

THE COBRA AND SCARAB: A NOVEL OF ANCIENT EGYPT

"… Rich, vibrant, descriptive language. Characters with depth, imbued with loyalty, courage and strength or touched with madness for power and evincing raw brutality. Treachery, betrayal, intrigue at every turn…"– *Amazon.com - Five Star Review*

Non-Fiction:

THROUGH THE STORMS: THE JOHN G. SLOVER DIARY

Edited by Glenn Starkey for the Alvin Museum Society

"…An important and valuable work…genuinely impressed with the completeness of the manuscript, as well as its organization…a work that, in my view, combines both the best of first-person observations and conventional historical narrative to understand Slover's experiences as part of the larger sweep of American history during that period."

—*Andrew W. Hall, author, historian, DeadConfederates. com - Civil War Blog, and regional Marine Archaeological Steward for the Texas Historical Commission*

For the veterans who returned to the condemnation of an angry nation and wanted nothing more than to blend into their country...

For the refinery and chemical plant workers who earn their pay while enduring acrid smells, chemical and steam burns, dangerous product releases, unit fires, site explosions and the deaths of their co-workers...

And for the real Jim Thurman... *Semper Fi.*

"At his best, man is the noblest of all animals;

separated from law and justice he is the worst."

Aristotle

CHAPTER ONE

Texas Gulf Coast
Monday, June 25, 1990, 4:30 a.m.

Jim Thurman lay watching the numbers slowly change on his bedside digital clock. Since his wife and son's death more than a year ago, setting the alarm had been unnecessary. Throughout the nights, sleep came in slivers of exhaustion, and only then between long periods of restlessness.

Turning the nightstand lamp on he squinted against its harsh light and looked away. The security guard shirt hanging from the closet doorknob caught his attention and his thoughts strayed. He had left police work for better benefits and pay, but now there was no family to support. No longer a need to remain. He touched his throat. His fingertips brushed the gold cross on his necklace; Susan's gift to their ten year old son, James, to commemorate his baptism.

Exhaling hard, Jim rose from bed.

Today's going to be different, he thought. *Today I bury the ghosts and rejoin the living.*

He showered and shaved, and the sight of his jagged stomach scar didn't evoke any further notice than a passing glance. He dressed in his uniform, strapped his gun belt on and settled its weight on his hips. From the nightstand drawer he withdrew a loaded 9mm pistol and two full magazines.

He could smell the gun oil on the Beretta as he slid it into his holster and shoved the magazines into their belt pouches.

Now, he realized, *comes the true test of the day.*

Jim walked down the hall and paused at his son's room. He turned the hall light on and stood in the doorway. His six-foot frame cast a deep shadow across the dust-laden furnishings. The memory of always looking in on his son before leaving for work passed before him with painful clarity. Gazing at the room, Jim touched his gold cross, turned the light off and left.

The truck engine revved slightly, its noise carrying through the early morning stillness. As he drove away the sound faded in the sleeping neighborhood, and within seconds, silence returned.

• • •

June 25, 5:40 a.m.

Years of traveling the same route had cemented every twist, bump and chuckhole of the roads into Thurman's mind. Fifty miles round trip and, although, the drive was tiresome at times, living so far west of Grainger City had its benefits. The air didn't hold a constant chemical stench and there were no worries about his house windows being blown out if a refinery exploded.

Dawn's yellowish orange hues stretched across the horizon as he drove onto the Grainger freeway. Jim glanced skyward, comparing it to the Texas Hill Country sunrises he intended to see within a few days. The decision had been made and he would stick to it. He had no choice. It was time to move on with his life if he wanted to retain any remnants of sanity.

Topping an overpass, the lights of the city and its industrial complexes came into view. Flare stacks from the refineries and chemical plants released their flames into the air like candles randomly stabbed across the landscape. Whenever they burned wildly at night, their wavering glows reflected off the clouds and consumed the skyline, giving the impression of a city fully ablaze.

There had been a time when Jim naively believed they were burning off excess gases, nothing to be overly concerned with, but as all his beliefs had been shattered, he discovered otherwise. Burning like a fire stack from Hell meant critical problems, an upset. Only the operators of that refinery process unit knew what was coming out—and hopefully being burnt before escaping to the atmosphere and the city.

An acrid chemical odor filled the air, stinging slightly at first smell then tempering out as his sinuses adjusted. Within an hour the light, sepia haze that always hung over the city would be visible. The rising sun would reveal how drab and dreadfully in need of cleaning or fresh paint every building was. Red streaks of rust on the refineries battleship gray structures were the city's only colorful sight.

Further down the road a large weathered billboard stood beside the road greeting motorists.

WELCOME TO GRAINGER CITY

Home of the World's Largest Industrial Complexes and Port

We Fuel America! Enjoy Your Stay

Jim had read it each day while driving to work and the last line always irritated him. There was nothing to enjoy. The city was crime-ridden and ugly. The air stunk and no one came here unless they had to. But the sign was basically correct. This place was big. Petrochemical complexes covered miles of city blocks, all built so only fence lines separated them. From these confines came the greatest percentage of gasoline and chemicals required daily by an addicted nation. And it all meant money.

Money was the invisible chain that tightly bound the community, its plants and workers to one another. Jim didn't kid himself, though. He wasn't any different than the rest. He had sold himself to the highest bidder, and the old joke of prostituting yourself to the company struck him with its harsh reality. Regardless of their multitude of dangers, the refineries paid too well when you had a family to feed. But the money no longer mattered to Jim.

Titan Oil's power encompassed the globe under countless subsidiary names. As if it were a living god, a board of directors worshiped the corporation, sacrificing anyone and everything for its continued existence. These high priests of business saw little wrong in their actions as long as the corporation prospered and their mega salaries were retained.

In the battle for eternal prosperity, Titan Oil's Grainger City refinery was valued as the corporate flagship of its fleet of complexes. The profit the refinery generated was too phenomenal for the average man to fathom. Within its fences lay a giant cement and steel jungle designed to dwarf all competitors.

The faint light of dawn painted the lot as Jim parked and sat gazing at the main entrance. He watched the off-going shift of security officers mill about inside the office, anxious to be relieved. A taste of bile rose in his mouth. At thirty-eight, he didn't care to play any more of their childish mind games. There was more to life, precious things, like cherishing each day you have with your family and trying to do what's right so you won't look back with regrets on wasted years. Unfortunately, the majority of Titan Oil's in-house security officers had not come to that realization and spent their days wrapped in petty jealousies and departmental bickering.

They would slit each other's throats for a sergeant's badge, he thought. A grin formed. *Hell, Sancho beat them at their own game, and didn't even get his hands bloody.*

Stepping from the truck, Jim brushed his uniform and adjusted the weight of his gun belt. Out of habit he withdrew the Beretta and looking at it with indifference, checked the weapon's magazine and safety. There was nothing special about the weapon as far as he was concerned. Everyone had to work with something in their daily business. His *something* in life

4

had always been some type of weapon, and lately, the way thugs kept jumping the refinery's fence to steal copper wiring and whatever was loose, a pistol was necessary. But opposition to Security carrying pistols was coming from the corporate level, and steadily growing.

Titan Oil lived in fear of courtroom publicity, especially the type that might come from a shooting, justified or not. Calder, the Security Superintendent, had tried to make brownie points by suggesting the department's meager arsenal of weapons be melted. He had even joked about making them into a statue of some sort for the Chairman of the Board. The lazier officers in the department whined over the discomfort of wearing a gun belt, and caught in the middle were the few officers who tried to do their job. Fortunately, Calder didn't know about all of the weapons the department owned. That was the one secret the officers truly kept to themselves.

With management talking out of both sides of its corporate mouth about protecting assets and employees, the task of counteracting the creeping apathy affecting the officers was becoming increasingly difficult. Management didn't care about Security, and deadly as any cancer, that same attitude had taken root and was spreading within the department's ranks.

Yeah, money isn't everything but its way ahead of whatever's in second place, Jim thought in disgust. *The company is more worried about their liabilities than our lives.*

Years of being a street cop gnawed at him. He didn't want his co-workers to die without a chance to defend themselves, but the corporation had ruined them. It was too late to salvage most of them. Politics at the refinery was sickening. Ass kissing had become a disease and complacency a plague. Self-pride had been exchanged for benefits and paychecks far beyond what police departments paid.

Thurman shook his head, holstered the 9mm and unconsciously touched his abdomen. He started for the gate office, more determined than ever to resign.

Decorative wrought-iron fencing accented the manicured lawns surrounding the two administrative buildings. The wide street leading into the refinery was lined with trimmed trees while an oversized corporate flag waved from a tall, custom-made pole in front of a building. In the main yard by the flag, floodlights illuminated a large circular sign bearing the corporate symbol of an old-fashioned oil derrick. All was designed to be pleasing to visitors yet the remainder of the vast complex was an eyesore to humanity.

To the left of the gate's security office stood the white, six-story 'Ivory Tower' engineer building, capturing everyone's attention because it was the tallest in the city. Sitting squalidly on the right was the renovated three-story 'Admin' building, built when the refinery was constructed sixty years ago. Even with its recent million-dollar facelift, the structure resembled an aging Texas prison building. Within its weather stained, red brick walls were the offices of the refinery manager Dave Simmons and an entourage of division managers who would willingly stab one another to have his job.

Jim looked ahead at the glass-plated fifty by fifty-foot Gate House, Security's main entrance office. Through it every visitor was processed before being allowed to walk or drive in through Derrick Road, the refinery's main street that bisected the twenty-four hundred acre complex.

Agitation scalded him. The Gate House—*the guard shack.* The name never ceased to amaze him. Three-hundred thousand dollars to build; two-hundred thousand dollars worth of radio, alarm, and camera controls inside; manned around-the-clock by former police officers yet the engineers in the Ivory Tower referred to the security office by the derogatory name to keep their caste system intact.

Titles and ranking in the refinery weighed heavily on the engineers' minds and they wanted all to know they sat at the top of the pyramid. The arrogance knew no end and even the size of offices with windows in the Ivory Tower were prime real estate, designating an individual's refinery prominence.

Jim saw Sancho Martinez strutting through the office like a general before the troops, ensuring everyone took note of his new gold badge. Jim scowled. Sancho's immaturity made him believe everyone was always against him. In truth, he was his own worst enemy. With a real name of Raul Martinez, he preferred the Hispanic nickname of a man who sneaks in the back door of another man's home while the wife is alone. A 'Sancho' kept the wife happy when the husband could not but if the rumors were true, though, Sancho couldn't take care of his own wife.

No, Jim, keep your mouth shut and turn in your resignation today. Find your friends, say goodbye, and leave. Tomorrow, this place will be nothing more than a bad memory.

His mouth formed a thin line as he crossed Derrick Road and entered the Gate House's side glass door.

• • •

25 miles northwest of Grainger City, Texas
June 25, 7:00 a.m.

The sun broke over the horizon into a cloudless sky, beating the ground with its blistering summer rays. Sitting in the driver's seat of the panel van, Tonya glanced impatiently at her watch. For the last hour they had waited along the tree-lined road for seven o'clock. Now, within a few seconds, it would finally arrive.

Next to her, Trey Richards sat with eyelids drooping, head cocked against the door. His receding hairline and scrubby goat-tee gave his face an elongated look, more so with his mouth agape. Tonya wished she could be so calm yet also knew he wasn't fully asleep. Richards was dangerous whether his eyes were open or not.

The rustle of clothes and jangle of automatic weapon straps caused Tonya to look in the rear view mirror at her teammates. They were hot and squirming about, unable to get comfortable in the van's cramped cargo space. She lightly drummed her fingers against the steering wheel and let her hazel eyes scan the wall of tallow trees and dense brush about them, hating the countryside and its miserable Gulf Coast humidity.

Murdock never left a stone unturned, she thought. *The location was desolate, perfect for their needs, and the closest town was several miles away.*

Richards' head moved, then his hand. The safety on his semiautomatic lightly clicked as it eased off. His dark eyes searched the terrain in front of them. Twigs cracked and brush swayed. Muffled footsteps grew louder from the undergrowth.

Inside the van the terrorists alerted at the click of Richards' pistol's safety. Zachary Caan broke from the waist-high grass and wild briar bushes, giving a thumb up signal as he approached.

"He's back," Tonya stated, opening her door and hurrying to the van's rear door. Trey Richards followed her.

Three men and a woman climbed out, stretching from built-up numbness, and inspecting themselves as they waited for Zachary. Their military trousers were bloused over desert boots and each wore a different styled shirt for comfort and pocket availability. About their waists hung ammunition pouches, grenades, and radios. While several carried Spanish, Austrian, and German semiautomatics, and Russian *Kalashnikov* AK-47's with double-taped banana clips, others bore smaller, more common automatic weapons from straps on their shoulders. But shoved between everyone's belt and stomach was a simple black ski mask.

Drenched in perspiration, Zachary's shirt stuck to him. He dragged a forearm across his face and wiped sweat from his brown eyes. A diagonal cut on his right cheek bled freely. He touched it with his fingertips, examining the blood as he pulled his hand away. Always maintaining a neat, soldierly appearance, Zachary dusted himself and swiped spider webs from his close-cropped blond hair.

"Well?" Kotter Ryan asked impatiently. "Can we go in?" He glanced at the wall of vegetation Zachary had come from.

A curt nod answered him. "There's six people like Murdock said, but they're too spread out. They would spot us before we cut the telephone lines. We'll go with Murdock's alternate plan," Zachary said, looking at Dutch Williams. "The trail brings us in on the backside. Takes time to get there. Thorn bushes are bad, but I'll radio you when we are in position."

Dutch, a towering, muscled figure of insanity, nodded and turned toward the team. Bushy beard, wild brown hair pulled into a ponytail behind his head, chest hairs stuck out from his shirt collar and prison tattoos showed on his wrists beneath his long sleeved shirt as he moved his arms. He motioned to a short, buxom woman standing by him as he talked to the team.

"All right, I'll take Peterson and drive Jessica in from the front as diversion. Martin, Kotter, Richards, and Tonya move in from the rear with Zachary to cut off any escape. Sweep the buildings and make sure the employees don't rabbit. I don't feel like chasing anyone through these woods this morning."

"Why not hit the office with a rocket, or drive in and shoot them before they know what's happening?" Kotter asked. His eyebrows drew downward, and he frowned as he glanced at his team members for support.

"Too many chances for errors." Dutch said, shaking his head. "Murdock doesn't want to risk setting fire to the buildings and some farmer reporting the smoke. If we drive in shooting, the employees might scatter into the woods like a covey of quail. Jessica will draw them outside into a group, away from their phones. Remember, they have radio contact with surrounding airports too." His eyebrows rose and he grinned wryly. "If you want to call Murdock and tell him you're changing his orders, don't forget to mention there is a chance of scrubbing the mission."

Zachary smirked and looked at the slender blond man who had asked the questions.

Kotter Ryan's eyes widened. He shook his head and his teammates grinned.

Pulling the radio handset off his belt, Dutch smiled and keyed it. "Adam, we have six ducks on the pond."

The silence grew thick as everyone listened for their leader's reply.

"Good hunting, Dutch. I'll be there by the time you are through." The voice on the radio was cold and commanding.

Dutch acknowledged and glanced at Zachary. "You heard the man."

Scanning his teammates' faces, Zachary nodded and started toward the thick briars. When the last man vanished into the brush, Jessica and Peterson climbed into the rear of the van. Dutch Williams settled into the driver's seat.

• • •

The seventy yards through the dense undergrowth seemed like a mile to the insurgents. Branches slapped their cheeks and ears, vines entangled feet, and sharp thorns scraped their clothes and stabbed their arms and legs. No breeze moved in the thick brush and breathing quickly became labored from the stifling humidity.

Zachary Caan retraced his earlier path and found his travel to be no easier. Behind him in a serpentine line, Kotter, Martin, Tonya, and Richards kept pace, teeth clenched from the pricks of needle-like thorns. Zachary slowed and moved through the brush like a panther stalking its prey. After ten yards, he knelt behind a tree and raised a fist into the air. Everyone halted.

Voices and laughter carried through the morning air. The team grinned, glad their wilderness trek was at an end.

Silently edging to the brush line Zachary motioned Tonya and the men to him. He pointed to their individual strike positions. Seconds later they stood at the corners of the buildings.

• • •

Jessica Carter and Bruce Peterson stared out the rear door of the van. When the radio transmission came across Dutch's handset, they smiled.

"Did you hear?" Dutch turned the ignition key and glanced in the rear view mirror.

Jessica removed her shirt, rolled it into a ball and shoved it in a corner. Unsnapping her bra, she threw it aside. A chill swept over her as the perspiration across her chest caught the morning air. She shivered and her melon breasts swung, nipples erect.

The former Green Beret's gaze was locked onto every jostle her body made.

Strands of sandy brown hair fell across Jessica's face. Seeing Peterson stare at her breasts, she winked at him, massaged them teasingly, and then grabbed the van's doorframe for balance.

Peterson smiled and slapped the magazine butt of his *Kalashnikov*, double-checking its seating. He braced his feet and looked back at the driver.

"Go!" Jessica shouted, and the van lurched forward.

CHAPTER TWO

Langley, Virginia June 25, 6:15 a.m., E.D.T.

Traffic moved at a snail's pace through the narrow gate, but Ben Dawson was accustomed to the daily congestion. His thoughts were drifting when the cellular phone rang, making him jump at its sharp bleep. He grabbed it yet immediately grew frustrated that the caller was not who he expected.

"Morning, Mr. McCall." Ben tried to be cheerful, hoping his disappointment had not carried through the phone.

"Sorry to bother you so early, Ben. I know you're on your way to work so I'll be brief."

Ben straightened in the driver's seat. The palms of his hands grew slick.

"No problem, sir. What can I do for you?"

"Beverly and I haven't heard from Alexandra in weeks. Is everything all right? She usually calls us on the weekends."

Breathing deeply to calm himself, Ben checked the traffic about him and gripped the steering wheel tighter.

"Alex is fine, sir. I talked to her the other day. She's been doing routine background investigations this month and should be returning in another week or so." He tried to chuckle. "I bet she snuck off somewhere for a short vacation and lost track of the days."

Jeff McCall's laughter eased Ben's mounting tension.

"You're probably right. With her crazy schedule, she deserves time to herself. I took today off to do that very thing. Tell her I called—and ask her to contact her mother when she can. Thanks, Ben."

"Yes, sir, I'll definitely give her the message."

The dial tone returned and Ben slowly set the receiver back into its bracket holder. He sighed in relief at being off the telephone call. *I would have to get a partner whose father is on the National Security Council.*

The traffic started moving again. He waved to the stern-faced guard at the gate and held his badge aloft to be seen. Receiving approval, he drove on toward his office, passing the formal sign that he never bothered to read any more.

CENTRAL INTELLIGENCE AGENCY

• • •

25 miles northwest of Grainger City, Texas
June 25, 7:25 a.m., C.S.T.

David Arnett stood on the flight line admiring his small fleet of Bell helicopters. The morning ritual was difficult to break. He poured the remains of his coffee cup onto the ground, never taking his eyes off the machines.

His first flight, riding with his crop-dusting father in an aged plane started the love affair. They had sailed over the countryside with the wind rushing through his hair, missing treetops by mere feet and soaring over rooftops. The cattle fled across the pastures and the ranchers shook their fists skyward. By the time they landed that day, flight had forever become a part of him. Football injuries kept him out of the military, preventing his ambitions of being a combat pilot yet nothing could hold back the dream of owning a flying service.

The first two years were an uphill struggle. He and Sharon had taken quite a chance in buying their first helicopter. It didn't matter that the bird wasn't new. He was as proud of it as if it had been. There were days when he wondered if he was drowning financially, but the risks paid off. Now his dream was a reality. After traipsing across oil fields and drumming business, their company began to grow. Ferrying men and supplies to offshore rigs became profitable enough to allow him to add a couple of employees to the payroll, and in time, buy more helicopters.

"They're topped off, boss." Neal wiped his hands clean on a rag. "As soon as I put the hoses up, I'll tighten the seat on our new baby." The mechanic stuffed the rag into his pocket.

David looked at the lone transport helicopter sitting off by itself and motioned to the tail rotor.

"When Larry and Henry finish, have them—" He spun to look at the road.

A white panel van raced out onto the landing field, circled erratically and skidded to a dust-clouded halt. The rear doors burst open. A half-naked woman leaped out, screaming hysterically as she ran with arms flailing the air toward the men.

David and the mechanic froze, unable to comprehend what was occurring, stunned by the sight of her partial nudity. Inside a hanger, Larry and Henry heard the woman's pleas. They threw their tools aside and rushed from the hangar to David. They scanned the field and saw her.

"Help me!" The terrified woman fled across the airfield, her breasts bouncing wildly. "They raped me…." She pointed back at the open doors of the van as she ran.

Neal raced David to the vehicle. Behind them, Larry and Henry struggled to keep pace, eager to capture the woman's assailants.

Automatic weapons held firmly against their waists, Bruce Peterson and Dutch Williams jumped from the rear of the van.

The mechanic was the first to see the AK-47's and tried to stop. Behind him, the running men collided into one another, almost tripping as they came to a halt. They were caught in the open.

Chest heaving, David spun about to flee. Thirty yards away, a paramilitary dressed man stood at a rear corner of the hangar, staring at him.

Zachary turned away from David Arnett and shouted to his team. "Let's go." The team moved forward, out into the open.

David saw armed men, crouched low, rush from behind the hangar. He glanced at the office and saw Sharon at the door. His wife held it partially open, watching in terror.

A pistol-wielding woman raced along the office wall toward the front of the building. David realized that within seconds the armed woman would round the corner and see his wife.

"Who are they, David?" Fear carried in Sharon's voice.

The bare breasted woman's hysterics ceased. She took a defiant stance with hands on hips out in the field and laughed.

"Get inside—" David's effort to rescue his wife was cut short by deafening bursts of automatic gunfire. He danced spastically in a tight circle as bullets riddled his body. His knees buckled and he collapsed in the dirt.

"No—No..." Sharon backed into the office, screaming in horror.

Having heard the woman, Tonya wheeled around the corner, arms extended and locked, pistol trained on the door. No one was in sight. She rushed toward the entrance, but the door swung open hard, making Tonya skid to a halt.

The cannon-like barrels of a rusted double-barreled shotgun protruded through the doorway and continued to grow.

An aged voice, weakened by grief, cried out, "You bastards killed my David!" A yellowish-gray haired man crossed the doorway's threshold in

16

a wheelchair. He rolled to the doorknob and struggled to lift an antique shotgun from his lap.

Martin Shanks rushed from the hangar and saw the handicapped man try to lift the shotgun and take aim. He shouted at Tonya, "What the hell are you waiting for? Get in there. Find that woman."

Arms trembling from the weight of the old *L.C. Smith* shotgun, the elderly man swung the long barrels toward Martin. Tonya ran past the wheelchair and entered the office. She glanced back at Martin and jumped clear. His AK-47 climbed as fire spewed from the muzzle. Spent casings streamed from the weapon. The shotgun clanked against the wheelchair's footrests and crashed into the dirt. The old man toppled from his wheelchair.

Having witnessed the murders of David and his father, Neal fled in terror. Dumbfounded, Larry and Henry glanced at each other then raced after him. A crossfire laid down by the insurgents trapped them. The brief staccato of gunfire echoed across the helicopter landing field.

David's death consumed Sharon. Grief and shock blended to hold her prisoner until the bawl of automatic weapons bombarded the office. Her senses returned. As she reached for a telephone, a pistol then an arm and the full profile of a woman appeared at the front door.

The change from bright sunlight to the dim interior of the office made Tonya squint to force her eyes to adjust. She scanned the office but saw no one. *The radios.* Her stomach tightened. A thankful sigh passed her lips when she located them on a corner table, power turned off. She yanked their cords from the wall and glanced at the telephones on the surrounding desks. Laying a receiver on the desk, she entered two numbers to block incoming calls and moved on.

Semiautomatic lowered to a forty-five degree angle, hands firmly gripping the weapon, Tonya crept to a long hall and scanned its length. Four doors were seen, all closed.

Tonya opened the first door slowly; the lavatory. She turned and opened a second; a janitorial supply closet.

The gunfire outside had ceased. The quiet filling the building became nerve wracking to Sharon. She eased David's chair away from his desk as she kept watch on the locked office door. A light *clunk* coming from the hall caught her attention. Her mind registered the sound—a closing door. Blinded by tears, Sharon tried to focus on the telephone's keypad. She raised the receiver and pushed buttons. The line was dead.

At the third hallway door, Tonya readied herself to shoot. Standing off to the side, she opened the door enough to see in. The room appeared to be a combination kitchen and meeting area. Again, she saw no one. Fury erupted within her as she looked at the final door down the hall.

Sharon wiped her wet cheeks and rubbed her eyes. She thought of escaping through the window, but it was still boarded. David had never finished repairing it from the storm that shattered the glass with a tree branch. Looking about the room, she searched for anything to use as a weapon. She saw her husband's cellular phone sitting in its charger on the credenza.

Tonya stood in the hall, straining to hear the slightest noise from within the room. Her fingers wrapped around the doorknob, tightened, and turned. It was locked.

Standing by the credenza, Sharon froze. She had heard something but couldn't place the sound. The doorknob moved. It had come ever so slightly, but it had moved. Sharon bit her bottom lip and squeezed David's phone until she feared it might break. She pressed the power button and watched anxiously as the compact phone digitally displayed its warm-up sequence.

Come on… Come on, she thought. The digital readout cleared and displayed a ready prompt. Sharon held her breath, glanced at the door, then depressed numbers. In the silence of the office, each beep of the entered numbers seemingly echoed like a gong.

Tonya closed her eyes and pressed her ear against the exterior of the office door. Her eyes flared as she heard the faint beeps and recognized them.

Sharon hit the last number and hoped she had not misdialed.

The hollow-core office door shook as it was violently kicked. It cracked and splintered about the doorknob.

A final *click* on the cellular phone told Sharon the connection was complete, and about to ring. The door was kicked so forcefully that it swung open and smashed against the wall.

The first ring on the cellular phone came, but it was too late.

Sharon's head erupted. Glistening brain matter splattered the wall. Tonya lowered her pistol, realizing a second shot was not necessary.

On the second ring, the cellular call was answered. A male voice spoke.

"Sheriff's department."

Walking across the room, Tonya gently lifted the phone from the carpet.

"I'm sorry, I must have dialed the wrong number," she remarked calmly, gazing at Sharon's corpse.

• • •

Zachary was helping Kotter drag the wheelchair away from the front door and out into the yard when the single pistol shot inside the building broke the morning quiet. They spun, raising their rifles. Tonya walked out into the sunlight and signaled success with a thumb up gesture.

"Search the area, make sure no one was missed," Dutch Williams ordered. Richards and Martin snapped nods and reloaded as they left.

Leisurely walking to the three men who lay dying in the dirt, Jessica Carter carefully looked them over. Finding vague signs of life, she pulled her pistol and shot each one.

Approaching from behind, Tonya tossed the topless woman's shirt onto her shoulder.

"All right, you've had your fun. Now get back to work."

Jessica holstered her semiautomatic, lightly laughing as she dressed.

"They never noticed I was wearing a gun," she remarked, brushing strands of sandy brown hair from her face.

"Look what I found," Zachary yelled, carrying a box of donuts as he strode from the office building. "Who's hungry?" He crammed a chocolate covered donut into his mouth and wiped his hands on his trousers.

Kotter Ryan trailed him. "Hey! They made coffee for us," he exclaimed, triumphantly raising a mug high into the air.

Stepping over corpses, the insurgents hurried to get a donut before Zachary devoured them. They joked and elbowed each other as they fought for the box, pleased with their performance as a team.

"Knock it off," Dutch said, looking to the road. He squinted against the glare of the sun and strained to hear the rumble of an approaching vehicle. It came again, only louder.

The insurgents threw their donuts into the dirt and took up ambush positions behind equipment, the hangar, and inside the office.

A faded gray panel van emerged into view from the tree-lined road and angled toward the office. It slowed, flashed its headlights and accelerated. Another van, identical in color and model, trailed it. Dust clouds billowed from the vehicles and drifted across the landing field.

Shoving the office door open with the barrel of his *Kalashnikov*, Dutch walked out into the yard. The remainder of the team appeared from their concealment and moved to him.

The first van came to a halt. A stalwart, stone-faced man, dressed in dark tactical clothes, opened the passenger door and stepped out. He paused, casually scanned the helicopters and corpses before turning his attention to the armed men and women by Dutch. His raven black hair was pulled tight to the rear of his head and bound, greatly accenting the ice blue eyes that stared at the world without emotion.

"You've done well, Dutch. You've all done well." Adam Murdock's words were complimentary yet his tone was hard. He glanced at his watch as he approached the former biker. "And with time to spare too. I like efficiency."

Behind the leader, an attractive blonde and two men, each dressed and armed like their counterparts, stepped from the van and looked about the area. Satisfied the airfield was secure, Kane Thompson nodded to Nicole Oliver and Doug Jordan. Jordan joined the team behind Dutch while Nicole walked toward the second van. She spoke briefly to the driver then returned to the team. Kane watched the van drive across the field and park beside a helicopter. When men jumped out of the vehicle and began to unload equipment from the van into the helicopter, Kane moved to Murdock's side.

Everyone on Adam Murdock's team held a unique talent; explosives, computers, weapons, ability to fly a variety of aircraft, or had a criminal record to fit the team's needs. But Kane Thompson was unique in himself. He was Murdock's constant shadow and a ruthless killer perfectly matched to be Murdock's right hand. Black hair cut in a military "high-and-tight," the forty-year-old former intelligence officer's body was rock-hard, and he appeared impervious to pain.

He casually slung the strap of his Uzi over his shoulder. Looking at the van by the helicopter, he glanced at Nicole with a warning stare before turning to Murdock again. She held a blank expression and nodded.

"They're unloading now," Kane said in a low voice.

"Good." Murdock sighed and glanced at his watch. "We have a few things to discuss." He motioned the team to follow and led the way across the field to the van Nicole had sent to the helicopter.

Jessica edged forward to be by his side. Shirt unbuttoned, its tails tied in a knot beneath her breasts; the open shirt provided ample view of her cleavage. She grinned as Murdock's gaze roamed over her full breasts.

"Nice," he commented, eyebrows rising. Jessica's grin spread into a wicked smile. She opened her shirt more, pretending to cool herself from the humidity.

Never slowing his pace, Murdock canted his head to her and whispered, "But I want my men's attention on fighting—not your teats—so if you don't want to lose them, button that shirt or I'll cut them off."

The order came in such a matter-of-fact tone that it stunned Jessica, making her swallow hard. Her smile melted. She fell back into the crowd and buttoned the shirt and tucked it in properly as fast as her fingers would move.

Tom Bowden and Vince Sefcik were feverishly stacking the backpacks filled with explosives into one of the choppers as quickly as Mike Galloway and Martin Shanks set them inside. At the rear of the van, Stoney Armstrong stood inspecting each before allowing it to be passed on. He heard the team approach and stepped around the door.

"Adam, I think some of these should go with you and—" Stoney froze as Murdock's hand rose before him.

Fire belched from the muzzle of Murdock's *Glock*. The 45ACP round bored through Stoney's forehead and split the rear of his head open like a fallen watermelon. Death came instantaneously. The slender young man crumpled into the dirt.

Galloway instinctively reached for his pistol and Kane was on him like a tiger, pressing an Uzi against his throat. The former intelligence officer shook his head. Brown eyes flared, Galloway grunted acknowledgment.

Holstering his weapon, Murdock gestured for Kane to release the man.

"Our employer has paid quite handsomely for this mission. Results are expected and I intend to give them. Failure is unacceptable," he said, searching the faces of his mercenaries for any signs of rebuttal. There were none.

Glancing at the corpse by his feet, Murdock shook his head in disgust.

"Stoney jeopardized our operation yesterday by going into Houston to score a little nose candy. He risked arrest, but more importantly, he violated one of my explicit rules—no drugs on the team. I do not tolerate disobedience, and no one will jeopardize this mission. Do I make myself clear?"

Their understanding was unanimous. Heads bobbed eagerly. No one wanted to end up like Stoney, and besides, this was a once in a lifetime opportunity. With the money Murdock was paying, they could retire and spend the rest of their lives like royalty wherever they chose in the world.

Kotter felt his throat constrict and mouth go dry. He shifted his weight on his feet; worried someone might mention his earlier suggestion of changing Murdock's attack plan.

"Excellent," Murdock said, stepping over Stoney's body. He started away, paused and pointed to the packs in the chopper. "Stoney was right. We'll need more."

Kane tapped his wrist for the leader to see. When Murdock nodded, Kane grabbed several backpacks and started for their van.

"It's time to go, people," Murdock stated, glancing at the team members who had accompanied him to the airfield.

Bowden and Sefcik scrambled from the chopper. Sefcik jumped into the driver's seat of Stoney's van and started the engine. Once Bowden, Shanks, and Galloway finished positioning the backpacks and supplies in the van, they climbed in. No one paid heed to Stoney's corpse as Sefcik drove them to the road. Jordan and Nicole ran ahead of Murdock to be in his van when he arrived.

"Dutch, wrap up our affairs here," and with a final glance about the field, Murdock strode to his van.

• • •

Richards and Kotter watched until the vans were lost in the rising clouds of dust. In silence they turned to begin their preflight inspections of the Bell helicopters.

Dutch moved the remaining panel van closer to the helicopters and the team unloaded their equipment. When finished, he carried a shoebox to Martin.

"Set the delays for two hours," he ordered, "And put Stoney with the others. It'll keep the cops busy for a few hours. They love to sift through ashes and find bones."

Martin Shanks' craggy face broke into a smile as he lifted two blocks of C-4 from the box. He loved explosives, their swirling fireballs, and destructive force. "No problem," he replied, face beaming as he looked at the five hundred gallon aviation fuel storage tank.

"Tonya," Dutch yelled. "Watch the road. Let me know if you see anything."

She waved and trotted off to the tree line.

Returning to the helicopters, Dutch waited for a lull in the pilots' activity.

"Can you fly them?"

No answer came. Richards and Kotter smirked as they continued their inspection.

"Caan, Peterson, and Tonya will ride with you," Dutch said, gesturing to Richards. "Martin, Jessica, and me will be with Kotter."

Still, no reply. Dutch started to speak again.

"We remember Murdock's instructions," Richards remarked adamantly, tired of hearing the wild-haired man spout orders.

Dutch checked the time. "Lift off at nine. Until then, be ready in case we have to leave sooner." Failing to get a reply, he shook his head in frustration and left.

Trey Richards waited until Dutch's back was turned then made an obscene gesture. Kotter smiled like a schoolboy.

• • •

Grainger City, Texas June 25, 8:30 a.m.

Driving along the narrow refinery street, Jim Thurman scanned the monstrous process units to both sides. Throngs of hard-hatted, sweating, contract laborers and company employees moved about the area. He was entering "Contract City" where every available opening had been filled with mobile home trailers for the dozens of contractors' staff and consultants working on the catalyst-cracking unit repair project.

While some of the people appeared undisturbed by him, others watched with suspicion, but all were curious about his presence.

Jim parked the polished blue Security truck and glanced over the stacks of intersecting pipes and towering vessels about him. Men covered the landscape like ants on fallen food at a picnic. With wrenches, chains and tools in hand, they climbed scaffolding next to the vessels, making their way over the metal leviathans. Out of this organized confusion, new construction and repairs were made, and to Jim it seemed remarkable that anything was ever accomplished.

The noise level throughout the refining complex varied from deafening howls to muffled rumbles. When a relief valve popped from the strain of over-pressured lines, its release roared louder than two jets on the takeoff, shaking houses blocks away in town. Even with earplugs and muffs, the thunderous roar of the refinery bombarded a man's eardrums. As noise battered the ears, the odors of hydrocarbons and sour water assaulted the nostrils, inflaming them, often bringing on headaches. Although the air was tested, the stated results were always the same: *Not harmful within certain limitations.* Yet it was those *certain limitations* that concerned the workers the most.

From contractors to Titan Oil employees, every crew had a radio hand-set slung off their hips like six-shooters in a Wild West movie. Listening only to their primary channel, one group didn't interfere with the operation of others. The sight of the blue truck bedecked with antennas made everyone believe Security was specifically monitoring their channel, eavesdropping on transmissions. That was farthest from the truth. Security could, but the radio traffic was so congested that the officers kept all channels locked out except their own.

The hard bash against the driver's door startled Jim. He whipped around and grew angry at seeing the brawny, barrel-chested construction foreman enjoying the fright he had created.

"How would you like a 9mm enema?" he yelled, rolling the truck window down.

Removing his dark safety glasses, Charlie Martin laughed. He ran a dirty handkerchief over his face, wiping away an accumulation of dirt and sweat.

"Jimbo, what the hell you doing coming around scaring the shit out of my people?" Charlie slipped his glasses on and readjusted his hard-hat into a World War II bomber pilot's salty, half-cocked angle.

Jim stepped from the truck and stood with arms crossed over his chest, glaring in mock anger. "I was coming to tell you I was leaving. But instead, I think I'll haul your ass out of here for being a bastard in a no bastard zone."

Laughter bellowed into the air as it rolled from the depths of the stout built foreman.

"Hell, I'll race you to the gate. They're working me to death around here."

Jim liked the man. They were ex-marines and an 'esprit de corps' existed between them. But Charlie had survived his island hopping days in World War II with few scratches, something Jim couldn't say about Vietnam.

Hands like bear paws; arms that looked as if they were carved out of an oak tree; skin tanned and leathery from years of labor in the sun, Charlie looked as hard as he was tough. He ran his crews with an iron-fist. No horseplay, just pure work from dawn to dusk.

Shaking his head, Jim slapped Charlie's shoulder. They were equals in height and strength, yet Jim's fitness had not come from a lifetime of construction work. It was born from a vow made years ago to never to feel weak and helpless again.

Opening a fresh packet of *Red Man* chewing tobacco, the foreman dug deep, shoveling a handful of the leafy strands into an already protruding cheek.

"What's this crap about leaving, Jimbo?" he asked, eyebrows cocked. "You really taking off?"

Jim nodded as he glanced at the workers walking past.

"I'm gonna miss you not coming around harassing me," the foreman said, a devilish grin breaking over his mouth. He spat a thick stream of tobacco juice on the ground and wiped his mouth with his handkerchief. "But I won't miss you like some people will."

He gestured to the office trailer across the street. Again, his grin appeared.

"Yeah," Jim groaned, glancing at the trailer. "I better tell her."

He started across the street but stopped when he heard his name called.

"Jim, if you ever need a friend…just call."

Gratitude inundated Jim. Their friendship went back years, and the roughhouse foreman meant every word. But in Charlie's tough world, men never thanked one another with words of sincerity. Jim simply nodded and waved goodbye.

• • •

Alex sat at her desk, smiling inwardly, toying with a pencil as she watched Jim's approach through the window. Her gaze traveled over the ruggedly built man, admiring how good he looked in uniform, taking in the thick head of dark brown hair she always wanted to run her hands through. *Those dark eyes*, she thought. She was intrigued by the faraway stare he took on at times when he unknowingly ran a finger down his stomach.

She had felt drawn to him like a moth to a flame the first time she stood close to him, caring little about the consequences, never questioning the attraction. That had been over three weeks ago, and still an excited anticipation and sexual desire surged through her each time they were together. A sense of guilt tore at her for having to deceive him, and she wondered if she could ever leave him when the day arrived.

Jim entered the spacious work trailer and looked at the empty desks along a wall. He tried to smile at Alex, but it came out wrong.

The blue eyes staring at him narrowed.

"Uh oh, this must be an official visit." A teasing grin formed on Alex's soft lips. She looked at his strong arms and forced her gaze to his brown eyes. Worry rose within her. She glanced at the thin gold chain partially in view about his neck, knowing he cherished the cross that hung from it. "Something's bothering you."

"I've got a lot on my mind."

"Are you thinking about your family?"

"You know about them?" His eyes shut and he shook his head lightly. "That's a stupid question. There's very few secrets in this refinery regardless of how big the place is."

She softly nodded and tried to remain relaxed.

Jim gazed at her a moment before speaking. He nodded. "I always think about them. They died in that car accident, but they didn't die in here," he said, touching his chest.

Alex watched him, admiring the Jim Thurman that laid beneath a hardened exterior the world saw. There was honor in his actions, bravery in his soul, and still a deep, moving love in his heart for a woman he could no longer hold.

She wondered what he was thinking. His expression told little and by his silence she understood the need to change his thoughts.

"I even know how you received that scar." She pointed to his abdomen. "The one you don't realize you always touch." Jim's hand rose to his stomach then dropped away. Curiosity painted his face. "Who have you been talking to?"

"Charlie," she replied, comfortable with the small lie. The foreman had spoken to her about Jim when he realized their friendship had grown in such a short time, but Ben Dawson, her partner back at the Agency, had supplied the real truth from Pentagon files at her request.

"Along with a Purple Heart, you were awarded the Navy Cross for bravery. Charlie says that's only second to the Medal of Honor. Your commendation said you prevented an ambush even though you were wounded by—"

"That's enough." He gestured for her to stop. "Don't believe everything you hear. I wasn't a hero. If I had to do it all over again, I probably wouldn't do what I did."

Observing the pain in his eyes, she apologized, furious with herself for having overstepped an invisible boundary.

"I'm resigning today, Alex. Leaving for…"

Hurt drove through her heart and blanked her mind. He talked yet she heard very little. Time seemed to stand still. Gradually, the world returned.

"Alex, I'm not good at goodbyes." Jim stumbled for words.

"Neither am I," she exclaimed, biting her lip. Her outburst surprised her. Hurt turned to anger and then guilt set in. What hurt most was realizing she was losing him forever and didn't know what to do. She turned away, not wanting him to see her face.

The trailer door opened and the sounds and smells of the refinery rushed in. Jim stood in the doorway, gazing at her, waiting for her to look at him, but she never did.

Alex watched the Security truck leave, furious with herself for a thousand conflicting reasons. Frustrated, she dialed an unlisted telephone number and sat back listening to the monotone ring. It was answered immediately.

"Ben, I'll be on the first flight out of Houston tomorrow."

Fingertips tapping the desk, she listened to her partner.

"No, I'm fine," she said. "I just believe we've wasted enough time on this. It's been a month. I've talked to everyone I can think of… our suspicions didn't pan out."

Alex shook her head as Ben talked. She interrupted him.

"No—you're not listening to me. I'm coming back. The problem's not here. It's at Langley."

• • •

June 25, 9:15 a.m.

The helicopters flew side-by-side, close enough for the pilots to make hand signals to each other. At an altitude of six hundred feet, the morning air was cool, almost cold to the passengers. It was far better than the stifling humidity that tried to choke them earlier in the thick brush.

The roar of the engine, combined with the strident thumping of the rotor blades, restricted talk, but the mercenaries had little to say. Each felt a rush of adrenaline coursing through them, making their hearts pound.

Dutch Williams leaned toward the open side-door and watched in fascination as the ground swiftly passed below them. The panoramic view was marvelous. He was transfixed by the contrasting topography of the land, spellbound by the way houses and livestock appeared. Flying over a highway, he observed the lines of vehicles traveling in opposite directions.

They're like ants returning to the mound, he thought. Looking at Jessica sitting across from him, he realized she did not share his enthusiasm.

Jessica's face vividly displayed her fear of heights, and the tightly shut eyes added humor to her appearance. With each jar and bounce that came from the helicopter, she squeezed her safety harness harder. Gradually, her lips curled inward until they could move no further.

The burly man twisted in place and waved to the co-pilot. Martin nodded, tapped Kotter on the shoulder and lifted his watch for the pilot to see. Kotter jerked a thumb in the air and looked out his side window at the chopper beside him.

Richards was staring back.

"Ground Control, this is Tango One, do you copy?" Kotter adjusted the volume on his radio, repeated his transmission and listened for a response. None came.

"Tango One, this is Ground Control. What is your status?"

Glancing at Martin, Kotter smiled. "Ground Control, we have full crews and are on schedule. No problems to report. Do we have a 'Go' situation?"

"Tango One, we have a 'Go'. I repeat, George Oscar. We're entering the city now. Give us fifteen minutes, we have heavy traffic. Approach as planned. Do you copy?"

The pilot checked the time then turned to look at the helicopter next to him. Richards raised his radio microphone. They acknowledged their leader in turn, then waved to each other.

Kotter banked sharply left. Richards followed, maintaining a constant, safe distance between the choppers. Changing course from south to east, they flew into the morning sun, bypassing the city. The next time their course changed, they would be in final approach with the blinding sun behind them.

The Bell helicopter angled onto its side and Jessica's eyes flared. Her mouth shot agape.

Dutch laughed at her spectacle of fear.

Enraged by his glee, she shouted vulgarities, but neither words nor laughter could be heard over the roar of the helicopter's engine.

CHAPTER THREE

June 25, 9:20 a.m.

The number of job requests from throughout the refinery regulated the activity level in the machine shop. Never were any two workdays the same. Rarely were two hours ever the same. For hours on end, ear protection was required from the screaming howls of metals being cut and shaved. Then, as quickly as the bedlam had begun, quiet would settle over the shop once the lathes stopped, allowing men to whisper and be heard.

A high-ceiling, massive metal building housing lathes and machinery capable of tooling Titan Oil's largest equipment, the machine shop was a favorite haunt of Jim's while on patrol. The machinists welcomed him. His arrival heralded the signal to take a break, to swap lies about life in general, and temporarily escape their mundane routines.

The powerful lathe spun the steel flange so swiftly only its blurred circular outline told what it was. As the cutting blade edged slowly inward, a steady stream of hot metal shavings showered the air. With every revolution of the flange, cooling fluid bathed the blade and splattered the lathe.

Standing off to the side, a short, stout man wearing an Astros baseball cap monitored the machine's progress. Bushy locks of premature salt-and-pepper hair, with more salt than pepper, hung in disarray from beneath the cap. Raising his head, he noticed machinists powering down their lathes. Curious, he looked around and saw Jim Thurman standing behind him.

"Hey, big fella, I thought you might be here," Tommy McLawchlin shouted as he pushed buttons. Once the lathe came to a complete halt, the former Army infantryman pulled the foam earplugs out and pocketed his safety glasses. Smiling, he turned and shook hands.

With a happy-go-lucky attitude, Tommy rarely seemed to have a bad day; even after all he had been through in some of the fiercest fighting in Vietnam. Always ready to stop and talk, he constantly wore a mischievous grin, but McLawchlin was the best machinist in the shop and when the time came to get serious, he was strictly business.

"You ready to get a cup?" McLawchlin asked, draping his shop apron over the lathe.

"Wish I could, but I don't have time." Jim glanced at the men milling about the shop floor.

The machinist observed his troubled look.

"Let's go for a walk," Jim said, starting for the door. They strolled out of the Machine Shop and turned toward the Security truck parked at the far end of the building.

"Do you still have my rifle and gear?" Jim asked.

Tommy laughed sheepishly. "It's all in my truck."

"I'll need to get everything from you."

"I was planning to use your rifle the next few days. After work we're heading to Brewster County. Remember Braun's uncle? Someone is stealing his livestock again. He called and asked if the 'War Dogs' could take care of the problem. Why don't you come with us? Probably bandits crossing the border like last time. We'll scare 'em off unless they want to get serious." Tommy spoke of running the paramilitary operation with a casual air. He lifted his cap, scratched his head then smoothed his hair before putting the cap on again.

'War Dogs' was a good nickname for the close-knit band of blooded veterans who worked at the refinery. They were warriors who had survived the worst Vietnam had to give yet upon discharge had returned to an America torn by bitterness against the war, and against those who had fought in it.

Like Jim, they had laid down their weapons in hopes of returning to a simple life, one with a wife, kids, and a job that paid half-decent. But Titan Oil had treated them like society's misfits because of a lack of college degrees and their combative past. They were members of America's lost tribe. The tribe that did what was asked of them, and then were forgotten to exist as best they could.

The War Dogs were survivors, though, proving themselves to be knowledgeable, industrious workers. Now they mostly took pleasure in hunting together, sometimes using their former military skills to help eradicate cattle rustling and robbery problems that still plagued West Texas ranchers along the border.

"Our trucks are already loaded with gear. C'mon with us. We could use you again," Tommy said.

"No, I'm cashing my chips in and heading out."

The news didn't surprise Tommy. They had discussed it on several occasions, and although he would be losing a good friend, he was glad for Jim. The machinist laughed and opened the passenger door of the Security truck. "Well, do you at least have time to give me a ride to the warehouse? I need to get some gloves, and it'll give us a chance to do some horse-trading. I sure like your rifle and that *Kabar* knife."

Jim nodded with a grin and walked around the truck. He stopped abruptly and looked to the sky. A sound had caught his attention; the same sound that always stirred his emotions and had haunted him since Vietnam.

Tommy waited until they backed out onto Derrick Road and started up the street for the warehouse. "What's wrong?"

"Nothing," Jim remarked, solemnly looking down the road toward the Gate House. "I thought I heard choppers."

"Damn, how can you hear anything in this place anymore? We're all going deaf." Tommy lightly shook his head and grinned. "Flashbacks, Jimbo. Yep, too many drugs in the sixties." He laughed, shrugged his shoulders and sniffed the air. "That or the fumes around here have finally eaten your brain."

• • •

June 25, 9:30 a.m.

The newly promoted sergeant looked at his watch. A haughty smirk spread across his face. Nine thirty. He had been sergeant for three and a half hours, and it felt great. Relishing the authority, Sancho Martinez leaned on the camera console, refusing to help with the activity in the Gate House. It was now all below his new station in life.

At the control desk Nolan Phillips sat with one shoulder raised, telephone receiver pinned to an ear. Juggling a clipboard laden with documents, he flipped through sheets of information, unable to locate what the caller wanted. The refinery radio blared unintelligible bits of conversation as it scanned the hundred channels assigned to the enormous complex.

Across the counter, unconcerned with the officer's frantic pace, an obnoxious salesman continued his endless barrage of questions as to why he could not enter. Nolan kept motioning for him to wait but the cigar chewing man refused to quiet. The computerized alarm system activated, malfunctioning as usual, sounding its annoying, high-pitched alert tone.

Sancho was within arm's reach of the silencing button. He glanced its way, listened to the bothersome tone, and his smirk stretched wider. His gaze lazily drifted to the pot-bellied officer at the control desk.

Phillips' knuckles turned white as rage set him afire. He threw the receiver at the radio and spun his chair around to face Sancho. The alert tone, combined with the ongoing activity, grated his nerves yet not as much as seeing the new sergeant's refusal to simply push a button.

"Hey, when Calder made you a fucking sergeant, he didn't break your fingers." Nolan walked to the computer and smashed the button with a hammer-like fist. The tone stopped. His glare made Sancho's arrogance drain away.

A snorting chuckle carried across the room. Nolan spun, temper flared to its peak. The salesman chuckled again, staring at Sancho. His unlit stub of a cigar rose and fell in short strokes from his lips.

Offended by the chastising and laughter, Sancho's bottom lip pooched out into a pout as he straightened from the console.

Primed for an argument, Nolan glared at the sergeant, waiting for the least word from him. Nothing was said. Teeth clenched, he stepped close to Sancho so no one else could hear.

"This company fucks us enough without you adding to it."

The Gate House side door swung open. Louie Johnson entered, wiping his brow, grumbling about the humidity and being ordered to work on his day off. Laying the traffic clipboard on the counter, the black officer looked about the room, sensing tension. He glanced at the street then turned to the men engaged in a stare down.

"It's hot out there you know. I had things to do today. I didn't want to be here." Johnson shrugged, believing he was the topic of their discussion. He knew he wasn't liked in the department and assumed it was because he had no law enforcement background as everyone else. But he didn't care. Calder liked him and had protected him the times he should have been fired, and that was all that mattered.

No one spoke. "Is that for me?" Louie asked, spotting the telephone receiver lying on the desk.

"No, it's not one of your dumb-ass girlfriends!" Phillips barked, eyes closing in exasperation as he took a seat in the control chair again.

Louie ignored him and faced the glass door to watch the cars entering and exiting the main gate.

Phillips picked up the receiver. Finding no one on the line, he hung up the phone, still irritated over Sancho's antics. The salesman impatiently tapped a pen on the visitor counter.

"Now, what do you want?" Phillips asked angrily.

Mumbling, Louie looked northward to the public street.

A panel van rounded the corner on to Derrick Road, heading toward the office. The blinding reflection of morning sunlight off the vehicle's windshield blocked its occupants from view. The van slowed as it neared the gate.

"Oh, man, what does this fool want?" Louie stood staring in disgust at the vehicle waiting in the entrance roadway.

"Why don't you go out, do your fucking job, and ask him?" yelled Phillips, throwing his hands up. "What? Do you think you're a sergeant too?" He snapped a fiery look back at Sancho.

Louie glared at Phillips. Grabbing up the traffic log clipboard, he arrogantly walked out of the office.

Spinning the chair, Phillips returned to his argument with the salesman. The man adamantly demanded entrance even though he wasn't on the approved visitor's roster.

Sancho briefly watched Louie stroll to the driver's side of the van. His gaze carried to the eastern horizon. Squinting against the sunlight, he observed two dots steadily growing larger. He leaned forward as if the movement would help his vision. The size of the dots increased. He strained to make out their shape.

Helicopters? Flying side by side—treetop leveland coming toward the refinery at a high rate of speed?

Curiosity rising, he walked out the door, slowing to a halt in front of the van. He looked skyward at the fast approaching machines, wondering if they were LifeFlight medical helicopters. The thumping sound of the rotors increased by the second. Out of the corner of his eye he observed odd movement and glanced at the black security officer.

Louie Johnson's eyes sprang wide, whites showing like the sails of a schooner. The deafening drone of the turbines and dull whop of rotors blanketed his pleas. His body shook, legs suddenly weak, refusing to obey him.

Sancho turned to the van. A gleeful expression spread over the driver's face as he raised a shotgun from his lap and aimed it at Louie's head. The blast was drowned by the scream of the helicopters directly overhead. The wide streak of fire spewing from its muzzle stretched through the air.

The bloody remnant of Johnson's head flopped backward. His body staggered, collapsing in the street.

Sancho froze, his mind denying what he had seen. Shock overwhelmed him as he stared at the driver's face. The cruelty in the blue eyes of the shotgun wielding man was like nothing Sancho had ever seen.

The choppers flew over the Gate House at thirty feet above the ground, engines screaming, consuming the sky. They peeled apart in synchronized aerobatics, angling on their sides, returning for another run.

Confusion wrecked havoc with Sancho. His world reeled. The van's engine revved and before the newly promoted sergeant could jump clear, the vehicle struck him.

Phillips' attention was on the helicopters. When he looked to the vehicle, it mowed Martinez down. Drawing his pistol, Phillips lunged at the glass door, kicking it open to shoot.

The van's side door flew back revealing a black-masked passenger. At point-blank range, a tactical shotgun rose and fired two shots, cutting away Phillips' left rib cage and arm. Spun hard by the force, he fell into the street, dying within feet of his fellow murdered officers.

Another blast rang out. The street-side window of the Gate House shattered into gleaming pieces. Chaos instantly dominated the office. Visitors ran into each other as they tried to evade the spray of lead pellets.

The cigar-chewing salesman stared out the demolished window. Paralyzed, he tried to scream warning, but he was too late.

The van started down Derrick Road. Three grenades flew from the vehicle into the building, sailing through the air as if in slow motion. They landed on the floor, rolled to a stop, and detonated. The explosion violently rocked the brick building, blowing out plate glass windows and chunks of the walls.

Having heard the powerful whine of helicopters' engines, employees streamed from the Ivory Tower and Admin buildings. They searched the sky, heads craned, hands shading eyes. When the shotgun blasts and grenade explosions erupted they fled in all directions.

The lead helicopter landed atop the Admin building while the second circled over the stampeding crowd. Rotors whipped wind through the trees, making them dance a wild dervish. Loose grass and debris caught up by the helicopter-made windstorm flew into the frightened employees, stinging their faces, blinding them.

A harnessed passenger, face masked, feet braced against the landing skids, leaned out the chopper and released a long burst from an Uzi machine gun.

Bullets slashed through the running employees, missing some, striking others. Ricochets off the concrete tore through flesh, leaving jagged wounds. Shouts of alarm intermixed with anguished screams and the monstrous roar of turbines spawned a greater hysteria. The hail of bullets seemed unending.

Lifting upward, the helicopter angled away, circling the Ivory Tower. Office windows were randomly shot out. The masked passenger emptied five magazines of ammunition before leaning inside, gesturing to another passenger. Engine noise increased and the helicopter rose to the rooftop.

As it set down, the passenger at the door unbuckled and pulled the ski mask off. Whipping her head, Tonya freed the long black hair from beneath her collar. Her hazel eyes gazed at the three men ready to disembark. Shouldering a military pack, she jumped from the helicopter, enthralled with the assault.

Removing their own masks, each man grabbed packs and canvas handbags and climbed out. They made straight for the stairwell leading down into the building.

Tonya took up an AK-47 and rushed to the roof's edge. She took careful aim on a car speeding out the main gate and slowly squeezed the trigger. The automatic weapon rocked in her hands until the last bullet was spent. Maintaining her position, she watched the car careen sideways into the wrought iron fence. It climbed atop the gate's electrical control box, showering the air with sparks. The car's fuel tank exploded, engulfing it in flames. Fiery debris rocketed across the roadway, blocking entry into the refinery.

Remaining at the rooftop's ledge, she reloaded the *Kalashnikov* with a fresh banana clip and surveyed the damage below. Glass from the Gate House windows littered the road. Three uniformed men lay dead, sprawled in swiftly spreading pools of blood. The car now burned like a bonfire, black smoke billowing upward into the sky. Bodies of men and women lay scattered across the parking lot and lawn between the Ivory Tower and Gate House. A few victims crawled away, bleeding, moaning, begging for help. Others lay still, never to move again.

Tonya slapped the end of the magazine to ensure it was fully seated and gave an approving look at the thoroughness of her handiwork. She eased her pack off and withdrew three glass jars.

Sunlight made the gasoline shine golden brown as she held a jar high. One by one, they were thrown as far out as possible. She watched them fall to earth and smash, splattering the flammable liquid over cars and pavement. Removing hand grenades from her belt, she pulled their safety pins and lobbed them into the air. They arched in flight, descending on the row of parked cars along the ornamental fence. She backed away from the ledge before they landed. The explosions came almost simultaneously. Cars erupted in flames, quickly spreading to the next because of their close proximity and the gasoline bath. Grenade shrapnel and flying pieces of car metal struck wounded people attempting to escape. With a last glance at the devastation, she shouldered the AK-47. Satisfied, she ran after her three teammates. She changed to the Uzi and grinned. The short weapon was better than the AK-47 for close-quarters combat.

• • •

Two blocks east of the attack, four men sat in a panel van on the shoulder of the public street bordering the refinery. From their vantage point, they could see the helicopters strafe, circle, and descend onto the buildings.

Tom Bowden turned from his window to look at the gaunt driver. He pulled his ski mask down and adjusted the eyeholes.

Acknowledging with a casual nod, Vince Sefcik eased his ski mask into position and signaled the men sitting behind him. Mike Galloway and Martin Shanks shuffled to the sliding door and placed their masks on.

Sefcik drove along the road's shoulder then turned onto the long refinery street leading to Gate Nine, the refinery's primary delivery entrance. He drove slowly, noting the people massed in the middle of the road by the small contract guard post. They gestured to the attack, gazes locked on the rising pillars of black smoke. No one had yet observed his vehicle's approach or its ski-masked occupants.

At one hundred yards from the gate, Sefcik eased to a halt. A tight-lipped grin formed as he watched the size of the excited crowd steadily increase.

The van's side door slid open and men jumped out. Galloway settled the weight of the rocket launcher comfortably onto his shoulder and peered through its sighting device. He brought the metal guard building into view. Martin Shanks stood beside him, his own rocket launcher aimed at a row of Titan Oil trucks parked to the right of the crowd. Standing watch, Bowden scanned the area, prepared to kill anyone who drew near.

"Fire in the hole." Galloway's warning came calmly as he applied pressure to the trigger. Shanks echoed his words. Two missiles streaked through the air, smoke trailing them as they shot toward the gate and the trucks.

The explosions instantly sent a violent tremor through the ground. A churning, blackish-orange fireball mushroomed skyward from the guard building, spewing jagged pieces of metal siding and shrapnel outward through the crowd. Trucks catapulted into the air and landed atop fleeing people. Fueled by ruptured gas tanks and blazing tires, walls of dancing flames spread about the delivery gate's entrance. Gray and black swirling smoke caught up by the wind stretched over the gate and blended with the rising fog bank of dirt.

Sefcik looked at the destruction, maintaining his vigil while the men climbed into the van. A blood-drenched woman, face heavily marred, staggered from the smoke, weaved and fell. To her right, a man appeared with dripping, crimson stubs for arms. He walked three steps and sank to the pavement. The smoke parted and a twisted mass of bodies lay across the gate's entrance.

Fiery ribbons streaked upward from the demolished guard post and engulfed trucks. The wind lifted the grayish-black smoke and soon the devastation came into clear view.

"Hold on." Sefcik pushed the accelerator to the floorboard. The van bounced over the wounded and dead, cracking and crunching bones as it drove through the burning delivery gate.

Entering the refinery, the vehicle turned toward Contract City, its masked occupants steadily shooting anyone they observed.

• • •

Within seconds of the attack, hysteria carried through the refinery with the speed of an earthquake's shockwave. Standing in the warehouse at the receiving counter with Tommy, Jim heard explosions. He fought his way through the door as a dozen people tried to exit at the same time. Shoving men aside, he burst into the parking lot and looked down Derrick Road to the Gate House.

Black smoke rose in contorted pillars of swirling clouds. Raising his gaze, he saw the helicopters atop the buildings. Their blades rotated slowly as they wound down.

Cars and trucks raced through the refinery. Employees and contractors fled on foot in all directions, screaming unintelligibly. A gray panel van with its side door open sped along Derrick Road, traveling deeper into the complex.

Tommy barely made it out of the warehouse when Jim shouted for him to take cover.

The outline of a man moved in the side doorway of the van. A rifle barrel came into view. The rhythmic staccato of automatic gunfire sang through the air as fire flashed from its muzzle.

Tommy flung himself to the ground. Three men behind him caught bullets in the chests. People ran without direction, but Tommy scrambled on hands and feet to the Security truck.

Jim never hesitated and drew his Beretta, bracing himself on the truck's hood. His sights were dead on the terrorist in the doorway and he was about to fire when an employee ran in front of him.

"Get down!" he ordered, leading the panel van with his pistol as it raced away. Men saw him taking aim and dove to the ground. Field of fire clear, he squeezed the trigger twice. He knew he had hit the van's sliding doors and missed the terrorist.

Swinging his truck door open, Jim grabbed the radio microphone. "Base, this is Unit Seven. Can you read me?" he shouted. "Nolan—Sancho—" There was no answer.

Frightened by all they had witnessed, hysterical people rushed to the Security truck. Their frantic questions to the uniformed man came out in an incomprehensible bawl.

Jim waved the crowd away, unable to hear any response on the radio. He keyed the microphone and called the Gate House again. The effort to listen was useless with the delirious throng about him.

Jim reached for his semiautomatic, unsure of what was happening behind him. He wheeled about. Charlie Martin stood with massive arms spread wide, restraining the mob from getting close to his friend.

A blood painted man, arms hanging listlessly, staggered toward the riotous crowd. He dropped to his knees in the middle of the warehouse parking lot. His pleas and moans were lost in the melee, but the sight of his burnt face and shredded clothes brought a temporary silence.

"Jim!" Charlie shouted. "A van went through Gate Nine. There's at least twenty dead and everything's on fire."

Jim slowly shook his head, believing a small army had invaded the refinery.

As men ran to aid the wounded employee, Jim took advantage of the moment.

"Leave the refinery. Jump the fence, but don't go near any of the gates. Go—Go," he ordered, pointing to safety. "I'm ordering a full evacuation of the refinery."

No more needed to be said. Tires screeched, engines raced, and vehicles left laden with people climbing in and atop them. While some people attempted to stop trucks for a ride, others ran, not waiting for a vehicle.

Jim tossed his pistol to Tommy. "Shoot any son of a bitch that even looks like he's carrying a weapon." He leaned into his truck and grabbed the radio's microphone again.

Changing the radio to the refinery-wide emergency channel, Jim pushed the coded sequence of buttons to activate the 'Oh God' button. Finishing, he realized all that remained was to push the red button and transmit his message.

The 'Oh God' button was Security's initial phase of the flagship's doomsday plan. It was designed to set off blaring horns and sirens through-out the complex. Every radio on the premises would key open and receive the transmitted emergency message. There were other locations that could activate the alarm, but he had to assume they were already under the ter-rorists' control. With Sancho and everyone else possibly dead at the gate, Jim knew he might be the only remaining person with access to the system. Another thought crossed his mind.

The system had only been tested twice in the last two years and he wasn't sure it would work properly. If the terrorists were professionals, they would immediately search for the radio and telephone rooms in the Ivory Tower. Controlling those meant all communication with the outside world could be severed. Every radio transmission could be monitored. This might be the last opportunity to warn the entire refinery. He pushed the red button and prayed.

For several seconds nothing happened. A sinking feeling filled his stomach, but his prayers were answered with a high-pitched squeal emitted over the radio's speaker. Jim knew he was going to get through. The squeal finished its cycle. The transmit light showed on the dashboard of the radio. He now had an open airwave to every Titan Oil radio in the refinery.

"This is Titan Oil Security—Emergency Transmission," Jim stated as calmly as he could. "Authority of the refinery manager, go to emergency shutdown of the refinery... I repeat... By authority of the refinery manager, begin emergency shutdown. Lockdown status—go to lockdown status. Evacuate as best you can... I repeat... Evacuate if possible. This is not a drill."

No sooner had he finished when the refinery's emergency horn and siren system activated, sending warbling blasts and blares into the sky. As operating units began to shut down, their own horns gave warning of what was being conducted. Jim breathed a sigh of relief.

Tommy raced back from the street. Ashen-faced, he looked at Jim. "Bad news, brother. Our friends in the van just turned toward A-5."

Shaking his head in disbelief, Jim turned to Tommy, face etched with apprehension. A single catalyst-cracking unit erupting would be disastrous, but the A-5 unit exploding was sheer terror; everyone's nightmare.

In the industry, Alkylate Unit #5 was discreetly referred to as A-5. Three city blocks cordoned off with fluorescent plastic fencing and elaborate lighting. It was a bomb waiting for the wrong person to flip the switch. Monstrous settler storage tanks; isobutane vessels; depropanizers; miles of interlocking specially treated piping; all were uniquely designed to work with and contain the lethal HF, hydrofluoric acid, necessary in the alkylation process to make high-quality gasoline.

Every processing unit in the refinery had its own dangers, and the potential for explosions always existed yet when the outcome was weighed, there were no comparisons to A-5. With other units there would be a blast, a massive fire that would sweep to surrounding units, more blasts and lives lost. The majority of damage would be contained locally, primarily within the city. A-5 was a different scenario all together.

A simple drop of HF on one's skin caused immediate deep-seated burns, a rapid destruction of tissue, decalcification of bone and a slow, systematic, excruciating poisoning of the body. Titan Oil knew the acid's dangers and avoided it in public discussions. The less that citizens knew about HF, the better for the corporation. Fear of a major acid release, though, existed in everyone's minds. Released in quantity to the atmosphere, the acid formed a toxic vapor cloud, gliding on silent wings of death, killing everything that lay in its path as far and wide as the wind blew. HF was a beast that knew no master once freed from the bondage of vessels and pipes, and it sought a hideous retribution for its imprisonment.

Both men saw the frightening truth in one another's eyes. Jim knew one thing that Tommy did not. Under a worst-case scenario with the vast quantity that the refinery had, if a total release occurred, Titan Oil estimated a massive acid cloud could be carried over Houston and on to Dallas from the predominant southeast winds off the gulf. Its swath of death would be genocide.

Tommy glanced at the men lying dead outside the warehouse. "You know if the Butane Farm spheres blow it will shoot A-5 into the sky like a rocket and—"

"Don't worry," Jim replied with a weak grin, "if this place goes up, we'll never know what hit us." He groaned and changed the radio to the A-5 Unit's channel. No one responded to his calls. Jim paused, trying to keep a level train of thought about what next to do.

The radio speaker crackled. A man's screaming voice came across, desperately crying for help. In the background, a commanding voice and the burp of automatic gunfire were heard. The radio went silent.

Jim closed his eyes in anguish, knowing what had happened. With the push of a button, he switched the radio over to the Grainger City Police Department frequency.

"Grainger City, this is Titan Oil. We have an emergency situation. Can you copy?"

He knew by now the blare of the refinery's warning system had carried over the city. With their phone calls and radio transmissions to the Gate House going unanswered, Jim realized the police would be rolling full speed, Code Three, to investigate... and drive into an ambush. He had to stop them.

"Titan Oil, this is Grainger City dispatch. All radio traffic is clear at this time. Go ahead with your emergency transmission," said a female dispatcher, anxiety thick in her voice.

Jim took in a deep breath, readying himself to give instructions. He caught sight of Charlie standing wide-eyed, mouth agape forming an oval. In the frenzy of trying to accomplish so much Jim had forgotten him. Now, though, seeing the foreman's comical expression, an odd urge to laugh came out of nowhere. It eased Jim's built-up tension. He glanced at Tommy.

"We've got to expect the worst."

The machinist nodded and looked toward the pillars of smoke rising from the main gate.

"I was sort of thinking that myself."

As if a valve opened and pressure was released within him, Jim calmed. His mind began to function as precisely as it always had during intense combat in Vietnam.

"Grainger City, this is Titan Oil Security. We are under attack by terrorists at this time. Do not come to the main gate or the delivery gate of the refinery. You will come under hostile fire. Unknown type of weapons involved. I see two choppers on our buildings and an unknown number of terrorists have entered the refinery. We have dead and wounded at this time but unable to confirm numbers. I repeat—do not approach any refinery gate. Do you copy?" Jim hoped he hadn't lost communication before he finished giving the police the basic information.

A long period of silence followed. The police were either having difficulty in believing what they had heard, or the radio was knocked off the air.

"Grainger City, this is Titan Oil. Did you copy?"

"Titan Oil, did you say *terrorist attack*?" the dispatcher asked slowly. A fast spreading fire; an operating unit exploding; people injured, maimed, killed; anything probably sounded plausible to her except a terrorist attack.

Jim knew he couldn't waste anymore time. "Notify surrounding plants to shut down all operations with us and prepare for hell to break loose. Sound the city disaster alarms. We may have a total HF release. I repeat— HF—Henry Frank—a total hydrofluoric acid release."

A formal sounding, masculine voice came on the radio.

"Titan Oil, this is Grainger City dispatch. We need confirmation before taking such action."

Angered by the unbelieving tone, Jim shook his head and squeezed the transmit button.

"Hey, fuckhead, go outside and listen to the damned sirens if you need confirmation. Better yet, why don't you drag your happy ass down here and get it blown away with the rest of us!" Jim threw the microphone across the cab of the truck, jumped in and slammed the door.

"Let's go, Tommy." He looked at Charlie. "Where's your truck?"

The foreman motioned to the far side of the warehouse.

"Stay clear of the main gate area and the A-5 unit. See that your people get out even if you have to drive through a fence, then get the hell out of here yourself," Jim yelled, starting the truck and placing it in gear.

"Where're you going, Jim? Maybe I can help."

"You've done enough already." Jim looked over the construction fore-man's head and saw the helicopters. A southeast wind pushed the black smoke spiraling above the buildings northward over the city. "I've been invited to a party and you haven't."

The paw-like hand of the foreman extended to Jim. They shook with the unspoken understanding that they may never meet again. Their squeeze was hard and strong.

Jim watched Charlie leave and turned to Tommy.

"This is doomsday, brother. I'm getting you out of here. You have a family."

Tommy adamantly shook his head. "And what are you going to do? You coming with me?"

"I'm going after them." Jim's dark brown eyes were cold and his voice rang with a cruel edge.

The machinist grinned, eyes scanning the refinery. His gaze came to rest on Jim with a granite stare. "Well, doomsday man, it looks like we are taking this one-way ticket to Hell together."

The security truck's engine raced and its tires squealed, seeking traction on the asphalt pavement.

CHAPTER FOUR

June 25, 9:30 a.m.

The video of last night's national news broadcast was poor. Lines crossed the screen and the sound garbled at times. The managers sitting at the rear of the Admin building's lavish conference room had difficulty hearing. They ordered the volume be raised. It was important to understand the popular commentator. His past criticisms of Titan Oil had stirred public wrath, creating additional headaches for the corporation. Now he was accusing the oil giant of orchestrating a future fuel shortage to fatten already overflowing coffers.

"That's bullshit." Walter Gunnerman, Division Manager of Reforming, swung a hand at the video. "Why haven't we bought this son of a bitch off?"

No one replied. They were too intent on the broadcast.

All newscasts were recorded and kept on file for two weeks before being erased. It had been standard practice for years, allowing management to know the complaints lodged publicly against them and to prepare a defense against the media's onslaught. Last night's allegation was so critical that the tape had to be reviewed before all other business this morning.

Having seen the tape twice, Danny Barton studied the stern expressions each leader in the room wore. Except for the refinery manager Dave

Simmons and his second-in-command Howard Russell, everyone was present. Even Clarence Calder, which made no sense to Danny.

They must need him to pour their coffee, he thought.

Leaning to one side, Danny watched the security superintendent try to impress a manager with his usual kiss up remarks. The public affairs man stifled a laugh when Calder received nothing more than an irate look in response.

Barton was no man's fool. He knew he was only present because of the broadcast. Once management finished watching the tape and decided upon statements they wanted released, the responsibility to call a local news meeting and declare Titan Oil's innocence fell to him whether he believed the statements or not.

The company had taught Danny to cast aside his naive ideology of reporting the truth. Years of working as a reporter had been flushed down the toilet the day he hired on in public affairs. Referred to as the flagship's mouthpiece, Danny's task was to paint rosy pictures and fertilize a garden of contentment with the local media. But Danny was a fast learner and the managers kept him overly supplied with fertilizer. He would either have to be content or find employment elsewhere.

The helicopter over the building hadn't been heard. The television's blare and the room's soundproofing blocked it yet the vibrations were felt as the chopper landed. Men rose in alarm.

Whipping curtains aside, Danny pressed his face against the windowpane. He looked skyward and caught a glimpse of a tail rotor. Hands gripped his shoulder, jerking him away. Managers anxiously tried to squeeze themselves into position at the same window to look out.

Shoved back by the crowd, the young public affairs man glanced at the other windows. No one had bothered using them. He ran to a window and swept its curtain aside, trying to see the helicopter again. It was gone. Leaning on the windowsill, he felt the aged building tremble.

An explosion? A dozen scenarios swept through his mind.

Pressing his right ear against the thick glass, Danny shut his eyes, hoping to detect any outside noise. Closing his other ear with a finger to block out the room's clamor, he faintly heard rhythmic tapping. The building shuddered again. He looked at Derrick Road below as he straightened from the window. People raced back into the refinery from the main gate area, fleeing for safety. Some limped, some fell, while others ran as if they were at Olympic trials.

"The Gate House," he yelled, turning to leave.

Having seen the terrified people below, division managers sprinted toward the door. The staccato rattling of automatic gunfire bellowed into the conference room when a door was flung open. One of the first men to run out into the hall was immediately thrown back. A manager caught him and held fast. The wounded man twisted in the arms that held him. His eyes rolled upward and body limp, he slumped to the floor. The front of his white shirt changed rapidly to red as bullet holes leaked freely. Walter Gunnerman lay dead on the carpet with eyes open, mouth agape, the focus of everyone's attention.

The deafening report of gunfire blocked the screams of secretaries being massacred in their offices. Masked terrorists raced down the hall, wasting no time in their brutal takeover of the third floor.

While division managers huddled by the door, Danny slipped behind the curtains concealing the entrance leading into the adjacent emergency operations room. He grabbed a telephone and dialed the Gate House's number. The call wouldn't go through. Danny hung up, gaze sweeping the room, knuckles tapping the receiver. He tried to telephone Calder's secretary at the security office inside the refinery. A recording stated the system was experiencing temporary problems.

A commanding voice in the room sent a cold shiver up his spine. Wheeling about, the last thing Danny remembered before all went black was a rifle butt coming at his face.

• • •

"Where is he?" Jessica looked into Dave Simmons' vacant office. The *Llama* semiautomatic in her hand held steady aim on Brenda Avery, the refinery manager's executive secretary.

"In New York. He… He's been gone for several days." Brenda's throat constricted. The mask hid the terrorist's face but the breasts showed that a woman pointed the gun. Brenda watched as the terrorist stared at her dress and jewelry. Something in the brown eyes scared Brenda even more.

"You're nothing more than a high paid whore." Contempt was thick in Jessica's voice. She smiled at Brenda's fear.

Fire belched from the muzzle of Jessica's pistol, then the terrorist turned to leave.

"Dammit, don't kill everyone you see. We may need them later. Bring 'em to that room," Dutch ordered from the door, motioning to the conference room.

Jessica nodded and left to search the offices again.

• • •

While Martin Shanks stood guard over the hostages in the conference room, Kotter Ryan verified the controls in the emergency operations room next door. Engaging switches, he observed dials and gauges move. Override control of the refinery's computers was almost complete. He grinned, pleased with the swift activation.

Dutch Williams entered, looked at Kotter, then to the control board. He checked the time.

Good, right on schedule, he thought.

Two shots rang out at the end of the hall. Dutch's head whipped in the direction of the report. He scowled. *That bitch!*

• • •

Being slapped on the face wasn't Danny's favorite manner of waking yet neither was being put to sleep by a rifle butt. He heard his name fade in and out of his mind. Bright lights shined in his eyes. He squinted and the simple movement flashed pain in his temples.

Reflex made him raise a hand to touch the source of his agony. His face felt pulverized. As his fingers brushed his nose, bone moved and shot bolts of pain throughout him. He forced his eyes to open partially. Blood covered his hand. Moving his lips made his cheeks feel afire. He hoped his skull wasn't fractured.

Another slap on the face jarred his senses. Danny knew if he did not show more signs of life, someone was going to beat him to death. He uttered a weak moan. The slapping ceased. Looking up, Danny saw Calder's pale face.

"Are you all right?" The security superintendent's lips quivered.

Danny stared at him, thinking the question was the most absurd thing anyone could ask.

"You idiot! Do I look it?" Danny winced at the pain in his cheeks.

"Shut up!" Martin brought his Uzi to bear on the hostages. His grip tightened and the hostages braced. The black ski mask hid his grin.

Helping Danny off the table and into a chair, George Ruddel, Manager of Projects and Construction, grabbed a shoulder to steady him. Danny remembered the rifle but little else until revived by the slaps. His ribs ached. He assumed he had been kicked, but how he came to be placed on the conference table remained a mystery.

Standing submissively along the window wall, in line as if awaiting execution, the flagship's elite echelon of management exchanged anxious glances. Each wondered who would step forward and risk a leadership role. Everything was different now. They were unprepared for such a contingency. Giving orders; being in charge; dominating everyone around them was all their training had ever consisted of. Now, though, frightened and reduced to a level of insignificance, each manager appeared concerned only with his survival.

A masked, brawny terrorist entered the room. Hair protruded from beneath his mask all about his neck. He stood staring at the hostages, arms resting on the AK-47 slung off his shoulder. Scrutinizing their faces, the towering man searched for the bravest and the most frightened among them. He pulled his mask off, swept a hand over his hair, and tucked the ski mask into his wide gun belt. The terrorist beside him did the same.

"Sit," Dutch commanded, gaze traveling the length of the room. The managers sank obediently to the floor. The wild-haired man shook his head and raked his coarse beard, glad to be free of the mask.

"What the hell do you want?" Paul Hawkins' insolent tone slashed the air. The elderly Division Manager of Refinery Maintenance glared at his captors.

Dutch watched him, knowing someone would eventually speak out, proclaiming himself king. Shifting his stare, the rough-hewn biker had no difficulty in finding the most frightened. Clarence Calder sat ashen-faced, trembling, eyes downcast.

"Hey, pecker-head," Dutch announced calmly, pointing a finger at Hawkins. "Come with me." The hostage followed him out into the hall.

They walked several steps before Dutch stopped. He wheeled and shoved the arrogant manager hard against the wall. The impact was still flooding Hawkins' body when Dutch grabbed his wrists and jerked them up to chest level. "Put your hands together."

Hawkins did as told.

Reaching into his shirt, Dutch removed a roll of duct tape and bound the hostage's wrists.

Hawkins' glanced from his wrists to his captor's face. Insanity painted the terrorist's eyes. Fear roiled the manager's stomach to the point of nausea.

"Move," Dutch whispered, gesturing down the hall.

All bravado drained from Hawkins. He walked meekly until ordered to halt at a janitorial closet.

"Hold this until I return." The terrorist wedged a fragmentation grenade into Hawkins' cupped hands.

The silver-haired manager blinked in disbelief. His gaze rose to meet Dutch's stare. Mouth like cotton, Hawkins ran his tongue over his lips. He looked at his hands again.

"No, no…please, no." The manager's head shook in jerky motions.

Dutch pulled the safety pin and tossed it into the air. It *clinked* and bounced along the polished hall floor. The grenade was live, kept only from detonating by the manager's fingers wrapped about its spoon. Opening the closet door, Dutch smiled and ordered Hawkins inside.

"If you move your fingers, the spoon will dislodge. When it does, you'll have about five seconds to bend over and kiss your ass goodbye."

The door closed. Darkness enveloped Hawkins. Returning to the conference room, Dutch stood in its doorway, staring at the seated men, sensing their fears. Three minutes passed, then a long, muffled scream, laced with terror, rose to a peak. Dutch glanced at his watch and mumbled a countdown.

The janitorial closet door exploded outward into the hall. The blast caused the hostages to flinch violently. The grenade's concussion rattled the room as the explosion bellowed throughout the building.

Lowering his arm, Dutch smirked and glanced back along the hall. Hundreds of bloody pieces of splintered wood and human entrails painted the floor. He turned to the managers.

"Your friend will not be joining us."

No one spoke.

"We control the refinery," Dutch stated, letting his emotionless stare sweep the room. "Your security force is dead. There's no one to rescue you. Do as you're told and I might let you live."

The hostages glanced at one another. Some bowed their heads and prayed silently. Others stared at their feet in shock. Calder lowered his head into cupped hands and wept like a frightened child.

Relishing the moment, Dutch stroked his beard and smirked. He paused, remembering Murdock's instructions.

"We are the Serpent and the Sword," he stated with a ring of steel, shifting the weight of his AK-47 on his shoulder.

Danny sat in his chair, studying the burly man. He had a talent for gauging people, reading their faces for what floated in their minds. It came in handy in public relations. He realized the terrorist had more to say and was waiting as if it were all rehearsed. Danny raised his hand. Pain pierced through him in hot streaks, racing from his ribs up into his head. He grimaced and fought the agony.

The terrorist nodded to him.

"Excuse me, sir, but are y'all a militia?" he asked, feigning ignorance.

Dutch stared at the young man for several seconds and shook his head lightly.

"Mercenaries."

Glancing at the floor, Danny sighed wearily from his passing pain. He looked up. The wild-haired man appeared to want more questions asked. The young public relations man played along in utter innocence. "Who would want to hire mercenaries to attack us?"

"The middle-east." Relief appeared in Dutch's eyes as he spoke.

Groans flowed from the managers' mouths yet Danny remained guardedly silent. He watched the burly man. The change in the expression confirmed to Danny it was scripted. He gazed at the terrorist.

You wouldn't last long around here... You can't lie.

Danny wanted to grin, but the fire in his cheeks and nose made him think otherwise.

• • •

June 25, 9:45 a.m.

Tonya stood guard while Bruce Peterson set an explosive charge on the stairwell door. She brushed a strand of black hair from her face and glanced at the bodies sprawled along the Ivory Tower's sixth floor hall. Contorted men and women lay in mounds, having died in mass as they tried to escape. They had waited too long, though, caught up in their shock and curiosity of what was happening. Tonya's bullets had answered their questions.

"There," the former Green Beret remarked, examining his workmanship. "That will stop any would-be heroes from storming in. Did you lock the elevators in place?"

Tonya nodded, not bothering to look at him. "And I put bodies inside with a live grenade under them like you said."

"Good," Peterson replied. "If anyone overrides the controls and takes the elevators down, the first thing they'll do is remove the dead." He grinned and gazed down the hall to the stairwell door leading to the roof. "Keep an eye on that. It's not rigged. If you need to, shoot the backpack hanging on the doorknob." Peterson held a fist up before him and flicked his fingers open, gesturing an explosion.

They walked the hall, checking each office they passed. At the communications equipment room they stopped to watch Richards. The pilot feverishly cut cables and routed wires into his own control box.

"Can we help?" Peterson asked.

Trey Richards motioned them away without breaking stride in his project.

"We'll be back. We're going to check on Zachary." No response came and they left.

Telephones incessantly rang in every office. News of the attack had not yet reached the outside world. Business was still believed to be as usual. Vendors continued to phone in, wanting appointments, hoping to make a sale, unaware of the takeover. The ringing grew louder, then silence fell with the abruptness of an axe striking a stump.

Peterson sighed a hard blast in relief, feeling better at Richards' control of the phone system. Only the disruption of the main computer and bypassing of unit controls remained, and sole mastery of the refinery would be theirs.

Patrolling the halls, examining avenues of approach, Peterson was satisfied with the securement of the floor. Explosives kept the stairwells well protected, elevators were locked out, and they had sufficient hostages. He glanced at his watch, pleased with their precision. Tonya followed him, pausing periodically, searching offices a last time for people hiding under desks. She had found one man on her last check, angering her at having missed him on an earlier sweep.

Zachary heard their approach and leaned out the door. Recognizing them, he unconsciously smoothed his close-cropped, blond hair and straightened his shirt before turning to the hostages cowering in the corner of the makeshift prison room.

Ten men and seven women stared in horror, traumatized by having witnessed co-workers be savagely cut down in a hail of bullets. Smears and erratic lines of makeup stained several women's faces where tears had been wiped away.

From the doorway, Tonya's hazel eyes watched them, mentally selecting six. Several of the younger women moved behind older men, seeking protection from their masculine presence. Two men eased behind the women, though, their gazes downcast, squatting slightly for anonymity. A redhead held her bulging stomach, pressing gently, squinting against the increasing aches of pregnancy.

Tonya walked away, amused by it all. Peterson's gaze followed her until she disappeared into an office with a view of the public street. He turned to Zachary and glanced at the prisoners.

"Any problems?"

Zachary shook his head and looked to the far end of the room. A bloody corpse lay crumpled on the floor. "Not anymore," he remarked wryly.

"We should be hearing from Murdock soon."

Zachary gave a half-nod and leaned against the wall.

• • •

Gently rocking in a high-backed leather chair, Uzi across her lap, Tonya watched the main gate and street below. The view was excellent despite plumes of twisted black smoke rising off of the tires of burning vehicles.

Peterson walked in and leaned on the windowsill, straining to see both ends of the city road in front of the refinery. Cars raced by, accelerating when the Gate House fires came into sight.

"I'm surprised the police haven't arrived by now," he said, half talking to himself. "There's usually an idiot or two that comes barreling in."

"Do you think they will?" Tonya's voice was unruffled. She gently stroked the Uzi in her lap as if enjoying its feel.

Turning his head slightly, he watched smoke curl upward from the gate. Brief glimpses of the dead officers in the street could be seen whenever the swirling smoke cleared.

"Soon," he replied. "If they do come, we'll go up on the roof and take a few of them out. Right now, the police station is probably getting flooded with calls."

Warbling horns, sirens, and whistles devoured the air. Peterson bolted upright and looked about him. Tonya jumped to her feet and followed Peterson to a window on the opposite side of the building. Their heads whipped left and right, attempting to place the source of the alarms. Vehicles sped through the refinery. Few people were seen and only then a flash of clothes as they disappeared into surrounding buildings.

Relief valves across the refinery began to pop from the sudden flood of built up pressures. Their releases roared louder than jets on the takeoff. Windowpanes shook from the impact of forceful concussions. Processing units were dumping their products into burn-off lines for the emergency lock-down. Flare stacks shuddered and streamed black, orange, yellow, and red fireballs high into the sky like spewing volcanoes. With every unit going into a critical shutdown at once, the lines were overloaded. Flares roared, intensifying, equaling the relief valves. The eerie spectacle displayed what one would envision the apocalypse to be.

Touching the window's glass, Peterson felt the penetrating heat of the thrashing flames. As the size of the flames continuously grew, so did the vibrations and warmth upon the glass.

"Someone gave an alarm," he stated angrily in a hissing voice.

Tonya heard him but could not force her attention from the fiery exhibition. A mushrooming cloud of black tinged, orange smoke skyrocketed from a flare stack.

"I'm glad we won't be around when this place blows," she commented nervously.

Peterson's tense gaze followed the massive rising cloud.

"Hell, I'm not too thrilled about being here now."

• • •

June 25, 9:55 a.m.

Angered by the squalling alarms, Murdock hurried through the halls to A-5's computerized control room. The windowless building was a reinforced concrete fortress, theoretically able to withstand the devastating forces of explosions yet the dulled din of refinery horns easily penetrated its cinder block walls. Internally partitioned with glass doors and half-glass walls, the clamor lessened as the mercenary leader entered the heart of the building.

Murdock glanced at the clock on the wall and lifted the refinery radio's microphone from the desk. About to speak, he paused, smiling inwardly at the horrified expression on the bloody man in the chair beside him. One of the five process operators caught inside the building when the terrorists burst in, he had been selected by Murdock to work the computer board. At first he refused, but Kane Thompson beat him into submission while Doug Jordan held the operator's co-workers at gunpoint and forced them to watch.

"This is A-5, do you copy?" Murdock released the transmit button and waited.

The operator looked at him curiously.

"A-5, I copy loud and clear." Kotter's transmission carried out of the loudspeaker across the control room. Murdock nodded in satisfaction at knowing the Admin building was secured.

Richards' voice came next from the Ivory Tower. "A-5, we copy loud and clear."

A smile crossed Murdock's lips. Total command of the refinery's systems had been achieved in less than thirty minutes, and without losses to his team.

"This is A-5, switch channels." Setting the microphone on the desk, Murdock pulled the radio handset off his belt. "Kotter, are you there?"

The radio crackled and the replying voice was barely understandable. Raising his head, Murdock glanced about the room. The building's construction hampered reception. "Richards, how do you receive?"

"You're breaking up but I can hear you," answered the man from the Ivory Tower's sixth floor.

A computer screen next to Murdock changed colors, flashing white lettered warnings across a sea of red. "Stand by," he said into the handset. Turning, he yelled to Jordan. "Call Kane."

Within moments, the retired intelligence officer arrived.

"Monitor this computer. I don't want anything to blow until we're ready," commanded Murdock.

The process operator swiped blood from his eyes in dismay and started to rise.

"I need to close some valves and release line pressures. If I don't—"

Kane shoved the injured man back into his chair and bent low to read the display on the computer screen. He pulled a small book from his pocket and flipped through its pages.

"Cut the charge to K93l then open lines M337 and M339 to dump tank 105," Kane ordered, reading his notes. "Close T774. Leave its contents at level eight."

Surprised by the terrorist's knowledge of the unit, the operator sat stunned, hesitant to move.

Kane's movement came so fluid that the operator never saw the semi-automatic until the muzzle was two inches from his nose.

"You have three seconds to do it or I will kill you and bring someone else in. One…" The mercenary cocked the hammer back, its click loud and distinct. "Two…"

Hands shaking, the operator hastily reached across the desk and pushed buttons on a console panel. Immediately the computer screen changed from red to blue, but retained its warnings. A low rumble commenced. The building trembled as flares vented A-5's built-up pressures of steam and isobutane.

"Swing cameras four and one around to the loading dock," Murdock said, standing with arms crossed over his chest. His ice blue eyes narrowed as he watched the monitors.

Hearing the order, the operator briefly closed his eyes. In the madness of the takeover, he had forgotten about the two tanker trucks ready to discharge hydrofluoric acid. The cameras panned until the trucks came into view. Zooming in, he observed a driver draped over a four-inch hose attached to the tanker. The second truck driver could not be seen. Shaking his head, the young operator found it all too much to believe. A nightmare had become reality. Pushing another button, he scanned the area with the camera, searching for his fellow process operators who had been out working on the unit when the attack came.

A pistol barrel viciously struck the side of his head, knocking him back into the chair.

"No one told you to do anything," Kane snarled, recoiling to strike again.

The operator groaned. His world spun in blurs as he struggled to retain consciousness. Murdock nodded approval of Kane's action. He let his gaze carry about the room.

"Where's Scofield and Briars?"

"Briars is with Nicole and Scofield's guarding prisoners."

The militant leader lightly massaged his forehead and stared at the ground. Eric Scofield and Nathan Briars were Murdock's aces in the hole for the attack. Having entered the refinery earlier under the guise of making a delivery, their radio reconnaissance reports had assured Murdock of a swift strike without interruptions. Letting Scofield watch over hostages wasn't a good idea, though. Fortunately, Nathan had a calming effect on him, but alone, the dishonorably discharged soldier sought revenge at every turn for his military dismissal. Killing the prisoners later wouldn't matter yet for now Murdock needed them alive.

"Have Jordan guard them instead. Tell Scofield to patrol the exterior of the building until I call for him," Murdock ordered.

Kane left immediately.

"Nathan. Nicole. What's your status?" Murdock released the transmit button on his handset and stood listening. Seconds passed without a reply.

A woman's voice answered. "We have the first two charges in place. No resistance—just people running everywhere. We should be finished in ten minutes. Even with the radio ear plugs, we can barely hear you because of the noise out here."

Murdock glanced at his watch, thinking as he listened. He was glad he had bought the throat mikes. They were cutting out most of the background noise in Nicole's transmission.

"Have Nathan set charges under the trucks at the loading dock. Are you clear?"

"We copy."

Murdock rolled a cushioned chair to the control board and took a seat. Laying his *H&K*, MP5, on the armrest, he rubbed his eyes. The short, black automatic weapon tilted and slid into his lap, catching itself by the protruding magazine. He collapsed the stock and let the weapon rest across his left arm. Touching his shirt pocket, he felt for the small remote control box. His gaze focused on the frightened man sitting at the computer console. Crimson streaks trailed down the operator's face from the deep gashes on his cheek and forehead.

"Put all fifteen cameras on scan and watch for anyone trying to enter the unit. If you see someone, tell me. If you see someone and don't tell me, and I see them, then you'll die in that chair. Do you understand?" Murdock's eyes glistened with madness.

The hostage's head moved slightly in confirmation.

Murdock picked up the handset again. "Kotter."

The man quickly acknowledged.

"Phone the media and keep monitoring the police channels."

"That's clear, sir. Everything is ready here. We have complete control of the computer and telephone systems."

When Kotter finished, Murdock checked with his men still roving the refinery in the van. Once assured they had encountered no problems, he ordered radio silence until further notice.

The young operator hostage lowered his head, angling it toward the terrorist leader to see him. Their stares met.

Murdock's malicious smile matched the evil in his eyes.

CHAPTER FIVE

June 25, 10:15 a.m.

The city was unprotected. Surrounding the refinery and blocking its bordering streets had drained all available manpower. When Chief Draeger's nervous voice came across the radio ordering access to Titan Oil be sealed off, the patrolling officers had no knowledge of the attack. The rumbling thunder and billowing smoke clouds rising into the sky made them believe another industrial accident was happening. But Chief Draeger rarely got as excited as he sounded this morning. When he did, his men knew it was going to be a long day.

Patrol units arriving to secure the refinery's perimeter were shocked by the bedlam of hundreds of terrified people climbing fences to escape. The sight of the mass exodus, coupled with the Chief's emergency order, stirred every officers' anxieties. For those closest to the main entrance of the refinery, the view of rising smoke columns and helicopters atop buildings was unsettling. Through binoculars they observed lifeless bodies across the landscape and realized why their Chief had sounded as he did.

The accelerator pedal was shoved to the floor. The blue and white police car couldn't go fast enough to satisfy Dan Draeger. Skidding around corners, weaving through traffic, he cursed everyone and everything that got in his way. As he neared the Titan Oil refinery, several news media vans were arriving and lining the roadway.

"Damn!" He struck the steering wheel with the heel of a hand. "How did those sons of bitches get here so fast?"

Dispatch briefed him within minutes of receiving the industrial emergency channel's distress call, and as he had burst out the door to his car, Titan Oil's warbling horns and rumbling flares provided more than enough confirmation. Acting as swiftly as he did, Draeger still hadn't been able to beat the media to the scene.

Driving past the camera crews and reporters searching for prime angles of the refinery's main gate entrance, Draeger realized two major problems confronted him. He needed to find out what was actually happening, and then try to prevent the press from turning it all into a three-ring circus.

Tires locked, car sliding sideways to a halt, Draeger kicked the door open. He barely had a boot on the ground when dispatch called him on the radio.

"Chief, we need to patch this one through." The communications officer's voice grew tense. "It's them."

The pressurized roar of burning hydrocarbons forced Draeger back into his car to hear.

"Go ahead. I'm ready."

The radio crackled as the linkup was being made. Once complete, a click told him the recorders were active at the police station.

"This is Chief Draeger of the Grainger City Police Department."

"We are the Serpent and the Sword," replied an apathetic male voice. "Listen and do not waste my time talking. Move your men back and allow the reporters through. I will give you two minutes to comply."

"I'm concerned about the media's safety. They could be hurt." Draeger hoped to initiate basic negotiations.

No response came for several seconds.

"Look at the roof of the tallest building." The emotionless voice spoke slowly and deliberately.

Pulling his binoculars from beneath the car's seat, Draeger focused on the rooftop, searching for whatever the terrorist wanted him to see. A helicopter sat unattended with no one in sight. Keying his radio, the Chief of Police kept watch as he talked.

"I see it but—" His voice cracked in abhorrence.

Four men and two women stepped up onto the rooftop's ledge, hands behind backs, struggling to maintain balance. A paramilitary dressed woman, her long black hair blowing in the wind, walked behind the hostages and prodded them with a pistol.

"Wait. Don't harm them. Tell me what you want." Apprehension squeezed Draeger's throat. He tried to remain calm yet every word had to be forced out. The brutality of the terrorists overflowed his mind. In thirty years of police work he had never encountered such an enormously hostile scenario. Gaze sweeping the vast complex, he felt as if he were laying siege to a city with only a handful of men.

"Please, don't harm them…Tell me what your demands are."

"You did not respond properly to our instructions. Instead, you chose to argue. We do not argue, Mr. Draeger, we order." The steel hard voice paused, then spoke again. "Observe the consequences of your action. You have forced us to do this."

"No, wait," Draeger shouted into the microphone. "Wait, please…" He pressed the binoculars to his eyes again.

The dark-haired woman atop the roof paused as if listening to instructions on her radio.

Draeger froze at seeing her grin and back from sight. He silently prayed she had not received the execution order, but from left to right the bodies of the hostages began to spasm. A flared crimson spray burst from their stomachs. The first man spiraled off the roof. The second bowed and fell forward as his legs went limp. The third man's mouth went agape when his bullet came. The roar of the refinery's flares masked their dying screams.

Oh, Jesus! Dan Draeger sat frozen, helpless in his car, watching as the hostages plummeted off the six-story building. He swung the binoculars back to the ledge. Two women and a man remained, faces scrunched as they wept and awaited their fates. The Chief of Police braced, anticipating their executions. His stomach soured and clenched into a gut-wrenching knot. In the shock of the moment, his trained mind had overlooked a harsh truth. One of the women was pregnant.

The executions halted. Draeger didn't know why. Maybe the terrorist had stopped them. All the Chief knew was that he only had seconds to prevent more deaths. He glanced at his car's radio microphone, confident the terrorist was watching him from the distance. Kicking the door open, he jumped out, left arm thrashing the air as he screamed into his radio microphone.

"Move those patrol cars back. Everyone, fall back. Release the reporters—let 'em go. All units, fall back!"

Bruce Peterson watched from inside a sixth floor office as police cars made a mad retreat.

A new blockade formed several hundred yards further down the road. News teams rushed past running officers left afoot. The network vans followed, bouncing hard over curbs until reaching the cleared roadway. Driving to the front of the refinery, they parked in the middle of the wide public street and intersection of Derrick Road. Film crews frantically set up to pan the entire location. Flames danced from the cars burning in the parking lots surrounding the Ivory Tower. Pillars of twisted black smoke rose at every turn, and corpses were strewn across the ground. All was against a backdrop of raging flares, roaring and rumbling with the power of a fleet of jets going airborne. It would all provide more than enough tragedy to consume the networks for months to come.

Draeger grabbed the microphone. He knew his officers had all heard the terrorist and witnessed the hostages' deaths.

"There's your media. Please take those people off the ledge." The Chief of Police choked on the hurt stabbing his heart.

• • •

Inside the A-5 control room, Adam Murdock wryly smiled as he lowered the telephone's receiver and pressed it against his stomach. He keyed his radio and spoke softly, "Peterson."

Static came, but cleared. "Yes, sir."

"How does it look?"

Peterson leaned against the windowpane and scanned the street below. Satisfied with the positioning of the police, he keyed his radio. "All clear, sir." He glanced at the growing pool of media. "Cameras are in position."

On the rooftop, Tonya stared at the backs of the three remaining hostages. She listened for her next order as she aimed at the spine of the trembling pregnant woman.

Murdock's voice came across her radio. "Tonya, do not kill anymore. Take them inside."

She replied in disappointment, but obeyed.

• • •

Lifting the telephone receiver, Murdock suppressed his delight. "Mr. Draeger, do not force us to resume executions. If we do, you won't like what you see. The Serpent and the Sword wants only justice for our Arab brothers-in-arms. We will make our demands known to you within the hour. Until then, you are to do nothing. Do you understand?"

"I understand," the police chief answered softly.

Adam Murdock laid the telephone receiver in its cradle and glanced at his watch. He shook his head lightly and held himself from laughing aloud at his thoughts.

Arab brothers-in-arms. What a crock of shit.

• • •

Draeger sat in the car rubbing his furrowed brow, evaluating his options, wishing he had retired months ago as he originally planned. His men had witnessed the murders and heard him talking to the terrorist. *The terrorists won the first round. What would they want next?*

A young rookie officer stood by the front of a squad car, staring in the direction of the Ivory Tower. Turning in shock, he looked at the chief.

"This is Chief Draeger. All officers are to maintain their positions. Take no further action unless directly ordered by me." A despondent mood flowed over him as he released the radio microphone button. He saw the rookie's eyes close and face lower in frustration of their helplessness.

I know how you feel, the Chief thought. Reaching across to his car phone, Draeger laid the receiver in his lap while he thumbed through a notebook. Finding what he wanted, he exhaled hard and dialed a series of numbers. The ringing on the other end of the line seemed to last forever.

"Federal Bureau of Investigation, may I help you?" The receptionist was cordial yet formal.

The dryness in the chief's throat made him swallow first.

"Ma'am, this is Chief Draeger of the Grainger City Police. Terrorists calling themselves 'the Serpent and the Sword' have attacked the Titan Oil refinery. I'm going to need your help as soon as possible."

"Sir, let me get one of our agents. Please do not hang up."

As he waited, Draeger motioned for a patrolman to approach. "Don't use your departmental radio, they're probably monitoring. Go back to the station and have dispatch telephone the state troopers. Tell them I'm ordering a complete evacuation of the city and we'll need their assistance. Give them twenty minutes and broadcast the evacuation notice across the inner-city frequency so surrounding cities will know what's going on. Once you do, hit the city evacuation sirens. I can't spare any officers so we'll have to see how the citizens manage on their own."

The officer nodded and glanced at the refinery before running to a squad car.

Draeger watched him, mind reeling from an onslaught of confusion. *Who the hell is the Serpent and the Sword?* He was shaking his head when a male voice came on the telephone line.

"Chief? This is Special Agent Hayes. What do we have?"

Draeger's gaze cut to the helicopter sitting atop the six-story building.

I could sure use a miracle about now, he thought. Taking a deep breath the Chief related the morning's events.

• • •

June 25, 10:23 a.m.

"What are you doing?" Tommy McLawchlin's anxiety carried in his voice. He turned to Jim as the security truck eased to a halt between two immense cranes. They were out of sight for the moment.

Thurman sat in silence, squinting against the glare of the sun, staring at the towering refinery units about him. The intensity in his gaze was as if he planned to assault them himself. He gestured for Tommy to be patient.

The Gate House, the Admin building and Ivory Tower, A-5, and Gate Nine from what Charlie had said—all compromised, Jim thought. Evaluating the helicopters and van he had seen, Jim estimated at least thirty terrorists were within the refinery's chain link walls. Working independently as they were, they needed their own radio network, and that, Jim hoped, would prove to his favor.

Trial and error had shown Security that unless a radio system has a repeater to magnify its transmissions and a high tower to work from, the refinery's steel piping and mammoth structures blocked most signals, often garbling the reception. The terrorists might be hampered to some degree.

Jim looked toward A-5 and saw the tops of its vessels. He closed his eyes momentarily to recall its layout. Fifteen surveillance cameras were atop poles around the complex, their lenses capable of zooming in on virtually every part of the unit. Under normal circumstances the cameras allowed process operators at the control boards to examine an acid leak before sending anyone to investigate. The terrorists would surely be using them for a different purpose.

Watching a windsock rise slightly then fall, Jim estimated the wind speed and direction to be ten miles-per-hour out of the south to southeast. The worst possible direction if a HF release occurred.

"A-5," he said softly, turning to Tommy.

"What?" The machinist continued to scan the area for terrorists.

"We've got to take A-5. They already have control of the Admin building's Ops Center and the Ivory Tower's communication room."

Tommy shook his head and looked at his friend. "I love the way you make it all sound so simple." He readjusted his baseball cap. "Why don't we just knock on the door –'Hello inside, may we have our unit back'?" The machinist raised a hand, fingers forming an imaginary pistol. "Shall I use full auto or semi when we go in?"

Thurman smiled. "Simmons is in New York so the only hostages they have in the Admin building are clerks and engineer managers. Hopefully, they won't harm the clerks." He grinned. "Whoever the terrorists are, they've done their homework and know exactly what to do to control this place. They're pros and A-5 is their trump card. Everyone dies if it blows.

Gut instinct tells me they don't intend to set it off until they are ready to leave—or their mission fails. If we take A-5, we might cripple them."

Tommy stared in dismay. "You're serious, aren't you? Two men with one pistol are going to assault a control room against an unknown number of heavily armed terrorists?"

Jim scanned the surrounding area, lost in his thoughts as if he had not heard his friend. The refinery was a miniature city, holding more people within its fences during the day than most Texas towns have population. Employees and contractors were everywhere and there was no way of knowing how many had made it to safety.

It will be a bloodbath, he thought. *We are easy prey for anyone with automatic weapons.*

He lifted his hands off the steering wheel. His palms were slick. Rubbing them dry on his trouser legs, he weakly grinned. "Yep, that's the plan. Don't worry. I'll get a gun for you."

The Security truck lurched forward, tires showering the air with gravel.

Thrust back into his seat, Tommy frowned and massaged his brow.

"Oh, that's good," he mumbled. "For a moment I was afraid you were going to try and find someone to help us."

• • •

The drab brown, one-story Security and Safety building sat in the heart of the refinery, its brick walls cracked from age, partially obscured by a futile attempt to landscape it with trees. Unfortunately, oil sprays and fallout from the chemicals in the refinery air had withered every leaf on their limbs, giving the building an appearance of a dying oasis in a sea of asphalt. Inside, though, the Security Superintendent had assured nothing resembled its pathetic exterior. Polished mahogany executive desks sat on the best carpets with black leather chairs in each office. Custom drapes covered the windows, blocking the sun from shining on the computerized office toys on the desks. The lavish furnishings were thorns in the security officers' sides because expenditures were always refused when they pertained to the department's true needs. Clarence Calder loved to press the thorns deeper into his men whenever the opportunity arose.

The building's interior was a labyrinth. Calder's whims of providing a team of safety and health engineers with larger offices in the building always involved moving walls and redirecting travel. Gleaming brass signs guided the few visitors that ever came. Regardless of the information listed, the superintendent's name always appeared at the top. He wanted all to know they had entered his kingdom.

Thurman parked at the rear of the building and entered with pistol drawn through a side door. He paused at a hall corner to listen, then followed the maze to an unmarked door. The building was deserted as he had hoped.

"My, my," Tommy whispered, eyebrows rising as he looked into each office they passed. "This place is certainly a well-guarded secret." He nodded toward a spacious corner office down the hall. "Who owns that piece of real estate?"

Unlocking the plain door, Jim never bothered to look. "That's a stupid question," he remarked sarcastically.

Tommy grinned and followed Jim into the crowded room. "So that's where Big Daddy Calder sits. If you're lucky, maybe the bastard is dead."

"The refinery couldn't be so lucky. Dick-heads like him are survivors. He's been complained on so many times that the corporation is embarrassed to admit he exists. They didn't fire him when they should have, so now they hide him here—in Security of all places—like they always do when they want to punish someone. Security is nothing more than an insurance write-off for Titan Oil," Jim stopped abruptly and stared at Tommy. He swung a hand, gesturing to the cramped office. "Look at this room. Compare it to the others in the building."

The machinist glanced at the small room and its badly worn furnishings. The paint on the walls had faded and showed marks and stains. A scarred, gray metal desk with a hard-backed, torn cloth chair sat against a wall by the door. Behind it, the file cabinets and storage locker appeared to have survived minor wars, and everything held a salvaged look.

Anger rose within Jim. "This is the sergeants' office...a fucking hole-in-the-wall." He paused and scanned the room. "Calder laughs when we ask to get a fence line camera repaired, but he will buy another thousand dollar chair for his office at the snap of a finger." Disgusted, he shook his head and clenched his teeth. "He better hope that the terrorists get him before Maddox does. I can't stand Calder, but Maddox hates the bastard with a passion."

"Sergeant Maddox? The guy who looks like Friar Tuck in one of those Robin Hood movies?"

Jim handed his pistol to Tommy and gestured for him to watch the hall. He spoke as he strode to a tall, doublewide storage cabinet. "Don't let Friar Tuck fool you. When that Tennessee ridge runner was a cop, he killed three men at a stop-and-rob after they shot him twice."

Silence fell as Jim slid his hand along the back of the cabinet. Finding the magnetic clip, he pulled a key from it. "Calder's one of those people who hates veterans and cops because of the crap we've been through. He's a safety hygienist by profession, and the closest he's been to danger is a paper cut in college. We had heard he screwed something up so the corporation put him in charge of Security a few years ago. That doesn't bother me as much as the way he talks down to us in order to make himself feel important."

Leaning out the door, Tommy looked to both ends of the hall. "Corporate is full of guys like that. If you're not an engineer, you're not in their clique—not smart enough to do anything except manual labor." He heard the cabinet doors rattle and glanced at Jim. "Calder's nothing more than president of the prick club."

Jim stood gazing at radio handsets, wiring, and ammunition boxes on the cabinet's top shelf. Along the next shelf lay new, black, bulletproof tactical vests yet the elongated compartment at the lower half of the cabinet held his greatest interest.

"You won't get any argument there. No, he mouthed off one day about cops and Maddox overheard him. I don't know what all was said, but Maddox told him to pray that none of us were ever killed."

"Sounds like something you would say." Tommy smiled, still scanning the hall.

Wide swathes of sweat painted Jim's light blue uniform shirt. He raked the shelves clean, dumping everything into a gray canvas, paramilitary bag. Radio handsets clunked as they fell atop each other, and boxes of ammunition cascaded into the bag in a steady stream.

Opening the lower compartment, Jim stepped aside and smiled mischievously.

"I told you I'd get you a gun," he said. Four pump shotguns stood in a row with six semiautomatics hanging on hooks around them. Bandoliers draped each of the 12-gauge Remingtons, and loaded magazines sat above the Berettas.

Tommy looked back at Jim. The sight of the armament took him by surprise.

"Wait a minute." He shook his head. "Calder's against y'all having guns... He bought all of this?"

A devilish glint shined in Jim's eyes.

"A little maneuvering on our part four months ago when Calder took a long vacation. Janie pushed the paperwork through by listing them as office equipment and only using their serial numbers." Jim smiled. "Calder's too arrogant to realize you can screw the troops, but you never piss off your secretary."

Opening another bag, Jim laid the weapons inside. He glanced at Tommy, enjoying the moment.

"It was her idea for us to buy everything. She even wanted us to have these so we would look good." Jim held a black baseball cap into the air. The Beretta trident arrow symbol was embroidered in red above the brim. "Want one?"

The machinist tipped his *Astros* baseball cap. "I'll stick with mine, thank you, but I will take a shotgun and pistol."

"Here, you'll need these too." Jim passed a tactical vest and radio handset to Tommy along with the weapons and ammunition. He stood and glanced at his uniform. The polished badge reflected the overhead lights. Taking a firm grip, Jim tore his shirt off and used it to wipe the sweat from his face and chest.

"No need to be a bigger target than I already am." He lowered his hands to find Tommy staring at the patchwork of horrendous scars across his hard-muscled chest and rippled abdomen.

Tommy shook his head compassionately, face mirroring the pain in his heart. "I knew you were shot, but…" The worst scar ran vertically from mid-chest to navel then horizontally to the left in a continuous jagged line.

No reply came. A dark mood enveloped Jim as he eased into an extra-large tactical vest and filled its pockets with ammunition. Settling the black cap onto his head, he took his pistol from Tommy, holstered it, and slung a shotgun over his shoulder. Never balking at the weight of the equipment bags, he bent and lifted them with one hand. Eyes consumed with cold rage, he looked at Tommy.

"The scar is courtesy of an NVA grenade. They tried their best to kill me. Let's see if these bastards can."

Watching his friend, Tommy observed the fierce warrior he always knew existed beneath the quiet giant's facade of control. The weight of the bags would have pulled Tommy over, but Jim's massive arms displayed no hint of being burdened. An expansive chest of rock-hard muscles kept the vest from fully closing, giving clear sight to the small gold cross hanging from his neck. Pockets laden with 9mm magazines, shotgun bandoliers crisscrossing his chest, Jim Thurman appeared more in his natural element now than in a Titan Oil Security uniform.

"I'm glad you're not after my ass," the machinist said as he walked from the sergeant's office. In the hall he paused to tighten the strap over the pistol in his vest's holster.

Jim started out the door then froze.

Tommy McLawchlin stood with shotgun braced against his waist, staring at Calder's corner office. He nodded in its direction.

The tension in the air hung thick and suffocating for what seemed like endless seconds as the two men strained to listen. Outside the building, the refinery flares still roared, vibrating the office windows and walls. A constant dull rumble could be heard, but wood bumped wood, distinctly telegraphing a *thunk* from the security superintendent's office.

Tommy slid along the wall, edging closer to Calder's open door, shotgun leveled and ready.

Equipment bags in one hand, 9mm in the other, Jim took the opposite wall and eased toward the posh office. They drew to a halt, gazes sweeping the room's interior, waiting for the odd noise again.

Calder's high-backed leather chair moved, faintly bumping the rich mahogany desk. Tommy stood at the door, shotgun trained on the desk's front panel. He nodded and Jim entered, careful not to interfere with Tommy's field of fire.

"Live or die," Jim declared, finger steadily drawing slack from the Beretta's trigger. He held aim on the desk's side panel. "Show me some hands."

A trembling left hand came out from beneath the desk, followed by a right.

"Jim?" The voice, weak and breaking, asked, "Is that you?"

"Hershel? Get out of there."

The hands lowered and pushed the chair away. Groaning from the strain of being curled into a tight ball for so long, Herschel Cannish gradually appeared. The lanky computer technician scraped his back on the desk drawer as he rose to his feet. He grimaced and stretched, but grew pale when he saw Jim's pistol and Tommy's shotgun.

"Calder...Calder wanted me to check his computer while he was gone this morning." Herschel's hand shook as he gestured out the window. "The flares started blowing, then everyone was running and yelling about dead people at the Gate House—so I hid. When I heard voices down the hall, I didn't know it was you. What's happening, Jim?"

Gold-rimmed glasses, an inch or so shorter than Jim in height, Herschel was so slender that Jim often kidded him about having to run around in the shower to get wet. Jim liked the baby-faced, twenty-three year old. He knew what Herschel lacked in courage, he made up for with his computer wizardry. Jim's first impulse was to get Herschel to safety, but an idea flashed through his head. He knelt and dug through the equipment bags.

"I don't like that look in your eyes," Tommy said warily from the door. "Thurman, are you listening to me?"

"You want help, don't you?" Jim glanced at the machinist. "After we take A-5, he can work the computers."

"No, Jimbo, you don't understand. We need combat vets, not computer geeks." Tommy's plea fell on deaf ears.

Herschel braced and spun toward Tommy. "Who's a geek?"

"Easy, tiger. He didn't mean anything by it. Here, put this on." Jim helped him into a tactical vest and zipped it closed. The vest comically engulfed Herschel. He shoved a pistol into the vest's sewn-in holster, draped bandoliers over Herschel's neck, and set a black baseball cap on his head. Strapping a radio handset into a pocket, Jim laid a pump shotgun across the technician's arms and stepped back.

The weight made Herschel weave. Jim warmly smiled, but drew solemn. It evoked the memory of a gangly young boy long ago proudly wearing his father's oversized uniform shirt and dragging a police baton behind him. The memory hurt.

"A lot of our friends are dead, Herschel. I need your help." Jim paused, glanced at Tommy and slowly let his gaze return to the baby-faced technician. He spoke softly yet deliberately. "Terrorists attacked the refinery. Right now, they're in A-5. We may be the only hope this city has of staying alive."

Herschel's mouth formed an oval cavern as his eyes steadily widened. The impact of Jim's words drained the strength from his arms and the weight of the shotgun became unbearable.

• • •

"This thing is hot," Martin Shanks stated, pulling the ski mask from his head. He sat in the cargo area of the van near its open door. Rubbing his craggy face and scratching his shaved head, he enjoyed the freedom from the mask.

Sefcik nodded and removed his own as he drove along the refinery streets. Tom Bowden sat in the passenger seat. He nodded to Mike Galloway sitting in the back beside Shanks. They gladly followed suit.

"How much longer?" Shanks reloaded a CAR-16 with a fresh thirty-round magazine and passed it to Galloway at the door. Beside him on the floorboard of the van lay a mound of empty magazines. He glanced out the open, sliding side door at the myriad of pipelines and odd-shaped vessels they passed.

"Fifteen minutes, then we double back and let Galloway do his bit." Bowden turned in his passenger seat and motioned to the athletically built explosives expert taking aim out the door.

Shanks grunted in reply.

"There's one." Sefcik accelerated the panel van. Fifty yards ahead, a wide-shouldered, brawny contractor stepped from a truck and started trotting down the narrow refinery street.

"Truck problems." Sefcik's gaunt face illuminated as he looked at Bowden. "Ten bucks says he'll try to jump in like the last one."

"Naw, he won't."

"Come on…we're getting close to him. Ten bucks?"

Torn Bowden frowned. "All right."

"Mike, you ready?" Sefcik grinned as he glanced in his rear view mirror at the terrorist by the door.

Galloway slid back and raised a thumb into the air. The muzzle of his CAR-16 held aim on the center of the wide, open doorway.

The distance between the van and the fleeing man closed quickly. Sefcik honked the horn and waved, but the mountainous contractor never slowed his loping pace nor looked back.

Bowden laughed and pointed. "Look at that old-timer run. Hell, he'll have a heart-attack before we get to him."

Refusing to lose the bet, Sefcik sped up. The van almost overshot the stout-built contractor when he stopped abruptly and turned to face the terrorists. Vince Sefcik hit the brakes and slid to a halt beside the hard-breathing man.

Hard-hat cocked at a salty angle, sweat streaming from his temples, barrel-chest rising and falling in labored rhythm, the brawny contractor threw his glasses aside and swiped his time-worn face with a dirty handkerchief. One cheek bulged and a sliver of tobacco juice seeped from a corner of his mouth.

Muzzle less than two feet from the man's chest, Galloway held his fire, caught up by the contractor's fearless gaze.

Charlie Martin stood his ground, coldly grinned and blasted Galloway's eyes with a thick stream of tobacco juice. His paw-like hands tore the CAR-16 from the terrorist's grip.

"This is how we did it on Iwo!" Within the blink of an eye, Charlie spun the bush gun in his hands and drove its butt into Galloway's chest. He charged through the van's side door at Martin Shanks.

Three deafening, fiery blasts came as one. Bowden leaped toward Sefcik to avoid being hit shot. Blood splattered the interior of the van and the old bull's brave charge ceased.

The craggy-faced terrorist released the trigger of his drum-fed shotgun and lowered the short-barreled weapon to his lap. A partial smile formed as Shanks admired the devastation his automatic shotgun had dealt so swiftly.

With chunks of flesh torn from his chest and his body pierced with needle-like nails, Charlie Martin was pushed from the van and left to lie on the street.

Shanks opened a green canvas bag by his boots and set the short, but powerful weapon inside.

Coughing and holding his chest, Galloway gradually sat upright and wiped his eyes.

"Shit, it burns." Galloway rubbed them harder. "That motherfuc—"

Angered by the outcome of his intended game, Sefcik shoved Bowden off of him and put the van in gear. "What the hell did you shoot him with?"

Bowden looked out the passenger window at the butchered body as they drove away.

"Flechettes," Shanks replied, holding one of the special close-quarter combat shotgun shells up for him to see. "They're packed with little nails."

"My eyes are burning," Galloway cried out.

"You idiot. If you had shot the bastard, your eyes wouldn't be burning now." Sefcik began to worry about Murdock discovering their antics. He turned the van onto another refinery street. A one-story building surrounded by withered trees came into view. Sefcik stomped the accelerator and motioned to the building ahead.

"Hold on, we'll go in there and let you wash your eyes. Murdock wants us to set charges so we might as well start there."

• • •

The gray panel van slowly came around the building and drew to a halt. Vince Sefcik slid from the driver's seat, gaze sweeping the vehicles in the parking lot as he cleared the door. He adjusted the sling of his *Heckler* and *Koch* 9mm submachine gun so the weapon hung level and ready from his shoulder. Finger loosely beside the trigger, he pointed to a well polished blue truck bedecked with antennas. It sat unattended in the drive lane.

Crouched, Bowden gripped his CAR-16 tighter and moved between several vehicles until reaching the truck. At the passenger door he swiftly rose to full height and shoved the barrel through the window. Seeing no one, he walked forward and laid a hand on the hood. It was still hot. He looked at Sefcik and gestured to the building.

Shanks grabbed a backpack and helped Galloway out of the van. Wiping sweat from his brow, Bowden climbed the steps leading into the building and waited for the others.

"That's one of their Security trucks. Someone might be inside," Sefcik whispered, glancing across the parking lot a last time. He returned his attention to the men. "Shanks, get his eyes washed out, then find the mechanical room and set the charges on a gas line. Bowden and I will search the building."

The terrorists nodded.

Sefcik paused before he entered the building. "Shanks."

"What?"

"Don't let any old men hurt Galloway again," Sefcik said.

A crooked smile broke across Shank's pockmarked face, but Galloway waved his hand in an obscene gesture to Sefcik.

• • •

"You can count on me, Jim," Herschel said timidly, garnering courage. When he turned to glare at Tommy, the Remington shotgun slid further down his arms, muzzle halting within inches of Jim's stomach.

Jim immediately clamped a hand around the barrel and shoved it away. He exhaled a hard blast and glanced at Tommy. The machinist shook his head and turned to the hall.

"It's loaded, Herschel. Be careful where you point it," Jim said wearily, releasing his hold.

Nodding, the skinny technician looked at Tommy and copied the way he cradled the shotgun across one arm. The weight felt better.

Tommy lightly snapped his fingers and maintained vigil on the long hall. He raised his shotgun as he knelt, aiming at a far corner.

In fluid movement, Jim grabbed the equipment bags and pulled Herschel away from the door. Setting the bags on Calder's mahogany desk, he motioned the technician to stay with them then rushed to Tommy's side.

The machinist kept watching the hall, sensing danger.

Jim tapped him on the shoulder and gestured to move into the office. He reached to close the door as Tommy eased past him and observed movement at the end of the hall.

A wiry, paramilitary dressed man spun around the far corner, automatic weapon rising in his hands. Fire flashed from its barrel. Spent casings flew through the air in a steady stream, striking the wall by the shooter. The submachine gun bombarded the hall with a staccato of gunfire.

Adrenaline gorging his body, Jim slammed the thick wooden door shut. The wall shook from its impact. He locked it as bullets riddled the exterior. For the first time, Jim was glad Calder had bought the exotic hardwood, solid-core door. He spun to Tommy. "One way out!"

Tommy snapped a nod and wheeled toward the wide windows.

"Get down!" he yelled, shouldering his shotgun.

Herschel dropped to the floor. The barrel of Tommy's shotgun barely missed his head as it swept through the air.

The first blast took out a large, jagged section of the west window. The next shot shattered it in an irregular pattern, but the enormous window required more to clear an escape route. Tommy continued to fire.

"Close the bags," Jim ordered, throwing them at Herschel. Their weight smashed the technician into the carpet. He recovered, heart savagely pounding against his chest.

The mahogany desk was beautifully crafted, wide and sprawling to provide its owner with the commanding appearance of holding a king's power. Sunlight magnified its rich, polished surface, and the contrast of white papers atop the dark wood only enhanced its grain. Solidly built, five deliverymen had struggled to carry the desk into the office. With file drawers full and a computer sitting atop one side, its weight was now far heavier. But Jim never hesitated.

Veins protruding from the side of his neck like thick chords, muscles rippling as his arms fought the weight, a guttural growl flowed from Jim as he lifted one side of the desk. A crystal lamp crashed to the floor. Calder's computer and monitor slid off the desk's scrolled edge and smashed into each other. The streamline, deco-telephone dinged loudly when it fell in an avalanche of papers.

When the desk crashed onto its front panel, Jim moved to one end and pushed. His boots dug deep into the carpet as he strained against the wooden mountain. At first the desk wouldn't budge, then it gradually began to slide. Herschel clutched the bags, stunned by the thundering shot-gun blasts and astonished at Jim plowing across the room.

With a gut-wrenching scream Jim slid the desk against the door as bullets splintered the exterior. Breathing deeply, Jim wheeled and grabbed Calder's high-backed chair.

"Move!" he ordered, but Herschel had already given the madman wide berth.

The black leather chair flew through the air, shattering a window. Shards of glass hailed the adjoining street. Jim tore the shotgun from his shoulder and used its barrel to smash the knife-like pieces along the window's ledge.

Tommy never slowed. He jerked the equipment bags from Herschel, threw them out the west window and climbed onto a two-drawer cabinet.

"Let's go!" he yelled, waving to Herschel.

The young computer tech stood frozen, confused by the swift destruction of the office and the automatic gunfire chewing the solid-core door. Jim rushed at Herschel and took hold of his vest. One moment the technician stood in the office, the next he was being catapulted through a window.

The shooting stopped. A muffled voice carried from the hall. "Clear the building! It's going to—" The voice faded and silence returned.

Tommy stood atop the cabinet. He looked at Jim in confusion. The realization of what was about to happen struck them.

"It's going to blow!" they yelled simultaneously.

Tommy spun and dove from the office.

Shotgun in one hand, Jim raced to the large window. He jumped onto a table and used it like a springboard to safety. Sunlight bathed Jim as he flew through the window.

The roof erupted in a deafening roar and the brick building trembled violently. Every window instantly exploded, spewing clouds of smoke, lashing streaks of yellowish orange flames and burning debris from the shattered openings.

As if shot from a cannon, the force of the gas line explosion propelled Jim far out into the street. He lay on the asphalt, his world reeling from the concussion of the blast. Hands pulled at his tactical vest, then more joined to drag him away.

The hands. Horror filled his mind. *No, God, not the hands.*

Day became night to him…

CHAPTER SIX

The hatred in the voices of the North Vietnamese soldiers carried through the night, weighing heavy in the stifling air. Terror blanketed Jim with thoughts of the suffering they were so capable of inflicting. Capture seemed inevitable. They were as relentless as a pack of starving wolves on the trail of a dying animal.

Blood trickled down his leg. The makeshift tourniquet had loosened again. Spasms of pain struck his body again, leaving him breathless and weak.

Above the dense, triple-canopy jungle, night turned into day as flares shot into a moonless sky. The enemy waited, listening, and watching, but all below the trees remained shrouded in black.

Machine-gun fire raked the jungle. Their tactics were changing. They wanted a quick end to a long search. He knew they would not leave until his head set atop a pole.

Irate shouts jolted him. Vines shook and branches rustled. Someone was moving toward him. From fear to hate; paralyzing tension to the suppleness of a leopard ready to pounce on its prey, he readied himself for the kill. He couldn't evade them. The Marine Force Recon team was long overdue and all hope of escape was gone.

Concentrating solely on the approaching footfall, Jim shut the world from his mind. His knuckles turned white as fingers tightened about the grip of his *Kabar* knife. An excited voice yelled from faraway, halting the footsteps. Anxiety flooded the hunted man, then the dull *whop* of helicopter blades cutting the black night filled his ears.

Listening to the helicopters drop fast into the prearranged landing zone, Jim let out the deep breath he had been holding. *They're here. Another minute would have been too late.* His weary eyes closed in thanks, then flared. *Recon will walk into an ambush.*

The whine of the turbines grew louder, blocking the noise of NVA soldiers running through the jungle growth. A North Vietnamese Army Regular squatted within inches of Jim, almost stepping on his hand. The extraction team was on the ground. He could not wait.

The razor sharp *Kabar* struck with lightning speed, driving deep into flesh. Reflex made the stabbed man squeeze his rifle. A burst of gunfire erupted from the *Kalashnikov*. Jim viciously twisted the knife and jerked the rifle free. The soldier's legs went limp. One last convulsive shudder and the soldier went down, the steel blade buried in his ribs.

Jim threw his head back, mouth agape. He struggled to stand and tried to fill his lungs but the suffocating humidity fought him.

The end of the chase had come. Mind blanking as cold rage coursed his veins, a sense of being dead yet alive, swept through him. He squeezed the AK-47's trigger and rocked from the recoil of automatic-fire. An animalistic instinct of self-preservation took control as he fired through the jungle foliage at the NVA. Shouts of alarm, intermixed with obscenities, poured from his mouth like froth from a rabid dog. Insanity dominated Jim Thurman's world.

Brilliant flashes of light blinded him. The earth shuddered and the night exploded. Bullets sang their lethal song, cutting the brush about him. His shoulder took a brutal smash, almost knocking him off his feet. American and Vietnamese voices screamed, piercing the chaos while machine-gun fire created a deafening blast in his ears.

The silhouette of a running soldier appeared against the backdrop of a fiery explosion. Bleeding, Jim turned and pulled the trigger of the AK-47. Empty. Without hesitation he grabbed the rifle by its hot barrel and swung. The rifle stock smashed into the soldier's face, shattering the skull with a resonant crack.

Arms shaking from the impact, Jim opened his hands and let the rifle fall. He stumbled over the dead man and started for the choppers, dragging his leg as he hobbled, teeth clenched against his agony. A grenade bounced and rolled to a halt yards away. Blinding light flashed as the ground erupted. Shrapnel unmercifully ripped his stomach, and the concussion flung him through the air like a rag doll in a tornado. Everything went black.

Jim's eyes refused to open but he could hear frantic screams. Hands held him in vice-like grips, pulling, dragging, and half carrying him through the jungle's growth. The monstrous whine of turbines meshed with the rhythmic clatter of machine-gun fire, consuming his mind with terror. Thrown onto a steel bed, he felt hands press against his stomach. Turbines screamed their eerie cries like a wounded mountain lion, and his body jostled.

The shaking slowed and the turbines faded. Again he felt himself being carried and tried to look, but his eyes would not open. Voices filled with urgency shouted at one another. Moans surrounded him, making no conceivable sense.

A radiant light, blinding even through closed eyes, bathed his body, then serenity flowed through him and all noise drifted to an uncanny quiet. He didn't understand why the anguish of his wounds was gone.

Squinting against the light's splendor, he opened his eyes and unexpectedly, felt compelled to move toward it. The warm, peaceful sensation the light emitted and the tranquility rapidly consuming him became breathtaking.

A gentle voice told Jim to look back and decide if he wanted to return or continue into the light. Turning, he observed himself lying lifeless on a hospital-ship gurney, unrecognizable from blood and dirt caked over his face. A doctor and nurse gazed at the massive wound of his brutally torn stomach. He heard the pronouncement of his death and watched the doctor grimace. Blood soaked bandages were laid back across the mutilated stomach and the doctor started to leave.

"I'm not dead," he cried out, but no one heard him. Confusion hammered him yet he knew he wanted to live. He felt movement, and the return began.

Life became an hourglass with the last precious grain of sand about to fall. Jim realized he must get the doctor's attention before all was lost. Trying to talk, his parched throat refused to make the slightest groan. One eye partially opened. His fingers reached out and wrapped themselves in the cloth of the doctor's shirt. His grip tightened. He had to hold on.

The doctor yelled and people rushed to the gurney. Hands dug deep into his stomach, making him scream a tormented cry of suffering into the air. The hands came at him again, again, and again.

Jim's head whipped in agony. His gaze fell on the cloaked, skeletal figure that stood beside him, relishing the misery. Skull craned back, its howl of gratification blended with Jim's dying screams...

• • •

"No—No...God, make them stop!"

"Jim, wake up. It's all right, Jim. You're all right."

The voice sounded familiar yet out of synchronization with Jim's oblivion. Hands held his tactical vest and jostled him lightly.

Squinting against the daylight, he shook the cruel fog from his head and looked at the men leaning over him. A weak groan escaped his lips and upon touching his chest, he found his body still intact. Breathing in hard pants he grabbed his gold cross necklace. The hands holding onto his vest released their grip.

Tommy stepped away. Seeing Jim alert, he sighed in relief, understanding too well the horrid journey his friend had just traveled.

"Did he have a nightmare?" Herschel anxiously asked.

"No, kid," the machinist replied softly. "He was walking through Hell again." Without a further word, he helped Jim stand and regain his balance. He glanced at Herschel.

"Find us some transportation, kid. Anything with keys."

"Steal one?"

Jim lifted his head, feeling stronger, and gently nodded in reply to Herschel's innocence.

"Somebody shoot me in the foot so I can go home," Tommy groaned. He watched Herschel trot away, bandoliers and oversized vest bouncing wildly on the technician's skinny frame. The shotgun appeared as big as the frail young man.

Jim raised his black baseball cap and wiped dirt from his face. Settling the cap on his head, he solemnly looked at Tommy. "Thanks."

The machinist held Jim's arm to steady him as they walked. He didn't look at Jim.

"I don't know what you're talking about, brother."

• • •

June 25, 10:30 a.m.

Alex stared out the window and let the telephone fall from her hands. It was as dead as the men she could see in the street outside her construction trailer in Contract City. Her gaze carried to the four jagged bullet holes stretched diagonally across the aluminum door. The bullets had passed within inches of her.

She pulled a cellular phone from her purse and tried twice to enter numbers. Anxiety flooded her. Her hands trembled. The phone bleeped from too many buttons being depressed at the same time. Breathing deep to calm, she steadied herself enough to complete the call.

One ring was heard, and then a second and third.

"Where are you, Ben?" she asked aloud. An office answering machine accepted the call and began its message.

Alex's fingernails drummed the desk as anger and apprehension swirled like a maelstrom within her. Patience worn thin, she waited for the final tone.

"Ben, this is Alex. Murdock did it. His men are driving through here killing anything that moves. I'll contact you when I make it to safety."

At the door, distracted by the sight of the bullet holes, she mindlessly turned the cellular phone off. She slid it into the rear pocket of her denims, and removed her keys and wallet from her purse. *Need to travel light*, she thought, casting the purse aside. She stood, collecting her wits, focusing on escape and evasion.

Brushing strands of shoulder length dark hair from her light blue eyes, Alex eased the door the door open and waited. No gunfire was heard. Bent low, hoping to make the least possible target, Alex raced from the office trailer. The roar of refinery flares pelted her ears and the stench of burning hydrocarbons stung her nostrils. Twisted clouds of black, gray, and white smoke passed overhead in clumps, blotting the sun at times and casting wide shadows.

She bit her lip and glanced to both ends of the street. Lifeless bodies were sprawled the entire length of the contractors' compound. The terrorists had traveled westward on their killing spree. Alex turned eastward and ran, her lithe body moving with the agility of a frightened deer.

• • •

Langley, Virginia

Ben Dawson walked out of the elevator and into a mad flurry in the lobby. Men and women rushed past him, anxious to return to their respective offices. He caught wisps of conversations and realized the news of the attack on the Texas refinery was spreading. Within hours orders would be flying and agency resources committed to the incident. He unconsciously touched the pager on his belt.

I only need a few minutes, he thought, hoping his division head had not heard the news. *But how could he have missed it?* Ben asked himself. *Every major network interrupted their broadcasts to splash the tragedy across the television. An emergency action recall of everyone was inevitable.*

Pace quickening, he broke through the main doors and quick-stepped across the parking lot. By the time he reached his car, he was at a light trot. He fumbled his keys and almost dropped them twice before managing to open the door. As he sat in the driver's seat, punching buttons into the receiver of the floorboard mounted phone, he grew angry at himself for having allowed Alex to talk him into letting her go to Texas alone. He had not liked the idea then, and more so now.

Completing the call, he sat impatiently listening to the monotonous rings.

"Where are you, Alex?" he grumbled, gripping the steering wheel to steady his nerves.

At six rings, a cellular phone company recording told him the party he was calling was temporarily unavailable. He depressed a button, clearing the call for another. A protracted sigh broke from his lips as he sought the courage to dial.

"I hoped I'd never have to do this," he said aloud.

The first ring made his stomach rise into his throat. Upon the second, he felt his stomach fall and gradually churn. When the ringing stopped and an authoritative voice answered, Ben grew nauseous.

"McCall."

"Sir, this is Ben." His fingers dug furrows through his blond hair. "Something has occurred that we need to talk about."

"What's the matter? Is Alex all right?" The anxiety in Jeff McCall's voice rose.

"I don't know, sir. That's why I'm calling."

"What do you mean you don't know?"

"Have you heard any newscasts?"

"Yes, I'm watching—" Silence came. "No, Ben, don't tell me Alex is involved with that mess in Texas."

"Sir, I'm still at work and can't say much. She was due to leave there this morning, but now I don't have contact with her. It's not like her to break communication. She knows better."

McCall's tone transformed from a worried father to the methodical operational control director he was known for being.

"If she's there on assignment, where's her backup? Is there a problem with extraction?"

Ben's next words came hard. He swallowed to get moisture in his cotton dry mouth. A backup team was standard operational procedure on high-risk missions; people ready at the snap of a finger to intercede and eject an agent from danger.

"That's the problem, sir. She doesn't have a team. I'm hoping she'll call you if she can't get through to me."

The quiet on the line disturbed Ben. He anticipated a fiery tirade, but none came.

"This wasn't authorized, was it?"

"No, sir," Ben replied.

"The last time we talked, she hinted at a cover-up." Jeff McCall was exceptionally calm and controlled under the circumstances. "Does the name Murdock fit into this?"

Ben's pause answered McCall's question.

"I'm leaving now, sir. I should be at a landline in less than ten minutes. Let me call you back."

"Meter's running, Ben." McCall's voice grew calloused. "Ten minutes tops, then my phone better ring."

Ben listened to the dial tone then set the car telephone receiver in its holder. Turning the ignition key, he glanced at his watch. The nearest store with a pay phone was miles away, and nine minutes remained.

• • •

June 25, 10:45 a.m.

Jim skirted the main portion of the twenty-four hundred acre complex and took a longer route along the rear fence to avoid detection. He hoped the terrorists were concentrating on the processing units at the front of the refinery and didn't care for the materials yards and storage buildings along this path.

The speedometer swiftly fell and rose as the Safety and Health truck slid around corners and hit long stretches of road. Herschel's eyes flared wide in time with the rising speedometer needle.

"Hey, kid. You did pretty good on your first auto theft." Tommy patted the dashboard and glanced at the technician sitting between him and Thurman. He frowned and cautiously moved Herschel's shotgun barrel away from him so it pointed toward the windshield.

No reply came.

"Yep, Calder only buys the best for other people," Jim remarked begrudgingly. "We baby ours until the wheels fall off, but the safety engineers get a new one every year."

Herschel's nod came in jerky motions. His gaze never left the speedometer. He choked when Jim cut across a gravel lot and steered toward a six-foot high, chain link fence.

"Jim…Jim…What are you planning to do?" the technician asked.

Tommy squarely braced his feet and tightened his handholds. There was no need to question Jim's intentions. He saw the employee parking lot ahead and knew in less than thirty seconds they would be in it.

"Lay that shotgun under your legs." Jim nodded toward the floorboard. When Herschel did as instructed, the security officer glanced at him. "Sit back and hold on."

Jim pressed the accelerator to the floorboard.

The young man's face turned pale as milk. His mouth went agape.

"Oh, shiiiiiiiiiiitttttttt!!" he yelled.

Fifteen feet before the fence, the truck struck a well-packed short mound of dirt. The incline threw the front-end of the truck upward and the racing speed shot it airborne. As the vehicle descended, the front wheels landed atop the fence, crushing it beneath the truck. The landing brutally jolted the three men in the cab, knocking them into each other.

Jim held onto the steering wheel. It flexed and the thought of it snapping free flashed through his mind. But there wasn't time to worry. All he could do was hope for the best.

The truck bounced twice, a tire exploded, and Jim fought for control. They careened across the lot and into a row of employees' vehicles before grinding to a halt.

Jim turned the engine off. No one moved. Each man sat staring out the windshield.

Tommy was the first to speak.

"Kid, I think we're going to need transportation again."

• • •

Mike Galloway knelt at the base of the towering vessel and taped the last of his explosive charges beneath a twelve-inch steel feed line. He activated its remote control and watched a green light blink.

"Sure wish I could be around to see this mother blow," he said, tilting his head back to admire the mammoth structure.

"You timed it pretty damned close in that building. We barely made it out. I don't want to be anywhere near this one when it goes off." Sefcik motioned to the unlit red bulb on the explosives and let his gaze glide across the congested catalyst-cracking unit.

"Let's go. If Murdock accidentally hits his button, you might get your wish," Galloway remarked.

They turned and started toward the van. The drawling blare of Grainger City's evacuation horns made them halt. Galloway looked northward, not knowing what he expected to see. Beside him, Sefcik stood tense, scanning the horizon. His gaunt features hardened as his hand rose, pointing to a fast approaching black helicopter. He shaded his eyes and tried to identify the markings on its side.

Martin Shanks raced from the van with binoculars and searched the sky.

"It says 'Eye Witness News' on the sides," he stated, lowering the field glasses. "Think it's legit?"

"Could be, but I'm not taking the chance." Sefcik looked to the van, tapped his shoulder and gestured skyward. The man in the vehicle waved acknowledgment and disappeared.

Sefcik keyed his radio handset. "Murdock, we have a black bird heading our way at low altitude, closing fast, distance less than four hundred yards. Lettering indicates a news chopper but unable to confirm further at this time. Standing by for your orders."

A long pause followed. Believing the transmission had gone unheard, Sefcik readied to call again when an iron-hard voice came from his radio.

"Put it on the ground and advise me."

"Clear, sir. Standby." Sefcik lowered his radio and glanced at the man walking from the van. When Bowden drew near, he motioned to the chopper. "Take it out."

Tom Bowden lifted the five-foot long guided missile system and settled its thirty-five pounds comfortably onto his shoulder. Although its ceiling range was ten thousand feet, the Stinger performed best on low-altitude jets and helicopters. The guidance system employed a 'fire-and-forget' passive infrared seeker, making it difficult to miss a target.

"Fire in the hole," Bowden said, acquiring the black helicopter in his sight ring.

The men near him were already moving clear.

The missile streaked through the air at supersonic speed, never wavering as it sought its prey. Bowden had barely lowered the launch tube when the missile struck. Warhead loaded with high explosives and fused for self-destruction upon impact, the helicopter exploded into a fiery orange and red ball, raining metal and flesh on the neighborhoods below.

Sefcik walked to Bowden and clapped him approvingly on the shoulder. He raised his radio and keyed it.

"Done, sir. No secondary explosions so it probably was a news chopper."

"Very well. Good work, Vince. Any other problems?" came the transmission.

"No, sir. Four charges are in place. We used the fifth to take out their security headquarters building. We're ready to move out."

"Excellent. Report to Dutch as planned."

Using silent hand signals, Sefcik ordered his teammates from the catalyst-cracking unit. They walked to the van, glancing back at the smoke thinning out into a long streak across the sky.

• • •

Dan Draeger was lighting a cigarette when he spotted the news media helicopter. "Those stupid sons of bitches," he exclaimed, angrily throwing his cigarette across the hood of his car. He spun and reached inside for his microphone. The explosion made him freeze. He didn't want to look. He knew what had happened. A bitter taste filled his mouth. He closed his eyes, unable to think for several seconds.

The car phone rang, but Draeger could only stare at it.

His stomach stiffened, instinctively warning him against answering the call. Forcing himself to move, he eased into the driver's seat and slowly lifted the receiver.

"Mr. Draeger, why do you insist on wasting lives? Did you assume we were not prepared for aerial assaults?"

The Chief of Police recognized the cold voice. His mind exploded with rage and a bloodlust swept over him. Dan Draeger found himself again wanting to be judge, jury, and executioner. The last time it happened, the killer had raped and butchered a child in a roach-infested, ten-dollar a night motel. He had been the first officer on the scene and discovered the eight-year-old girl's remains. The brutal image would never leave him. But three days later, when he found the killer and shoved a pistol barrel in the pleading man's mouth, he dealt justice in his own fashion. Now, the same urge had returned yet Draeger held himself in check, knowing he had to wait.

"Mr. Draeger, what part of our last conversation did you not understand? If you persist in angering me, I will be forced to commit some very unpleasant acts." Arrogance lay heavy in the caller's voice. "Am I clear?"

Biting his tongue, the Chief of Police desperately wanted to tell the unknown man what fate awaited him when they met. The terrorist spoke again in a venomous tone.

"I can't hear you, Mr. Draeger."

"Yes, I understand. But those were reporters in that helicopter, not police."

Laughter came. "Then it's no great loss, is it?" The laughter that followed was deep and heinous.

"How did you get this number?" The Chief of Police hoped the terrorist would slip and provide information about himself.

"You're insulting my intelligence."

"No, curious. Earlier you called me and had to be patched through on the radio. If you had this number, why didn't you call me direct."

No reply. At last the terrorist answered calmly.

"Fear, Mr. Draeger. I planted the seeds of fear in your entire department and fertilized it in one simple act."

The Chief of Police remained silent, realizing how well prepared the terrorists were.

"Enough of this chit-chat. Listen carefully because your car phone isn't recorded and you'll have to repeat everything I say to the feds." Without waiting, the terrorist related his demands.

• • •

Jim glanced at Tommy with a blank look and turned his back to the drifting wisps of smoke on the horizon. There was nothing to say. The news station should have known better than to risk lives for the sake of a story. Now their pilot, reporter, and cameraman were names on a growing roster. It might be a ratings game for the media, but to the terrorists it was a deadly mission.

The city's evacuation horns continued their eerie howl, cycling for several minutes before silencing. Herschel looked to the far horizon and glanced at the raging flares of the surrounding process units. Ashen-faced, eyes moist, he shook his head. "I'm scared, Jim… plain scared."

"Me too," Jim replied. He laid a consoling hand on the computer technician's shoulder. "Get the bags out of the truck for me and don't worry. We're all scared."

Studying the rugged built security officer, a piecemeal grin broke in the corner of Herschel's mouth. "Thanks."

"For what?"

"For lying." Herschel turned to the truck and walked away.

Tommy walked to Jim and stood by him.

"He's a good kid. Take care of him for me," Jim said, watching Herschel labor under the weight of the bags.

"No problem, but where are you going?"

"I want to recon the area. While I'm gone, get the hunting equipment from your truck, especially my rifle and *Kabar*. Anything you think we can use. We may be locked in here for a couple of days and will need supplies."

"Wait and let me go with you?"

Jim shook his head. "I move faster alone." He pointed to several trucks parked inside the refinery fence then gestured to the south. "Take one and meet me at Warehouse Seven. Go in through the backside. I won't be gone long. When I return, we'll decide what to do next."

Reaching across to the radio handset protruding from Tommy's vest pocket, Jim turned it on and changed its channel. He motioned Herschel to them and adjusted the technician's handset.

"These are prototypes of a new system we were evaluating. They're higher megahertz and use several transmitters we had installed. Factory reps told us a standard scanner only catches the transmissions in blurbs. I'll stay in touch and meet you both at the warehouse."

Herschel and Tommy watched him cross the downed fence and search several refinery trucks before finding one with keys. A cloud of dust hid him from sight as he drove away.

"Get us some wheels, big boy. We have a lot of work to do," the machinist said, already looking across the parking lot at his personal vehicle. He glanced at the wavering shotgun barrel in Herschel's hands and scowled.

"Be careful with that thing."

CHAPTER SEVEN

June 25, 11:00 a.m.

Alex prided herself on staying in good physical condition, rising early each day to jog several miles. This wasn't a jog, though. It was a race for her life and the stifling humidity, her tight denims, and heavy boots were rapidly depleting her endurance. She thought she had acclimated herself to the Gulf Coast weather yet she could feel her strides shortening, and breathing becoming labored.

Two blocks ahead, a truck drove off a side street and angled toward her, weaving between corpses as it traveled through the refinery's little city of contractors' trailers and aluminum buildings. Alex dove behind a pump motor, heart thumping against her chest, anxiety grating her nerves. She moved to a vantage point and waited. The truck drove past, its driver leaning forward, scanning the processing units near them.

"Jim!" The whine of the pump's spinning shaft masked Alex's shout. "Here, Jim!" She leaped to her feet and chased after him, arms flailing the air.

The sight of the brake lights shining brightly brought a smile to her face, but Jim jumping from the truck and running to her did more. His arms wrapped about her and washed away her fears.

Affectionately brushing sweat-soaked strands of hair from her face, Jim stared into the glistening blue eyes. Lost for words, he led her by the hand to the truck.

Sitting beside him clutching a rock-hard arm, his strength electrified her. Alex observed the abrasions on his cheek and the dirt smeared on his cap and vest. Anguish stabbed her at the thought of him being killed, and she knew then how deeply she had come to love him even though he may not love her.

Sweat trailed down Jim's chest as he anxiously scanned the myriad of pipes and machinery they passed. The terrorists were near. He could feel them.

"You can't stay with me. Terrorists have hit us and this place could blow any minute. I'll help you over a fence then I want you to run—get as far away from here as you can."

Alex frowned and started to protest.

"No," Jim said. "You're going. End of discussion."

Knowing she needed to contact Ben, Alex accepted the order with a weary sigh.

"Can you get me near my car?" There was so much she wanted to explain to Jim, but now was not the time. She watched him nod and let her gaze flow over his hard-set jaw. Her fingers tightened about his arm.

The route to the contractors' parking lot took longer than normal with Jim taking alleyways and roads further around the units. Seeing him glance at every shadow that could conceal a gunman, Alex remained silent. She never questioned their direction, trusting completely in his actions. Passing beneath a pipe rack, she recognized landmarks and realized he was also scouting the refinery.

Jim grimaced and skidded the truck to a halt.

"What's wrong?" Alex watched him walk to the front of the truck and kneel. She followed then stopped.

Charlie Martin's shredded corpse stunned her yet seeing Jim's head bow, hands squeezing into knotted fists, tore at her heart. She stepped closer and touched his shoulder.

"I'm sorry. I know he was your friend," she said, realizing nothing could ease his grief.

Seconds passed before Jim stirred. He looked at the dozens of miniature nails imbedded in Charlie's body and carried his friend to the bed of the truck. Concealing his emotions behind a stoic face, Jim covered Charlie with a tarp and briefly stared at the shrouded body.

They drove in silence to the fence bordering the parking lot. Jim reverently laid the Iwo Jima veteran on the ground and draped the tarp over him. Alex watched. She realized Charlie's death had reopened deep wounds within Jim.

"Keep this. You might be the only contact we have with the outside world." Jim gave a security radio to her and glanced at the orange windsock atop a pole. The breeze held at a constant southeasterly direction. "If our plans go sour, I'll try to call you. Tell the police to evacuate and stay clear of the wind's path."

"We?" Brow knitted, Alex stared at the cold rage glowing in Jim's eyes. "What plans?"

He didn't reply.

A bit of sunlight reflected off the gold cross at his throat. She let her gaze roam across his Spartan body. His tactical vest was half-zipped, strained by a muscled, shirtless chest. Shotgun bandoliers draped his shoulders while ammunition pouches bulged on the vest. The Berettas on his belt and secured in his vest all spoke of war.

You've been acting like a love struck schoolgirl, she thought. *The man is standing here with revenge in his eyes, armed to the teeth, and you ask him what he plans to do.*

"It's time for you to go," he said, turning her to the fence. His hands wrapped her waist.

"Wait—wait." Alex spun and passionately kissed him. As they parted, fear of losing him enveloped her.

Scaling the six-foot chain-link fence came easy. Jim effortlessly lifted her to the top rail and held on until she swung a leg over it. Once on the ground on the other side, she put her fingers through the fence to touch him.

"I need to tell you something," she said in desperation.

"No," he replied, gently covering her fingers with his. "You need to go." The solemn look in her eyes disturbed him.

"They're not terrorists. They're mercenaries. The Venezuelan government hired them to destroy Titan Oil's refinery and lay the blame on the Arabs. It's part of an eighty billion dollar plan to break away from OPEC and control the American oil market."

"Mercenaries?" Jim stood dumbstruck. "How would you know that? No, wait…" Backing from the fence, he shook his head. "Who do you work for—the FBI?" He stared into her blue eyes. "That's why you were so friendly to me when we first met, isn't it? You wanted information about the refinery." His voice rose, anger fueled by a sense of betrayal. "Charlie never told you anything about me. You read it off some damned FBI file. Is this all a big game to you? Is the cavalry supposed to ride over the hills now and save us?"

Pointing to Charlie's shrouded corpse, Jim glared at Alex. "Well, it's too late to save him."

Tears rimmed Alex's eyes at the fury she observed in Jim's face. Strength waning, she held onto the fence for support. She searched her soul for the courage to explain more knowing she risked further wrath from him.

"I'm with the CIA." Alex bit her bottom lip and gestured in the direction of the refinery's office buildings. "Their leader's name is Adam Murdock.

He was one of our best black ops agents until he went renegade. I don't know how many people he has with him, but they're mercenaries."

Jim felt his guts being ripped from him. Her words resonated in his mind. His mouth opened, but no words came. Turning to the truck he thought of Tommy and Herschel, of warning them about who they were up against and the futility of trying to prevent a disaster. The bloodstained tarp covering Charlie caught Jim's attention. Fury rose within him.

"Jim!" she shouted, but he wouldn't stop. "I'm sorry I couldn't tell you."

The truck door slammed shut. She shook the chain-link fence. "Jim, damn you, listen to me!"

The engine revved and gravel showered the air as tires sought traction. The truck fishtailed, straightened, and sped back into the refinery.

• • •

The searing heat of the day broiled the refinery, transforming the thick humidity into a miserable steam bath. Glancing across the horizon, Jim hoped to see thunderclouds building as they frequently did near noon, but he only saw black smoke billowing from roaring flares. The raging fires matched his mood. He forced Alex from his mind and tried to concentrate on the problems he faced.

Driving through the refinery, he looked at the massive, odd structures standing like metal leviathans along the street. Towering furnaces; flare stacks stabbing the sky; crude oil and gasoline storage tanks looking large enough to encompass a football field; reactors sitting in rows like missiles ready for launch; and around them all were miles of pipe resembling jungle vines struggling to reclaim to the land.

The green of vegetation was gone, and only the dull gray of a morbid prison painted the landscape. Brownish red streaks of rust covered the giants' sides like old wounds left unclean. Everything held a futuristic wasteland appearance with humans fighting to revive it.

How can something so vitally necessary to a nation as an oil refinery be so ugly and dangerous, he asked himself.

Jim shook his head, not really wanting an answer. Titan Oil supplied the largest daily percentage of gasoline to America. Without doubt, he knew the fine balance of life would be thrown into an immediate, catastrophic upheaval if the flagship were destroyed—and that did not take into consideration the disastrous loss of lives if explosions released the full storage of hydrofluoric acid and hydrocarbons. The entire scenario grew more apocalyptic than he dared envision.

Passing a catalyst-cracking unit's control room, Jim observed very few bodies sprawled about it. *I wonder if everyone inside is dead or if they managed to barricade themselves in before the terrorists—no, mercenaries—attacked.*

His wondering ceased when he saw a panel van parked behind the concrete building. No one ever drove onto a process unit unless the unit was down and major repairs were underway. He had driven through the units, but knew the danger spots to avoid. Contractors did not. Their engines could ignite vapors, and their vehicles blocked emergency fire lanes. Everyone that crossed onto Titan Oil property knew driving onto a unit was taboo… *Everyone except terrorists.*

Slowing the truck, pistol held across his lap, Jim glanced about the 'cat cracker,' the catalyst-cracking unit. Charlie had mentioned a van going through Gate Nine. *But why are they here?* His bottom lip curled inward, tongue wetting it as his gaze swept the steel jungle.

The stock market. Jim's thought surprised him. Something as simple as a cat cracker being down for repairs affected nation-wide product availability, and that started the dominos' falling. Foreign crude oil purchases rose and stock prices soared. The market was emotional and brokers bought and sold more on fear than fact.

He realized more reasons existed for the attack than to throw the stock market into upheaval. If what Alex had said was true, Venezuela wanted sole control America's flow of oil, to open and close the supply valves as it wanted, and at whatever prices it desired. There had been bad blood for years between *OPEC*, the Organization of Petroleum Exporting Countries, and its original member Venezuela. If this attack succeeded Venezuela would turn America against the already hated organization, create havoc within its membership, and reap unlimited rewards.

Jim was shaking his head in dismay when a bullet shattered his truck's rear window and traveled through the front windshield. His right cheek and arm stung sharply as glass fragments showered him. When the window exploded, he had felt the air being sliced mere inches from his head. There was no need to question what had happened. He had found more terrorists, or they had found him.

The shot came from behind him, fortunately, with enough angle for the window to deflect the bullet's true aim. Stomping the accelerator, Jim raced through the cat cracker unit, taking an emergency fire lane to get to the far side. Machinery, piping, and tanks became blurs. Clearing the heart of the process unit and seeing a street ahead, Jim opened his door, grabbed his shotgun, and decreased speed. He held the door ajar with his boot and readied himself to jump. An empty, smooth-paved area appeared and he went airborne. The truck traveled on, bounced over a curb, then veered right and crashed into a fire hydrant. A geyser of water shot skyward and rained across the truck and street.

Jim's legs folded and he tumbled uncontrollably across the pavement. Head swimming, knees, elbows, and knuckles scraped raw, he struggled to his feet and scanned the area. Bullets ricocheted off a storage tank and zinged over his head. He lost his sense of direction and ran deeper into the unit.

Back pressed against a towering vessel, Jim flexed his hands to ward off the burning sensation in their skin. Brief streaks of pain raced from his elbows and knees, but the adrenaline pumping his heart helped him ignore the anguish. He slid around the vessel to glance over a row of pumps and bumped into the scaffolding secured against it.

I hate heights, he thought, head tilted back to see the top. Black smoke steadily drifted overhead, giving an appearance of the towering vessel swaying. *It looks like one of those redwood trees in California.*

Jim groaned and began to climb, never stopping until he reached the ninth tier.

"No…no…no," he muttered rapidly, taking a vise-like grip on the scaffold rails as he peered over the edge. *What in the name of hell were you thinking, Thurman? That's at least eighty or ninety feet down.* He glanced at the tiers above him and decided he was high enough.

Kneeling slowly onto the thick, oak-flooring planks, he surveyed the area and watched for movement. Fingers white from his deathly grip on the railing, he breathed deep to relax.

"Okay, where is it?" he whispered, looking about the scaffolding. A sigh of relief passed his lips when he found the spare safety harness that workers always kept near when working so high off the ground. No one survived falls in a refinery. Too many men had already learned the hard way. Falling meant striking one of two things, concrete or machinery. If the concrete didn't kill them, then the sudden stop on machinery did.

Easing into the safety rig, Jim double wrapped the eight-foot safety line around a rail and clicked its end onto the scaffold. He breathed easier yet could not rid himself of the tension spreading throughout his body.

Jim looked to the south. Three blocks away sat Warehouse Seven. No sign of Tommy and Herschel, but he did not expect any either. They would be inside. Glancing westward into the unit, Jim thought he saw a head and crouched lower onto the scaffold flooring.

Two armed men ran between the equipment, pausing at corners to search before moving on again. From his aerial perch, Jim studied their movements and observed militaristic traits. A third man, his shaved head defining him better in the shadows, gestured for them to sweep the area to the south.

Hair prickled along the back of his neck. Jim sensed he was being watched. The disturbing sensation gorged his mind. As his gaze swept the ground behind him, bullets chewed the scaffold's flooring. Wood splinters speared his arm and instinctively, he threw himself away from the line of fire.

Landing atop his shotgun, Jim overcompensated to retain balance. The edge of the narrow board flooring appeared and before he could stop his momentum, he rolled off the planks.

The pumps at the base of the scaffold flew upward and the horizon cartwheeled. Jim's stomach catapulted into his mouth and his body locked, petrified from fright. His boot struck a rail, spinning him head over heel. Glimpsing the sky at his feet, his mind floundered in the horror of his free fall. The shotgun's barrel struck his forearm and clanked against scaffold railings as it sailed past him to the ground.

Jim winced as he violently hit the end of his eight-foot safety line and spun upright. The additional six feet of line sewn into the harness to cushion a fall instantly tore free. He felt himself careening toward the concrete again. A teeth-rattling jar struck Jim as the line abruptly popped and bounced him to a dangling halt fifty feet above a menacing hunk of steel. Breath knocked from him, he gasped, eyes flared in shock. It took several seconds for him to recover, but it gave the terrorists valuable time to draw near.

Jim swung through the air, realizing he was at their mercy. The harness straps brushed against the scaffold and his fingers touched metal. His frozen senses gradually thawed, allowing his mind to combat the fright of the fall. Grabbing a rail, he pulled himself around until his boots bumped a scaffold cross-arm. He toed himself onto a plank and climbed to safety. Heart pounding wildly, Jim looked at his trembling hands and grasped the gold cross at his throat, clutching it gratefully.

Unbuckling the harness, Jim observed a terrorist thirty yards away with rifle braced against a slender vessel to take aim. A new anxiety took hold of Jim, forcing him to move. Muzzle flashes spewed from the terrorist's weapon. The air about Jim grew thick with bullets thudding into wood, boring through the scaffold's aluminum railings, and ricocheting off the mammoth vessel by him.

Protected by the wood planks, Jim dropped and crawled to the far end of the scaffold. The barrage of gunfire ceased and Jim prayed the terrorist was reloading. He swung out and hung off the side of the framework, willing to chance being shot to get on the ground. Releasing his hold, he dropped from one scaffold level to the next, using his immense strength to reach out and grab rails to slow his descent. The ground rushed at him, but he was in control. By the time his feet touched cement, his anxieties and fears had transformed into black rage. He landed beside the shotgun, furious at the world.

• • •

Tom Bowden came around the vessel, his *H&K MP5* at waist level, barrel sweeping the base of the scaffold. Ready to unleash a full magazine he scowled at not seeing anyone.

"Did you find him?" Ten yards away, Mike Galloway had climbed several rungs on a vessel ladder to scan the sea of machinery. He glanced at Bowden and swung to look behind him.

"No, but he's here. I—"

Powerful hands wrapped themselves about Bowden's head. A brutal crack bellowed through his mind. The snap of his neck came so swiftly that he never heard the guttural voice behind him say, "Here I am."

Bowden's abrupt silence made Galloway turn. "Hey, Tom?"

No reply came and no one could be seen.

The athletically built terrorist jumped off the ladder, automatic weapon rising as he moved toward the scaffold. A black cloud overhead blocked the sun and cast a deep shadow throughout the cat-cracking unit. When it drifted past, the sun's glare made Galloway squint. The silhouette of a giant moved before him, its cold eyes staring from a granite face.

Galloway felt the CAR-16 being torn from his hands. The giant spun and sunlight blinded the terrorist. Steel smashed Galloway's face and his feet were kicked out from under him. He crashed to the cement, head striking the corner of a pump. Daylight faded then returned. When it did, Galloway found himself being stripped of equipment.

The unknown mountainous man straightened, seemingly rising to the clouds.

"How many men are with you?" he asked, voice calm and iron-hard.

Blood ran freely from Galloway's nose and trailed into his mouth. He coughed and tried to spit, but it only cleared his lips and flowed down his cheek. Steel brutally cracked his chin. When the world ceased to spin, Galloway saw a shotgun hanging from the stranger's right hand. Its muzzle brushed Galloway's nose and swung toward his groin in a slow arc.

"How many men are with you?" The icy stare in the brawny man's eyes never wavered.

Galloway tried to shake his head. The muzzle brushed his nose again and swept back toward his groin. It halted below the belt, two inches above Galloway's trousers.

"This is for Charlie."

The shotgun's blast blended with the terrorist's agonizing scream for mercy.

Jim racked a fresh round into the shotgun, never removing his gaze from Galloway's face. The terrorist writhed on the ground, mouth open, hands flailing the cement about him. Blood gushed from the cavernous hole in his groin and swiftly spread into a wide pool about him.

"Be glad I don't have more time. You wouldn't die so quickly," and having spoken, Jim walked away, relishing the sound of the terrorist's cries.

• • •

Sweat dripped from Martin Shanks' chin as he knelt beside fifty-five-gallon drums stacked on pallets. His eyes burned and he dragged a forearm across his craggy face to clear them. Nerves taut, he lowered his CAR-16 onto his leg and swiped a hand over his shaved head. Clenching his teeth, he leaned around the drums to look down a walkway and then glanced at the scaffolding twenty yards to the north. The shotgun blast and the scream had come as one, drowned in the maddening bawl of machinery.

The maelstrom in his stomach became a twisted knot. *Where is Galloway, Sefcik, and Bowden? Why didn't they shoot?* Shanks looked at the scaffolding again, recalling the tactical dressed man he had seen. *Where did he come from?* There were too many questions and no answers.

Sweat stung his eyes again. He lowered his head and rubbed them, shoulder resting against a drum for support. Metal touched Shanks' right ear and he froze.

"How many men are with you?"

The cruel tone sent a chill up Shank's back. He tried to turn his head and felt a pistol's muzzle drive into his ear.

"Hell, I don't know."

The Beretta bucked as fire belched from its barrel. The 9mm, silver-tipped hollow-point round bored through Shanks' head and into the drum. Crimson, pinkish brain matter spattered its side, and a stream of emerald green industrial detergent spewed from the bullet hole.

Shanks's body slid down the side of the barrel and onto the concrete.

"Wrong answer," Jim said, watching the detergent splatter the corpse's back. He grabbed the mercenary by the collar and dragged him to a wide walkway canopied by scores of lines of pipe.

• • •

Vince Sefcik scowled and lifted his gaze from the gruesome hole in Galloway's groin. Unconsciously, his hand lowered and touched his trousers to confirm his own family jewels were still intact. He scanned the ground. His lips formed a taut line as he realized Galloway's CAR-16, pistol and equipment were missing.

Leaving at a bent trot, Sefcik glanced between the long rows of whining pumps as he moved toward the scaffold. He held his automatic weapon ready to spray the area at the least sight of anyone.

As Sefcik approached the towering framework of rails and boards, he glanced from the higher tiers to ground level. It was then he saw Tom Bowden sprawled chest down, colorless face turned skyward. He smirked and shook his head, but frowned when he looked about the immediate area. Bowden's weapons and equipment were gone.

Never giving his actions a second thought, Sefcik spun in the direction of the van.

To hell with this... Murdock told me to go to Dutch and that's where I'm going.

At first he grew lost in the maze of machinery. Once he regained his bearing, his speed increased. He scanned the unit, vaguely searching for Shanks, more interested in spotting Bowden and Galloway's killer. Clearing three alleyways, Sefcik's confidence mounted. He turned into a walkway canopied with pipes that he remembered led to the van. A cocky grin edged upward from the corner of his mouth, and then it fell away.

Gaunt-faced, Sefcik raised his gaze to the naked man hanging in the center of the wide walkway. Martin Shanks slowly swayed and revolved five feet off the ground, an electrical extension cord stretched from his neck to a two-inch pipe overhead and was tied off to another pipe.

Stepping closer, Sefcik stared at the gory chasm that replaced Shanks' left ear. The body gradually turned and Sefcik's eyes widened. A finger-painted message wrote in blood across Shanks' stomach read: LEAVE OR DIE.

The mercenary wet his lips, gaze sweeping the area. Again, the unknown killer had taken his prey's equipment. Looking at Shanks, Sefcik lightly shook his head.

I don't know how I'll explain this to Murdock, but right now, leaving is the best advice I've had all day.

Sefcik raced to the van, anxious to be clear of the unit. Without searching the vehicle's interior, he jumped into the driver's seat and sped toward the Admin building.

• • •

June 25, 11:40 a.m.

The Grainger City police waved Alex through their barricades after briefly questioning her escape. The answers were truthful yet not complete. Having seen so many frightened workers climb the chain-link fence and flee, the officers accepted Alex's tale and ordered her to leave the city. She acknowledged with sincere anxiety and drove three blocks before stopping.

Parking off the road, she scanned the neighborhood. Families appeared, stricken by hysteria, arms laden with personal possessions as they dashed to their cars.

Alex watched an elderly woman lead children along a sidewalk and realized how drastically people were affected by the brutal plans of madmen. *These are people, real people, not the figures and estimates I've always read on paper. We sit in offices and send men like Murdock on covert operations as if it were a chess game, and when the pieces fall, people die—innocent people.*

The reality of her profession reared its ugly head and she didn't like what she saw. Activating her cellular phone, she dialed Ben's office number. He answered on the first ring.

Ben's voice bordered on panic. "Where are you?"

"I'm parked on a street in Grainger City. I'm not hurt, but listen, I have radio contact with security in the refinery. Can we get our people in on this? We can coordinate with them."

"Whoa, Alex. Nothing has changed around here. No orders have come from upstairs. Whomever knew about this is keeping it buried. You can forget agency assistance."

Alex sat silent, staring at the raging flare stacks along the horizon. Every refinery and chemical plant in the city was fighting to control their emergency shutdowns.

"Hello? Alex? Are you there?"

"Uh, yes, sorry. All right, I understand."

"You're agreeing too quickly, Alex, and that bothers me. What are you going to do?"

"I'll call you later. Don't worry, I'm fine," she said, disconnecting the call before Ben could argue further.

Wearily rubbing her forehead with the cellular phone, Alex recalled the hate in Jim's eyes. She hurt at the thought of him believing she had used him. Dialing a private number, Alex listened to it ring three times before a deep, commanding voice answered.

"McCall."

The sound of her father's voice lifted her spirits.

"It's Alex. I need your help."

Jeff McCall wouldn't discuss anything further until assured of her safety. His questions came fast and direct, and once satisfied, the tension in his voice relaxed.

"Ben called and briefed me when he couldn't contact you. How did this slip through the agency's fingers? It doesn't make sense that Murdock of all people would go unnoticed."

"He didn't. We heard rumors of him assembling a team of psychos and discovered the truth. After the field report arrived at Langley, it vanished." Alex paused, momentarily embarrassed at explaining the full sequence of events to her father. "One of the secretaries Ben sleeps with told him about seeing the report. She said it disappeared. That's what started it all."

"So you and Ben decided, on your own, to violate policy and run your own investigation?" Jeff's tone was a mixture of anger and admiration.

"Yes, sir, but everything we suspected came true. The only missing link is who at the top hid the report?"

Silence came on the telephone. Waiting for her father to speak strained Alex's patience.

"What's the situation in the refinery?" he asked.

Alex explained what she had observed. She spoke of Jim and what she believed he was going to do, intentionally avoiding her feelings toward him yet her father was too experienced at seeing through veils.

Jeff McCall chuckled. "If I didn't know better, I'd say my daughter believes more is at stake than national security."

No reply came, making Jeff McCall chuckle again.

"After Ben called, I phoned my office and set a few wheels in motion. We have a SEAL team in Louisiana. They've been planning to raid another offshore rig to demonstrate how vulnerable we are to hostile foreign governments. By now they should be heading your way. Are you carrying an agency radio?"

Alex exhaled in relief and faintly smiled. Her father always had answers for her every dilemma. "Yes, sir. Ben made me bring everything that could fit in a suitcase."

"All right, this is what I want you to do."

He spoke non-stop for several minutes, detailing necessary actions, pausing only for confirmation of her understanding. He continued until the foundation of his plan was firmly established.

"Venezuela has been rippling the water with OPEC, but now they've made it a tidal wave with international repercussions. We're talking about a serious threat to the nation if Murdock completes his mission." Jeff McCall paused and groaned lightly. "My God, the plan fits that animal like a glove. Ever since he pulled off those black ops in Nicaragua, his ties to South American leaders have only strengthened. You would think they would be leery of a man who was fired from the CIA for being too ruthless, but that only elevated his status in their eyes."

"What about Langley?" Alex bit her lip.

"In all of my years in the intelligence field, I've never been confronted with a situation like this. You, my dear, are caught in the middle of one gigantic spider web."

"I know. Whoever wanted this kept quiet must be pretty high up and powerful to be able to pull that report." Alex massaged her forehead as she looked about the area.

"First of all, whoever it is, is willing to go to any extreme to achieve their goal—sacrifice people for their own motives—and that means he wouldn't think twice about eliminating you to ensure your silence. No loose ends. And second, whoever the person is, is not simply high up, but must be at the top to have received the intelligence and control its dissemination."

"Bill Haverty?" she asked, finding it hard to believe the DCI, Director of Central Intelligence, might be involved.

"He came to mind because of the influence he wields, but his track record doesn't fit the profile. Off hand, I'd venture to say it might be his second or third in command. Those men actually have as much clout as he does, sometimes more. They've been known to keep private files and black-mail politicians and co-workers to retain their positions. I can't exactly call and ask Bill about all this, can I?"

"Dad, I don't care what happens to me anymore. If the refinery explodes…"

"Your Mr. Thurman may be killed along with everyone else."

"It's not just him. This has made me feel guilty about who I am and what I've been doing."

"Well, don't. One madman in the intelligence community doesn't mean the system totally failed. It means we need to clean house better and safeguard against something like this happening again. Right now, I need to make more calls. Damn, I wish you had come to me in the beginning."

Alex breathed deeply, feeling the world crash down upon her.

"I love you," she whispered.

"And I love you too. Now, go somewhere safe and remain by your phone. I'm going to stoke a fire under a few people and see what happens."

Disconnecting the call, Alex lifted her gaze to watch the billowing black clouds drift across the sky.

No need to stoke any fires here, she thought.

CHAPTER EIGHT

June 25, 11:40 a.m.

Jim scowled. The creaking door and sunlight flooding the interior of the massive warehouse had announced his entrance. He breathed deep as his eyes adjusted to the dim light. Stacked crates came into better view, but the ringing in his ears from the cat cracker process unit and refinery flares persisted.

"Where in the hell did you go? Dallas?" Worry carried in Tommy's voice. Shotgun cradled in his arm comfortably, the machinist stepped from behind Jim.

Angry at not having detected Tommy's presence, Jim walked away, arms laden with weapons and equipment.

Tommy followed him. "I never thought anyone would ever be able to sneak up on you, but I did." His signature grin became a proud smile. "C'mon out, kid. It's just Jimbo."

"Stop calling me a kid. The name is Herschel," the technician replied gruffly. He adjusted his oversized tactical vest and cradled his shotgun across an arm as Tommy had.

"How are you going to shoot anyone with the safety on?" Tommy took Herschel's shotgun and raised it up before the technician's face. He frowned and pressed the safety button behind the trigger guard. A small coloring of red appeared. "We've already talked about this once. If you want to run with the pack, you've got to learn the howl. Now remember, look for red on the safety. Red, shoot someone. No red, you can't shoot anyone. Okay, kid?"

The master and his apprentice, Jim thought. He grinned as he walked to the center of the warehouse. In a beam of sunlight cast through a rooftop window, he knelt and laid the equipment on the floor. Keeping a green canvas bag for himself, he stood and turned to Tommy. The light illuminated his haggard appearance.

"Sweet Jesus!" the machinist exclaimed, gazing at his blood-smeared friend. Stepping closer, Tommy held his breath as he inspected Jim's wounds for any needing immediate attention.

The raw skin of Jim's knuckles and elbows glistened in the sunlight. His trousers were torn at the knees and splotched with dried blood. Flecks of human entrails stuck to his vest and were visible on strands of Jim's hair. Glass cuts were on his cheek; wood splinters showed in his arms, and smeared across him from head to toe were varying streaks of blood, dirt, and grease. Tommy only found raw scrapes and minor cuts. He backed away with a stern look.

Knowing a barrage of questions was about to be unleashed, Jim gestured to the mound of weapons, grenades, and equipment. "I borrowed a few things and left a message for the mercenaries."

"Mercs? Here?" Tommy's eyebrows drew together. He braced at his thoughts. "Wait, I don't want you having to explain twice."

Nodding to Herschel, the machinist motioned to the equipment on the floor. "Bring those. We'll be needing them." He turned and started toward the warehouse office at the end of the long building. "Mercs," he grumbled. "I was hoping you had some *good* news for a change."

Jim followed, picking splinters from his arms, glad to be with Tommy and Herschel again.

The skinny technician adjusted the set of his glasses and watched Tommy and Jim leave. His mouth became a thin line. "Carry this, kid. Watch out, kid. Look for the red color on the button, kid… I'm about to lose my temper with him," he mumbled, grabbing the weapons and equipment. He drew still when he realized he was holding a grenade.

At the warehouse office, Tommy knocked twice on the door and grinned at the confusion in Jim's eyes.

"I brought your rifle and *Kabar.*" He opened the door and entered the room. "And look at what else I brought. They came to the parking lot after you left."

Five men mingled about the office, sitting, standing and waiting for Jim to appear. When he walked through the doorway, they gazed at him with wry smiles.

Seeing them moved Jim beyond words. *The War Dogs.* His eyes brightened. He scanned their faces and observed their backpacks set across the room, rifles and pistols balanced atop them.

"Tommy says your back is against the wall," Jake Pierson said, standing with arms crossed over his chest. He shook his head lightly when he glanced over Jim Thurman's battered condition.

A lump developed in Jim's throat. His pride in the men swelled. They were ready to do whatever was necessary, without question, and ask nothing in return.

Sam Garrett and Joshua Allen; former Marines; one a sniper, the other in Force Reconnaissance, now Garrett was a process operator on a cat cracker and Allen, a welder in the machine shop. Bob Fischer and Fred Braun; former Army Special Forces; experienced in missions behind enemy lines; both worked in the instrumentation and electronics department called I&E. Jake Pierson was retired Navy. He had been one of the early SEAL team members and now was a machine shop foreman. Including Tommy and himself, and even Herschel, the needed experience and expertise was there.

131

They'll make one hell of a team, Jim thought. Clearing his throat, he told them of Murdock, his CIA past, and the mercenary team that followed him for Venezuelan money.

"I found explosives under a unit feed line. We can assume they are planting them on every unit, especially A-5."

As Jim talked, a visible resurgence showed in their eyes. The dregs of civilian life were quickly being shed as they returned to their true selves. Thanking men of this caliber would be an insult so Jim continued.

"I want each of you to fully understand that our actions are not sanctioned by any authority, and we can rely on no one except ourselves." Jim waited, providing an opportunity for questions. There were none.

Herschel entered, glasses sliding down his nose, equipment on the brink of falling from his overburdened arms. Sweat painted his face as he looked about the room.

"Here, let me help." Tommy gently pushed Herschel's glasses back into proper position and stepped away. "There, that's better."

Herschel frowned. "Thank you," he said in a strained voice.

The War Dogs laughed and motioned him to a table.

"Come on, kid. We'll give you a hand," Jake said.

The technician's face flushed. "My name is Herschel." His admonishment only brought more of their laughter.

Jim watched the men spread equipment across the table. His grin faded into a staid expression.

"They'll do a good job," Tommy stated confidently, following his friend's stare.

"I'm not worried about that. I was thinking about how they've already risked their lives once and I'm asking them to do it again." His voice was low, as if talking to himself. "Remember when people used to say all vets were crazy and didn't care about anything." Barely moving a finger, Jim gestured to his team. "They care enough to gamble against a stacked deck."

Glancing at the floor, Tommy's gaze slowly rose. "Between me and you, Jim, do you think all the cards are against us?"

Jim's head gradually turned. His expression answered.

Tommy shrugged. "Well, it won't be the first time we've been dealt a sorry hand."

As Jim listened, his eyes shifted to follow Sam Garrett. Raised in the piney woods of East Texas, the slender man always appeared to be calm. Quiet, slow speaking by nature, Garrett enjoyed working by himself. It was one of the traits that made him such a good sniper in the Corps, staying behind enemy lines for extended periods.

Joshua Allen and Garrett had served in Vietnam the same year. Their paths crossed several times when Allen's recon team pulled Garrett out of growing hot spots. Now the two were close friends, spending most of their off time together. Over the years Allen had added a few pounds and standing next to Garrett made it obvious yet beneath the apparent weight was the strength and stamina of a mule.

Bob Fischer and Fred Braun were evenly matched. Brown hair and eyes, average height and build, nothing to really make them stand out in a crowd. Sometimes they kidded with people, other times they were as silent as church mice. The two had traveled into Laos and North Vietnam, living off the land more than they wanted to recall. Their missions had provided memories that more than justified their moments of silence.

Tommy saw Jim intently watching Jake Pierson, the shop foreman. "What's the matter?" he whispered.

Jim's face grew difficult to read. "As tough as that old boy is now, I'd hate to have crossed him when he was younger."

Hearing the remark, Tommy smiled. "He's still hell on wheels. Women, fighting and drinking… I don't think it really matters which comes first as long as he gets them all fairly regular."

Both men tried to hold back their laughter, but Pierson had noticed them looking his way. Rising from his chair, standing splayfooted with hands on hips, he stared at them. Close-cropped gray hair, broad shoulders with a thin waist, Pierson looked fit enough to tackle any two men in the room. His defiant stance made the dancing lady tattooed on his suntanned forearm clearly visible.

"What's so fucking funny?" Pierson asked. He looked at Tommy with eyebrows drawn down hard, forming a crooked line.

"Uh, nothing, Jake," Jim remarked. "I was swapping lies with Tommy. That's all."

The machinist breathed softly, knowing how quick Pierson was to rile and fight. Tommy nodded to the former SEAL and grinned stupidly. "Just talking trash, Chief," he said, calling the shop foreman by his retired naval rank.

Pierson wryly smiled and Tommy swallowed gingerly.

"Here, don't forget these." Struggling under the weight, Herschel set Jim's security bags on the table.

The men retrieved their personal packs and equipment from a corner of the room. Returning to the table, they dumped the contents and stripped from their clothes. Herschel dodged the shirts and trousers thrown playfully at him. He feigned anger yet his eyes glowed at being a part of the team. Within minutes each stood in their paramilitary hunting clothes and began sorting through the pile of confiscated weapons.

"What's it like up front?" Joshua asked, laying one of the CAR-16 bush guns aside to use. "Did you see them?" He jungle wrapped two banana magazines with duct tape as he talked.

The short automatic weapon was exactly like the M-16, only shrunk. Joshua loved its short length and firepower for close quarters combat. Taping the thirty-round magazines together, one inverted from the other, once one emptied, he could hit the release, flip the magazines and shove the next one home. The weapon would be ready to fire in record time, and experience had taught Joshua how valuable fast reloading was.

"Aerial assault on both buildings. Their choppers are still on the roof-tops. I radioed A-5 and heard gunfire when someone tried to reply. They're in there. I met a few of them on a cat unit." Jim paused. "They gave me their equipment." He grew quiet as he checked his pistols and reloaded several magazines. "One of the mercs left the party early. Too bad he didn't bother looking through his van. I had found some explosives on the unit and placed them under the driver's seat."

The team laughed, enjoying the camaraderie.

Joshua clipped a tactical belt on and slid a 9mm into its holster. He filled the belt's pouches to capacity with magazines for the CAR-16 and pistol. "These any good?" he asked, holding one of the compact, security handsets up before him.

Jim removed the wiring from Joshua's radio. "They were supposed to be for my department." Unraveling the attachments, he properly posi-tioned each man's radio wires.

"Ear plug with a swing down mouth mike. Keeps your hand free. Put your vest on and place the radio in one of the top pockets."

Joshua strapped the radio in tightly. The bulletproof assault vest had *Velcro* pockets all around, allowing for every conceivable piece of equip-ment needed to be carried without restricting movement.

"Not bad," he said, flexing his shoulders and arms. "And brand new too." His words transmitted over the handsets being passed along the table.

"Voice activated. If the button on the side of the earplug is in, you trans-mit and receive. Out, you can only listen." Jim tossed ammunition to each man and strapped the sheath of a menacing looking *Kabar* knife onto the side of his leg below the knee. He withdrew the razor sharp knife and sliced the strings on a long, well-wrapped bundle. The cloth fell away, displaying a scoped, bolt-action, *Remington* 30-06 rifle. Ensuring it was loaded, he set it aside and opened the green canvas bag stolen from the mercenaries' van. Inside was a short, pistol-gripped, automatic shotgun with a twenty-round drum magazine attached. Loose shells filled the bottom of the bag. Jim inspected one. *Fletchettes.*

This is what killed Charlie, he thought. He chambered the round and loaded the drum so every other round he fired would deal a cruel death.

Jim looked at Tommy's shotgun. He leaned closer, surprised that earlier he had not noticed the barrel was cut shorter.

"When did you do that?"

"Before you arrived. I found a hacksaw in one of the maintenance trucks. I've always liked a sawed-off shotgun," Tommy stated, dropping number four shotgun shells into a right-side vest pocket. He rummaged through an open ammunition box, took a handful of slug rounds and placed them in a pocket on the left.

The commotion within the room settled. Jim turned and gazed at the War Dogs. Six granite-faced warriors stood ready, waiting for him to give their orders. The looks in their eyes spoke silently of men who would willingly go beyond the call of duty for a just cause, but their weaponry proclaimed them to be a merciless death squad.

The team carried shotguns, knives, semiautomatic pistols, and the confiscated automatic weapons with enough ammunition to lay down a formidable field of fire on any battleground. And always was an added personal touch to their equipment.

Tommy stood somberly with his sawed-off pump shotgun cradled in his arm. His vest pockets bulged with ammunition, and shotgun shell bandoliers crisscrossed his chest. He wanted no additional weapons other than a 9mm pistol and survival knife.

A shotgun hung from Garrett's left hand as if it were a natural part of him. Strapped onto his belt within easy grasp was a curved *Kukri* carried by the infamous *Gurkha* regiment. Garrett had grown accustomed to the large knife in Vietnam. He enjoyed its heavy feel in hand-to-hand combat.

Pierson tucked a garrote into an empty vest pocket. He smiled when he saw Jim stare at the twisted strands of piano wire with small wooden handles. Pierson's smile held no humor, though.

Fischer and Braun had brought their own rappelling ropes from their trucks and wore them draped over their shoulders. Joshua Allen slid the strap of a short bundle onto his shoulder. Only he knew what the bundle contained.

Loosening the sling of his rifle, Jim hung it diagonally across his back. Handing Fischer a pair of binoculars, he glanced at their faces. The final moment had arrived.

"Jake has the explosives experience so he'll come with Tommy and me to check the butane spheres. We have to locate and isolate any charges before we hit the A-5 control room. Allen, you'd better come along too. We may need an extra pair of eyes because we're going to be close to A-5," Jim explained, shifting the drummed shotgun into his other hand. "Your guess is as good as mine about where they have planted explosives in this refinery, but we have to clear the spheres and A-5 first."

Herschel's skinny arms weakened under the constant weight of the shotgun. The barrel wavered and lowered toward Tommy.

Casually reaching across to the weapon, Jim raised its barrel and nodded in a fatherly manner to the technician.

"Garrett, Braun, and Fischer will provide cover for Herschel while he disrupts the main computer in the Admin building and takes control. If we find explosives at the spheres, we will clear them and send Allen to join Garrett's team. Once Herschel has computer control, just start killing."

Herschel's nerves tingled from the fear streaking through him. *Start killing?* The technician glanced at Jim's cold eyes. *He says it without a hint of remorse.*

Herschel looked at the shotgun cradled in his arms. *Red means shoot. No red, no shoot. Oh. Jesus, that means to shoot people–Herschel, this isn't a computer game where you get five lives to play with.*

"We'll call you as soon as we break into the computer bank," Bob Fischer stated. "Herschel may not be able to take full control because the mercs have been playing with the system. He can at least make the system appear to have malfunctioned."

"Sounds good enough for me," Jim replied. "Use any vehicle in the refinery that you can find. When you go to the Admin building, approach it from the blind side. I don't want anyone taking any unnecessary chances. Understood?"

Everyone nodded. Their stone-faced expressions showed no signs of fear or regret over accepting the assignment.

"Herschel."

"Yes?" The computer technician swallowed the lump in his throat.

Jim's eyes showed a trace of warmth. "These men will take care of you. Do exactly what they say, and do it fast."

The technician swallowed hard. "I will, Jim."

Jim grinned faintly as he patted Herschel's shoulder, then his eyes grew cold again.

"We're too old for bullshit speeches, and we know the odds are against us. If we succeed, a lot of people will live. There won't be any parades or thank you's after this is over. All I care about is that each of you stays alive. Remember, these bastards die and we live. Do whatever you have to do, but that's how it's going to be," Jim stated.

No one spoke. Each man kept his thoughts to himself.

"Good luck," Jim whispered. He looked at them, never wanting to forget the faces of the men who had come to his aid. As he walked away, he lifted his gold cross and kissed it.

The team stood in silence for a few seconds, watching him leave. They glanced at one another, wanting to say something yet not knowing what.

Jogging to catch up, McLawchlin, Pierson, and Allen reached Jim as he was about to walk out of the warehouse. Herschel knew if he didn't move now, his fear would never allow him to move again. He started the long walk to the door. Braun, Fischer, and Garrett followed.

Still, no one spoke.

• • •

June 25, 11:45 a.m.

Hearing the door open, Murdock swiveled his chair around. Nathan Briars entered rubbing both ears, complaining of how the high noise level outside the building bothered him.

Murdock swung back to the control board monitors. "Is everything ready?" he asked over his shoulder. No response came from Nathan.

A computer monitor changed screens and flashed new pressure readings in colorful warning. Propping an elbow on the armrest, he ran his fingertips in small circles over his chin, studying the numbers. Deciding to ignore them, he looked at the camera monitors.

"Where's Nicole?" he said, speaking louder.

Nathan rubbed his ears harder, but the constant ringing in them continued. "We finished. That woman…"

Nathan's abrupt silence made Murdock turn.

A scowl moved across Nathan's face. He shook his head, lips curling slightly. "That woman is crazy. I think she gets off on this shit."

The man's glower amused Murdock. He wondered if Nathan had intentionally brushed her ass and received a pistol in his face for it. Nathan was right though. Nicole did get off on the danger, and she was about half-nymph crazy. She had rules about when and where she dropped her pants.

Those rules were very few though. Murdock knew firsthand from the nights she left nail marks down his back.

"I called her and she said she would be in soon. She said something else, but I didn't understand. Is there a problem with her radio?" Murdock asked.

"I don't think so. She's staying outside to walk around and smoke. Damn noise outside gives me such a headache that I can't even think… I had to come inside for a few minutes." Nathan squinted hard, hoping it would give him relief. "I didn't see one person out there. This place is ours."

"At least for another hour it is. We made an example for the authorities to see. That bought us adequate time. They're too frightened now to attempt anything, especially anything that may jeopardize the hostages' lives. I'll let them believe they have begun negotiations. After that, the authorities will coordinate their efforts and stop arguing over who should be the boss. I'll make more demands about the plight of our Arab brothers, let them believe we are misguided sympathizers, then we'll pull out." Murdock glanced at the large faced clock on the wall, his blue eyes gauging the time. "Another hour should be all the media needs to make the Serpent and the Sword a household name from coast to coast. When all of their attention is focused on saving this place and they believe we're Arab sympathizers, we'll leave in the choppers… Then, *boom*, this place can go up."

The process operator's head whipped around. He looked at the mercenary leader in disbelief.

Murdock read the operator's expression and smiled patronizingly. "Don't be so naive as to think the Delta Force or FBI hostage team will come to the rescue. It will take at least two hours before they can assemble and start heading this way. We're leaving before they can get organized."

"Maybe there are other counterterrorist groups you don't know about," blurted the operator before realizing how it sounded. He winced, anticipating another pistol slap for speaking without permission.

Murdock threw his head back, his laughter carrying in the room. Slowly, he grew quiet. The smile drained from his face. He stared deep into the operator's eyes.

"I never said I was a terrorist. I'm simply a business man."

• • •

June 25, 12:05 p.m.

The high dirt firewall surrounding the sphere tank farm provided ample cover for the War Dogs crawling on their bellies. Edging their way to the crest of the mounded dirt, they laid motionless, surveying the area. Being heard was the least of their concerns. The clamor of roaring flares blocked out any noise they could make. Being detected by unseen mercenaries standing guard was their main worry.

Having parked their stolen truck blocks from the spheres, the march to A-5 had taken the four men longer than they wanted. Dark of night would have allowed them to move faster and easier, but with a midday sun breaking and shining through gaps in the refinery's clouds of smoke, their every movement was held to a minimum.

They continued their vigil, spread along the firewall, waiting to see if they had been detected.

Heat cast from the burning pillars of hydrocarbons combined itself with the harsh summer sun. The refinery was quickly becoming an oven. Sweat drenched their bodies and soaked their clothes. Lying in the dirt, the wet clothing covered them with a light film of mud, adding a natural camouflage to their appearance.

Jim' earphone sounded. The voice on the radio was Jake Pierson's.

"Front right, Jim. See that smoke? That's a cigarette."

At first Jim missed the brief puffs. Looking again, he realized someone stood behind a wide concrete support leg of a butane sphere tank. Jim scanned the area. No one else was seen. Directly to his right, fifteen yards away, lay Allen. The man watched the rising cloud of cigarette smoke like a lion waiting for his prey to walk out.

Thirty yards of open distance lay between them and the mercenary. Jim wondered what the best course of action should be to make the kill. Risking a shot in the refinery was one thing, but shooting a round off in this sphere tank farm was far too dangerous. He looked up at the spheres. They were like giant golf balls atop concrete legs. If one blew, the blast would detonate the remaining twenty spheres. He remembered an engineer saying that even if one exploded, it would clear a two-mile square area. Now, knowing someone was standing underneath a sphere, smoking a cigarette, created a despairing feeling in Jim.

"Thurman, I can take her," Allen radioed calmly, watching Jim from his position further down the firewall. He waited for approval.

Trusting Joshua's ability, Jim raised a finger and dropped it in the direction of the terrorist.

Allen slid back below the crest of the mound to remove his long, slung bundle. With practiced ease he set a short steel bow onto a rifle stock and adjusted its mounted scope. The bow's string took two hands to retract, but he pulled until it locked into position. A short, aluminum arrow was laid on the crossbow's track, and the weapon was ready. Crawling to the top of the dirt wall again, Allen drew still as he watched the wisps of smoke through his scope.

Surprised by the sight of a crossbow, Jim stared briefly before turning away. A hand swung out from behind the concrete leg, flicking a cigarette butt high into the air. The smoker was through. Allen now only needed the mercenary to walk out, giving him a shot.

The passing seconds lingered on. Jim waited for the mercenary to change positions. A rifle barrel appeared, then an attractive blonde walked out.

Pausing long enough to scout the area, unaware of being watched, she rested an arm across the AK-47 hung off her shoulder. She started casually toward A-5's control room.

Jim's tongue wet his lips. He kept watching, wondering when Allen would attempt the shot.

Loose fitting military clothing couldn't hide the woman's healthy build. Her stride told of an inattentive attitude. Stopping beside a framework of timbers holding electrical panels, she leaned against it and rested her head on the wood. She touched the wiring at her throat and spoke. Frustration showed on her face as she looked at the radio clipped on her belt. Tapping it several times, she frowned as her head lifted.

The cross hairs in the scope quartered her forehead. Breathing shallow, Allen had followed her from the first moment she came into view. He wanted her pace to slow before firing. Now, she gave him the opportunity.

Allen exhaled softly. His finger applied continuous pressure to the trigger as his breathing stopped. The woman looked directly ahead. Her eyes narrowed, squinting, trying to discern what she saw. Watching her through the scope, Allen knew she had seen one of them. Her eyebrows rose. Allen observed the whites of her eyes spread in his lens. Her mind had registered danger.

The warning came too late, though.

The whiplash of her head against the wooden boards took Jim by surprise. He knew Allen was taking aim yet when she stared in their direction and identified their position, Jim readied himself to shoot her. There could be no more waiting. But Allen's arrow had driven through her brain, pinning skull to wood.

Nicole's body danced in spasmodic quivers as if she were being electrocuted. Without hesitation, Allen shot another arrow through her head, nailing her solidly to the wooden bulkhead.

Dispassionately, Jim observed the woman's hands thrash open and closed. When the fingers flexed a final time, Jim looked at Allen. The man glanced his way, no more disturbed than if he had killed a rabid animal.

"Jake," Jim said over the radio, looking along the firewall at the former SEAL. "Find those explosives and let's get the hell out of this place."

Pierson acknowledged with a thumb's up signal and crawled over the crest, disappearing behind concrete leggings. Allen laid his crossbow aside and waited until Tommy cleared the high wall of dirt before following. Together with Jim, they scurried to the dirt firewall closest to the A-5 control room.

They laid still and scanned the area for any of the woman's friends. From his vantage point Jim observed three of the long box, unit cameras pan in half-circles. The salt from his sweat stung his eyes and burned. He tried to wipe them clean and only irritated them more. Accepting the discomfort, he turned back to watch the cameras.

"What do you think?" Tommy asked, staring at the process unit.

"We haven't heard from Garrett's team at the Admin building."

Jim's head shook slowly. "Unless they ran into problems, we should be into the system by now. They might need more time," he replied. He touched the button on his earplug to transmit and monitor. "Hello, Braun, can you hear me? Herschel? Fischer, are you there?"

No one answered.

Although his eyes kept searching A-5, his mind was preparing a backup plan.

Something must have gone wrong or one of the three men would have responded, he thought.

When the two bundles of explosives were shoved in front of his face, Jim felt his heart skip a beat. He took a deep breath and turned to find Pierson lying beside him. The smiling man proudly held the explosives up for his teammates to see.

"Crude but effective. No trip switches or secondary wiring. Just a simple remote detonation device," Jake explained, pointing to various wires.

"Did you disarm them?" Tommy asked nervously, eyes focused on the explosives near his face.

"No, I only disconnected them from the spheres. If one of those bastards has the master control and runs a test to see if they're receiving signal, I don't want it to alert them," answered the shop foreman.

Tommy McLawchlin's stomach felt jittery. Pierson made sense, but knowing the charges were live bothered Tommy. The machinist turned his head away. Keeping lookout was better than seeing the explosives and worrying about them detonating at any moment.

"Tommy, you and Allen stay here. Jake and I are going down the street to the control box on the telephone pole. We have to do something with those cameras or else we're not going to be able to move through the unit. We'll dump the charges somewhere," Jim said, already sliding off the wall. He took one of the bundles from Pierson and left.

Pierson's smile never faded. He glanced at Tommy and Joshua and extended his hand, offering them the explosives. Allen shook his head vigorously. Tommy recoiled from the bombs as if they were snakes, then glared at Pierson.

A mischievous expression spread over Pierson's face as he spun to follow Jim.

Tommy watched him for several seconds before returning his attention to the A-5 unit.

"Fucking prick," he muttered.

CHAPTER NINE

June 25, 12:10 p.m.

Alex parked in a softball field four blocks from the refinery. The location was good. Trees hid her from the view of passing emergency vehicles yet she could still see Titan Oil's flares in the distance. After a quick glance about the area she walked to the rear of her rented car and lifted a large, leather bag from the trunk. She grunted as she knelt with it to the ground.

The sides of the bag were tautly stretched. Alex barely pulled at its zipper and the leather parted. She paused, glanced at the street and surrounding park, and rummaged through the clothes.

"This should do," she said, inspecting a dark jump suit as she held it up before her. Draping it across her shoulder, she dug deeper into the bag until her fingers touched metal. A hint of a smile crossed her lips. Her fingers dug again and wrapped about a hard plastic case. She smiled, glad that Ben had pestered her into bringing the additional equipment. Laying the jump suit on the bag, Alex stood and listened to the constant rumbling of the flares.

The morning had passed like a whirlwind and Alex felt exhaustion taking hold of her. Her shoulders slumped and she exhaled hard, not knowing if the feeling came from her worries over Jim or the combination of fatigue and suffocating humidity. By her feet lay an agency radio handset, ammunition, shoulder holster with a .45 semiautomatic, a baseball styled cap, comfortable work shoes, and a navy blue jumpsuit with FEDERAL AGENT embroidered in reflective yellow letters across the back.

Gathering the equipment, she walked to the driver's door and dumped them in the seat. She glanced at the radio Jim had given her, hoping to hear his voice again and know he was still alive. The radio was on the car's dash. Its silence stirred her fears. Jim's last transmissions had come in blurbs, and from it she knew a terrorist had been killed and his men were moving to a different location.

She turned the agency radio on, clicked a button and waited. Holding Jim's radio, she keyed it and watched the agency radio scan frequencies until it found the transmission. When the scanning stopped, she locked the frequency into her radio and turned Jim's radio off, no longer needing it. If Jim talked, she could hear him, and talk to him *if* he would answer. Remembering the fire in his eyes, she wasn't sure.

Alex looked at her watch and calculated the SEAL team's flying time. Pressing buttons on the agency radio's keypad, she set the channels to scan between Jim's frequency and the SEALs. A police car raced by the softball park and was followed closely by an ambulance. Alex's heartbeat quickened. The sight of the ambulance only magnified the tension within her.

Dark shadows spread among the trees as clouds blocked the sunlight. The change in lighting broke her thoughts and she realized no more time could be wasted. She looked about the area and undressed. Using her shirt, she wiped perspiration from her face and breasts, then threw her shirt, denim jeans, and contractor work boots into the backseat floorboard of the car. The jumpsuit fit Alex well, tight enough to compliment the flowing contours of her athletic body yet loose enough to allow freedom of movement. She brushed her dark hair and zipped the jumpsuit closed almost to the neck, not wanting sight of her cleavage. What she had to do required a formal atmosphere. The last thing she needed was interference from overactive male hormones.

The agency radio handset crackled and Alex stopped to listen. She glanced at her watch and waited. Still, nothing more was heard. She put the shoulder holster on, ensured the pistol was loaded and adjusted the holster straps into place. Changing the radio's frequency, she depressed the transmit button and held it. The encryption activated. She spoke when a light beep was heard.

"SPECWAR, this is Eagle's Nest Talon Five on Twilight. Do you copy?"

The few seconds of silence seemed like hours. She gazed at the radio, hoping the intelligence network satellite had captured her transmission. The SEAL team was under orders to monitor the operational channel around-the-clock. That did not worry her. They would listen. What did, was if the radio malfunctioned. She had checked it before leaving Langley yet there were always unexpected problems to be considered.

She looked away, ready to attempt another try with the code her father said was used by National Security Council control officers. The radio squawked. They answered.

"Eagle's Nest Talon Five, this is SPECWAR's Dark Angel."

She sighed in relief.

"Dark Angel, this is Talon Five. Be advised hostile insertion at Grainger City Titan Oil has begun. Stand ready at this time. Be prepared for hot LZ. Recon intel to follow ASAP. Do you acknowledge?"

The encryption delay bothered her. She waited. Their transmission came confirming the orders. Alex closed her eyes in silent thanks.

Now came the hard part. Getting to Jim.

• • •

June 25, 12:16 p.m.

Dan Draeger rubbed his brow and looked along the police barricade line at the anxious faces staring at him. He knew his officers wanted to do something, anything, and were waiting for the slightest order. Draeger had nothing to tell them, though. He too was frustrated at the sense of helplessness blanketing them. This was their city, their refinery yet the feds were refusing to even acknowledge their presence.

"Paper-pushers," Draeger muttered, seeing four suit-coated FBI agents standing off to themselves, talking, pointing, and nodding toward the refinery. "Must be nice to never get your hands dirty and always come out the hero, even if it takes finding a scapegoat for your mistakes." His anger rose and he walked away.

A half-circle of city and county officials were formed around the televisions at the rear of the Industrial Emergency Response van. Draeger approached quietly, knowing they were monitoring news broadcasts of the attack. It was standard operating procedure in every major emergency event, but the chief knew the primary reason was to save their political careers. When the emergency ended, the finger pointing would begin. Knowing what the media had said forewarned the politicians of the public's anger they could expect.

"We have a special bulletin," the anchorman stated from his wide-countered desk at the Houston news station. "A state of emergency has been declared in Grainger City. All persons are being instructed to evacuate and the Department of Public Safety has ordered all highways going into Grainger City closed. Cities in the surrounding areas are assisting in the evacuation to allow it to flow smoothly."

Andrew Cannon, the Mayor of Grainger City, curtly nodded his approval of the report and waved a stubby hand at the television. The slender, balding aide by his side failed to see the political blessing and continued to watch the broadcast. Cannon's head turned, brow rising.

"Sorry, sir," Terry Keel mumbled, reaching out to the television. He turned through the channels, glancing nervously at the mayor until a stern nod came. A weak smile edged across the aide's mouth as he returned to the mayor's side.

Draeger's lips became a taut, thin line as he watched the slender flunky shrivel under Cannon's glare. He looked at the arrogant political kingpin, knowing the mayor's ego was swelling each time he heard his name, or saw himself on a broadcast. Andrew Cannon's wife was the trump card in his claim to fame. Her family was considered 'old money,' owned a handful of banks and had their fingers in every big money deal in the county. Marrying into the family had instantly established Cannon in political circles, but on his own, the short, squatty-framed man was nothing more than a spineless leech.

Keel lowered his gaze to the ground and Cannon, satisfied with having exerted his authority, returned his attention to the reporter on the broadcast.

A staunch-faced man stood on Derrick Road with the refinery's burning entrance as a backdrop. Gesturing to the fires behind him, he related the news of security officers and employees killed in the initial onslaught of the attack. He gestured to the roof of a building and explicitly described the cruel executions he had witnessed. The pitch of his voice rose and fell as quickly as his expressions changed. Pausing, he glanced at his notes.

The scene switched from a close-up of the reporter to the main gate's charred Security building. Zooming in for dramatic effect, the cameraman allowed viewers to see blackened, blown out windows and smoking debris. The picture swung to the street where uniformed bodies laid near a burning car climbed half-atop a crushed, wrought iron fence. Cutting away from the dead officers, the cameraman panned the parking lot to show more corpses and blazing vehicles. The burning tires cast a wide veil of black smoke across the sky, adding horror to the refinery battlefield.

Film footage of three men being shot in the back and falling to their deaths from the sixth story building appeared on the television. The reporter went into elaborate detail of the bloody carnage he could see from the mandatory press location. Speculating on demands he assumed would soon be made, the thin, graying man described the deafening noise of the refinery's flares and gestured to the terrorists' transport helicopters. The sight of bodies and fire consumed the television's screen again.

"That son of a bitch," Draeger growled. Rage raced through him. A few officials turned to him and nodded their agreement.

The reporter appeared proud to be relating the atrocities on national news. Draeger's abdomen tightened at the thought of families recognizing their loved ones and learning of their deaths by seeing the broadcast. There was no excuse for the networks to show this footage before proper notifications could be made, but that seemed to be the norm for media these days.

The broadcast displayed maps of evacuation routes before the film footage returned to the bodies sprawled across lawns, parking lots, and at the refinery's entrance, all under a broiling sun.

Draeger's eyes closed softly as the corpses were shown. He walked away from the Industrial Emergency Response van, toward his police car, not wanting to see anymore. Now he wished he hadn't come to see how much of a media circus the attack had become.

"Goddamned reporters," he said, hating the constant televising of the dead.

"Dan... Dan."

The police chief stopped and looked back, knowing all too well who had spoken.

Lighting an imported cigar, Andrew Cannon blasted a cloud of smoke into the air and glanced at the gathered politicians.

"Dan, when this incident is over, I intend to personally form a committee to investigate what could have been done to prevent these senseless deaths. I'll be looking to you for strong input on how your department can correct its mistakes and better protect our citizens in the future."

Draeger clenched his teeth to avoid speaking out. *My department's mistakes*, he thought. *You're a sorry piece of shit.*

The police chief's hands closed into knotted balls. He exhaled hard, looked at Titan Oil's roaring flares and let his gaze carry across the surrounding landscape. His eyes came to rest on Cannon with little emotion, but his words held a sharp edge.

"Stay away from my people, Andy. I don't take kindly to them being used as scapegoats."

The cigar fell from Cannon's mouth and stifled laughter erupted from the men about him.

Dan Draeger stared at the mayor a moment longer before walking away.

• • •

Vince Sefcik moaned in relief when the chopper atop the Admin building came into view. He didn't know how he would explain Bowden, Shanks, and Galloway's deaths, but for now he did not care. He was alive and that was all that mattered. His courage grew as he drove closer to the Admin building.

They had screwed up and let some amateur get them. Amateur? No, whoever did it killed three veteran mercs and left a message for me to find. No, that wasn't an amateur. He shook off the mental image of Shanks dangling from a pipe and began to plan what he would tell Dutch. A hint of a grin formed on his lips. *With them gone, though, that leaves more money for Murdock to divide among us once the mission is over.*

The gaunt mercenary parked the panel van and entered the three-story Admin building through a rear door. The air-conditioning felt good after being out in the refinery. He paused at a corner, glanced along the empty hallways, and pulled his radio handset from his belt.

"I'm here."

"Where are your men?"

"Dead. We got separated and I think some employees jumped them. Everyone was gone when I found their bodies." Sefcik released the transmit button and waited. His mouth was dry and he ran his tongue over his lips.

Dutch's response carried little concern over the news.

"I'll let the others know. Check the first floor then come up."

"That's clear," Sefcik said, glad the former biker had bought his story. He looked to both ends of the long hallway. A sign on the wall told of the offices and their room numbers. An arrow beneath the words COMPUTER ROOM pointed to his left. He decided to check it last, then turned right and started his room-to-room searches.

• • •

The Titan Oil truck slowed to a stop one block west of the Admin building. Fischer turned the ignition off and leaned on the steering wheel as he stared at the chopper on the roof. The sight of it and the black smoke swirling across the sky drove home the reality of their new war.

Fred Braun quietly opened the passenger's door and stepped out. He glanced about the area then turned to Garrett and Herschel sitting in the bed of the truck. "We'll hoof it the rest of the way."

"What do you think, Herschel?" Garrett asked, jumping over the side. He landed as softly as a cat and looked back at the pale computer technician. "If we get you in there, can you override the system and take control away from them?"

Apprehension kept Herschel from smiling. He tried to imitate Garrett's athletic jump from the back of the truck, but landed on the ground with a hard thud and almost dropped his shotgun. The oversized tactical vest shifted to a crooked slant on his slender frame. Face flushed, he straightened the vest, frustrated at his clumsiness, desperately wanting to prove himself to the team. Drawing a deep breath, he nodded and cradled the shotgun in the crook of his arm. "I'll do my best."

Bob Fischer walked around the truck and stood beside the technician. A slight grin edged up one corner of his mouth. "That's all we ask." He glanced at the shotgun then looked directly into Herschel's eyes. The grin melted, replaced by a grim stare. "If you have to use that thing, don't stop to think…just hold tight, pull the trigger and keep pumping."

Without waiting for a reply Fischer walked away, taking point on the patrol. "And be sure to reload," he added.

Garrett glanced at Herschel, made a friendly nod, and followed Fischer toward the Admin building. Fred Braun motioned Herschel to go next, then he trailed the patrol.

Don't think. Hold tight... pull the trigger. Keep pumping... Reload. The instructions kept repeating themselves in Herschel's mind, but Tommy's voice rose above all. *Red, shoot. No red, no shoot.*

Herschel glanced at the safety button on his shotgun, pressed it and observed red appear on the opposite side of the trigger guard. He sighed and lifted his head to find Garrett watching him as they walked. Once assured that Herschel's shotgun barrel was pointed to the sky, the former Marine sniper returned his attention to the patrol.

The noon heat relentlessly beat them and the thick, muggy air made their breathing labored. Their tactical vests became ovens and sweat trailed down their faces and dripped from their jaws. The closer the patrol came to the three-story building, Herschel's stomach drew tighter. By the time they reached the outlying landscape of the Admin building, it had become a knotted ball.

Fischer led them between hedges and tall oleander bushes until the patrol was within twenty feet of a door. He dropped to the ground, made hand signals, then slithered through the brush. Garrett and Braun knelt, motioning Herschel down with them.

The passing seconds grated the technician's nerves raw. When Garrett touched Herschel's shoulder and gestured for him to follow, Herschel felt his heart pound savagely against his chest. Braun gave him a light shove and Herschel was glad because he didn't know if he could have moved on his own.

They broke from the brush, crouched low, and raced to Fischer's position at the southwest corner of the building. Fischer whispered to Garrett and pointed to the panel van parked midway of the building. A slow nod came in answer, then Garrett leaned toward Herschel and Braun.

"Stay alert. Someone might be out here watching the parking lot," he said softly. "We're going inside through a maintenance entrance in the air-conditioning room."

Sliding along the wall, the four men crept toward the door, wary of the windows above them and the adjacent parking lot. At the air-conditioning maintenance room, Fischer eased the door open and slipped into its darkness. Seconds later he appeared and signaled them on.

Deafened by whirring motors and fans, they walked around the massive cooling units, eyes strained against the dim light. Another twelve feet and they halted at the maintenance door leading into the computer room. Herschel's gaze lingered on the doorknob as if he expected it to magically turn.

"We'll be back," Garrett whispered into Herschel's ear.

The technician nodded and watched the three men swiftly stream through the door. Sweat trickled down his face, and his palms felt sticky as they clamped tighter on the *Remington* shotgun. He closed his eyes.

Keep pumping. Reload. Red, shoot. Don't think. No red, no shoot. Pull the trigger. Hold tight. The instructions spun in Herschel's head in a maelstrom of horrifying visions. A hand brushed his arm, sending scalding streaks of fear throughout him. Herschel opened his eyes and exhaled hard, glad to see Braun.

In the past two years, Herschel had spent many an hour working in this room. Standing at the computer room door now, looking across the rows of computer banks and printers stretched along the computer room's fifty-foot length, he felt overwhelmed by it and the task before him. Jim was counting on him. Jim trusted him. Herschel entered the room, each step feeling heavier than the next.

"I'll be watching the parking lot. Garrett and Fischer are at the other end. If we yell, you clear out right then—don't wait," Braun ordered.

Herschel walked into the computer room and closed the door behind him. After being outside in the humidity and broiling heat, the sixty-nine degrees in the computer room felt like an Arctic front to Herschel. He shook involuntarily from the cold, adjusted his black baseball cap and straightened his tactical vest. Walking along the rows of computers, he reviewed the flashing warnings on monitors and glanced at the steady stream of paper flowing from the printers. A fierce shiver shook him as the frigid air chilled his sweat soaked body. He looked about the room for its primary computer terminal.

"There you are," he muttered. A smile of satisfaction appeared as he hurried to the south wall. Grabbing a swivel chair, Herschel positioned himself before the computer and laid the shotgun across his lap. The hair prickled on the back of his neck. He paused, spun his chair and realized what disturbed him. The door leading into the computer room from the Admin's offices was directly behind him. From the chair he could look over the top of a tall printer and see the outside hall through the door's small window. There wasn't time to waste in searching for boxes to stack and block him from view. Shaking his head, Herschel swiveled back to the computer.

"Remember me, sweetheart?" he mumbled, attempting to log into the refinery's mainframe system. The data rapidly scrolling up the monitor's screen refused to halt. He exhaled in exasperation and struck a key hard. The pause came. "That's my girl!"

Herschel's concentration intensified. He watched the monitor, and the outside world faded as he keyed in the backdoor password that the Titan Oil programmers thought only they were privileged to know.

"Oh, y'all are good," Herschel remarked. He read the commands on the screen that the terrorists had input from the third floor. He smiled with pride. "But not as good as me."

• • •

Twenty feet to Herschel's right, Sam Garrett walked out of a storage supply room and looked about the area. His brow drew downward. He held his CAR-16 at the ready as he looked down a row of computer banks and saw Herschel feverishly typing and talking to himself.

Garrett smiled inwardly and returned into the computer supervisor's office.

• • •

Looks like a hurricane came through here, Sefcik thought. Folders and papers were spread across every office floor and overturned chairs were by desks. *No one had to tell these people twice to haul ass.*

The gaunt mercenary cracked a grin and looked down the hall where he had come from. Holding his *H&K* automatic in the crook of his left arm, he drew a cigarette from his shirt pocket and leaned against the wall. He lit it, took a deep drag, and softly moaned in satisfaction as he exhaled the smoke.

The silence throughout the first floor reminded him of a ghost town as he glanced westward in the long hall. Taking a last deep drag, Sefcik snuffed the cigarette out on the wall, flicked the butt through the air and started toward the computer room, shifting the *H&K* into his right hand again.

How do people work every day in a place like this? Sefcik shook his head, amazed by the sea of five feet high partitions that formed a maze with the dozens of cubbyhole cubicle offices. He looked over the short walls as he walked. Scenic pictures of snow capped mountains and forest lakes cut from magazines and calendars were thumbtacked to the partition walls of every office.

Yep, they sit in these rat-holes and daydream about being somewhere else.

Sefcik's eyes narrowed. The thought of his sister having wasted years of her life in a hole like these at Titan Oil's corporate offices enraged him. *Fifteen years and they give her a pink slip so the CEO can get a pay raise off the money he saved by kicking people out. Downsizing. I wish that fucking CEO was here right now.*

The mercenary's fury fed his need for retribution, further justifying his acceptance of Murdock's offer and the end it held for Titan Oil upon completion. He turned and saw the small window on a door five feet away. Above it was neatly painted letters: COMPUTER ROOM.

The window was too small to stand off to one side of the door and peek through to see the whole room. Sefcik pressed his ear to the door. No voices, only the faint whirring of powerful computers and *thwacking* printers. The mercenary realized the room was soundproof and well insulated. The whine within would mask his entrance. He glanced at the doorknob and looked through the face-wide window, scanning the room's far left and right as best he could. Computer banks and printers blocked the majority of his view. His left hand gently wrapped about the doorknob.

Movement caught Sefcik's attention. He froze. It came again, this time as Sefcik looked through the window. A black-capped head bobbed on the far side of a computer.

"Who are you?" he whispered, intently watching the unknown man.

The mercenary glanced across the interior. No one else was seen. *Probably some geek who's afraid to leave his baby.* He weighed the chances of bursting in and making a quick headshot, or missing and having to chase the computer operator throughout the room. Sefcik observed the man sit upright and raise his slender arms to stretch. The set of the baseball cap was straightened and the arms lowered.

No, I can barely see his shoulders.

Decision made, Sefcik slowly turned the knob. Cold air and the high-pitched whine of computers rushed over the mercenary as he quietly stepped inside.

• • •

Herschel drummed his fingers on the terminal's keyboard and waited for his entered commands to alter the programming. The solid clunk of the door closing behind him shot paralyzing panic up his spine. He stared at the monitor, hoping to see the reflection of who stood at the door. His first thought was to callout Garrett's name, but his mind screamed *no*. A second later Herschel's worst fear became reality.

"Stand up, slow and easy." The voice carried a deadly ring.

Stomach rising into his throat, Herschel slid his hand off the keyboard. Forearms on the chair's armrests, hands dangling, his fingertips brushed the stock of the *Remington* shotgun on his lap. The safety. *Is it on or off?* Any moment the terrorist would recognize the tactical vest. *How can I stand without dropping the shotgun?*

"I said get up, punk." The mercenary's tone grew harsher.

Herschel clenched his teeth, afraid of being shot, afraid of dying. His life flashed before him, making him realize he had always lived in fear of someone, something, and envied men like Jim who stood against the odds. He closed his eyes, ashamed of the sensation consuming him. The cruel voice struck a raw nerve. *Bully* bellowed through Herschel's mind.

He's just another bully on a different school ground.

"Let's go, nerd." The words came with a tone of repulsion.

The baby-faced technician mentally snapped, breaking the chains that had bound him for so long. A hand wrapped about the stock while the other curled about the slide on the barrel. The chair spun to the left and as it did, Herschel rose with the *Remington* braced against his hip. He never heard the first explosion nor felt its recoil. His mind screamed.

Pull the trigger, keep pumping, don't think…and hold on tight. Herschel blindly obeyed every command.

Sefcik's eyes flared as the cannon-like barrel ten feet away swung toward him. Confusion stunned him. *A skinny kid in an oversized tactical vest with a shotgun?* But his confusion ended with the fiery blasts that erupted from the shotgun's muzzle.

The first shot barely cleared the printer and tore through Sefcik's stomach. The second, third, and fourth shots walked up the mercenary's chest, mangling Sefcik as they smashed him against the door and splattered the wall with a crimson spray.

Walking around the printer, the technician fed shells into the shotgun as Tommy had shown him. He paused and glared at the bloody corpse on the floor.

"The name's Herschel, ass-hole!"

Garrett and Fischer raced toward him, breathing hard, their weapons swinging across the room as they looked for danger. At the east end of the computer room, Braun dove through the door.

"It's all right, Fred!" Garrett shouted. He waited until Braun acknowledged before walking to Herschel.

The fury in Herschel subsided and the color drained from his face. His arms sagged from the weight of the shotgun. Garrett reached out and took it from him before it fell. He remembered how he had felt long ago on his own first kill.

Nerves tingling, stomach churning, a tidal wave of nausea swept over Herschel. He spun to a large plastic trashcan and vomited until only dry heaves came. When he stood and spit the bile taste from his mouth, Garrett gave him the shotgun and nodded in understanding.

"Let's go, Herschel," the former sniper said with respect.

A weak smile crossed the technician's lips as he turned to follow Garrett. Remaining in the computer room any longer was not an option.

CHAPTER TEN

June 25, 12:20 p.m.
Langley, Virginia

The fatherly appearing man randomly stopped at tables ringed with employees. He smiled warmly, spoke briefly, and patted their shoulders before moving on across the wide cafeteria.

Seeing him enter, people eased their plates aside. Ties were straightened, clothes were brushed, and hands groomed hair into place. Everyone wanted his personal accolades and the envious looks from co-workers that always followed.

Suit coat draped over an arm; shirt sleeves partially rolled up; identification badge hanging crookedly from a pocket; he looked more to be an insurance salesman than one of the most powerful men in the national security structure.

When not lunching with high-level government officials, it was almost certain he would make an appearance in the agency's cafeteria. The route and number were constant and the routine rarely varied. Escorted by plain-clothes security, he cut a zigzag path through the employees seating area, exchanging pleasantries to bond loyalties to him. Once ten people were met, he moved on, waving and nodding, until reaching his reserved table and the waiting, preordered meal.

Behind the endearing smile and his old style, plastic frame glasses was the calculating mind of a man dedicated to the protection of his nation at all costs and means available.

From fighting Nazis with Free French forces on Office of Strategic Services secret missions, and onto the formation of the Central Intelligence Agency, "Fighting Bill" Haverty had steadily moved through the ranks. Under the tutelage of the most prominent leaders in the intelligence field, Haverty had spiraled upward from an unknown Army Captain to his present position as DCI, Director of Central Intelligence.

He was as much at home in the political arena as he was in the planning of black operations. Through creative innovations he had established a private armed force to be used as covert problems arose. Quietly referred to as 'Bill's Animals,' they had grown into a clandestine army of trained mercenaries, hidden away until summoned and unleashed by their master.

As allegations of torture, assassinations, and illegal involvement in foreign coups were lodged against the CIA, Bill Haverty dauntlessly stood as the bastion of American intelligence before congressional committees. Crying havoc over the proceedings in the interest of national security, he always succeeded in portraying the accusations as paranoiac attacks on the patriots who daily risked their lives for freedom's sake.

It was this well-known aggressive side of his temperament, coupled with a valorous military service record that earned him the bold title of "Fighting Bill." But to the unknowing who observed him sitting quietly in the cafeteria, enjoying his customary order of chicken-fried steak drowned in white gravy, he looked more apt to enjoy a day's fishing than plotting the overthrow of a foreign government. Bill Haverty daily perpetuated his facade with employees and politicians alike.

Finishing the last bite of steak, Haverty wiped his mouth and stretched in the chair. Next came the ritual debate whether dessert was in order or not.

Judy will kill me if she finds out, he thought, knowing how rigidly his wife monitored his health. The last medical examination had shown minor problems with his heart. *Oh hell, you only go through life once,* thought the grinning DCI, enjoying the violation of her many rules. *What she doesn't know won't hurt her, and I guess I can trust these folks.* The thought made him glance across the sea of people charged with keeping national secrets. He smiled. *The Russians would tell her before they would.*

"Gene." Haverty gestured for a stiff-backed, wide-shouldered bodyguard to step closer. "Have one of the ladies with food service bring me a nice piece of cheesecake." He winked mischievously.

"Yes, sir," the bodyguard answered.

"And tell her to pour on the blueberries," Haverty remarked.

The bodyguard nodded and radioed the request to another agent standing with the cafeteria's manager. Receiving acknowledgment, the solemn-faced bodyguard returned to his position by the wall.

While Haverty waited he played a favorite game of guessing what job the unfamiliar people in the cafeteria held within the agency. Doing so sharpened his powers of observation and filed their faces in his mind for future reference. Hoping to find an interesting subject, he let his gaze glide across the room, careful to avoid direct eye contact with the employees around him.

There's a new hire, he thought. A frail, fidgety man sat by the cafeteria's doors intently watching everyone who passed. *He's bound to be in Personnel. No, probably an accountant.*

The sight of the Deputy Director's perturbed expression as he walked through the door disrupted Haverty's recreation. The usual collected, formal demeanor of his second-in-command was gone. Haverty watched the man's head wheel, eyes avidly searching the room. The Deputy spotted Haverty's security detail and then the DCI.

"Here you are, Bill." The silver-haired food attendant set a plate of cheesecake in front of him. She was as old as the DCI and as much an institution to the cafeteria as he was to the agency. The lines on her face displayed years of service to all too often unappreciative people. But the kindheartedness of her smile was genuine, projecting an honesty the DCI appreciated.

"Does Mrs. Haverty know you've been eating chicken-fried steak and cheesecake?" She straightened the agency identification badge on his shirt pocket. "That's not exactly low-fat." Her Arkansas accent gave the reprimand a friendly tone.

Haverty shook his fork in mock anger. "Maggie, if I ever thought you might tell Mrs. Haverty, I would have you transferred by this afternoon. Now go harass someone else. Go on, let me enjoy my meal." He narrowed his eyes, pretending to mean every word. When she smiled, he smiled with her.

Maggie saw the Deputy Director hastily approaching them. She glanced at Haverty. "If you want to enjoy it, you better eat fast. Here comes 'old stiff neck.'" Not waiting for a reply, she turned away.

The DCI twisted in his chair to look at her. "When are you going to start showing some respect to that man?" he asked, talking to her back. "I still might transfer you."

Maggie laughed and waved a hand over her shoulder as she returned to the food line. Shaking his head, Haverty realized she had spoken the truth. Duncan Stewart was an 'old stiff neck.'

Conservatively dressed at all times, he rarely removed his suit coat for fear of presenting an improper image to the employees yet Stewart was an expert in his field and as Haverty's right hand, could be trusted.

The Deputy Director took a seat with his back to the majority of employees. He glanced at the nearby security detail and watched Haverty take the first bite of dessert.

"Does Judy know you're eating that?"

Haverty's fork clanked loudly as he dropped it onto the plate. Sitting back in his chair, palms resting on the table, Haverty groaned and looked at the Deputy Director.

"No one can bring me good intelligence on the Chinese yet everyone can tell me about my diet." He pushed the plate away in frustration. "What is it, Duncan? You didn't come here simply to prevent me from eating cheesecake."

"We need to talk," whispered the Deputy. Worry filled his eyes. "We have a situation." A nervous urgency to say more showed on his face.

"What situation?" Haverty casually moved his plate aside.

"A leak."

The Director frowned. "Another damn mole?"

"No," Stewart replied, vigorously shaking a hand. He leaned across the table and whispered, "I'm talking about the report concerning one of your former animals."

Haverty nodded subtly.

"McCall at NSC knows about it and went straight to—*him*. We need to go to your office. Right now, every major network is televising the attack in Texas."

"That bastard," Haverty said through clenched teeth, hands squeezed into tight fists. For the past two hours he had been locked away in a covert ops meeting within one of the many security 'bubbles,' a thick *Plexiglas*, double-walled, elongated room with radio waves piped between the walls to block electronic eavesdropping. Short of World War III breaking out, no one ever entered and disturbed such meetings.

Edging forward, Haverty never removed his eyes from the man across the table. The glare of a king whose orders had been disobeyed painted his face.

"I erased the paper trail on that report. How did McCall get it? Who leaked it? No... wait." Haverty groaned as he sat back in his chair and lightly tapped the table. "His daughter, right?" The tapping increased.

"That's the least of our worries," the tense Deputy stated. "Bill, we need to go to your office."

Their plan had unraveled. The President wasn't supposed to find out until Haverty briefed him, pretending the intelligence was freshly received and they were acting upon it before the FBI. This was supposed to open doors for more funding, increased manpower, elevate them over the FBI, and help expand operations, and more. But with the President now knowing they had sat on the report, Duncan Stewart wondered if it was going to be every man for himself in this fiasco.

The Deputy Director observed people beginning to stare at Haverty, puzzled by his visible irritation.

Sensing a noose closing about his career, Bill Haverty left the cafeteria oblivious to employee farewells. He returned to his office by a different route, caught up in his thoughts.

Duncan Stewart followed the DCI's security detail, wanting time to think. Passing through the main lobby, his gaze swept the area. He paused to read words inscribed on a wall, words he had read many times, and like always, thought of the hypocrisy they bore for the secretive agency.

AND YE SHALL KNOW THE TRUTH.

AND THE TRUTH SHALL MAKE YOU FREE.

John, VIII: 32

• • •

June 25, 12:20 p.m.

The mammoth three story wooden structure was old but the cooling tower had faithfully served A-5 for years, churning and supplying thousands of gallons of water for its operation. There were other backup water systems yet this tower carried the primary responsibility of being the cooling system for the unit. With all of the modern technology the refinery used, the cooling tower acted as nothing more than a radiator did for a car.

Set out by itself in a vast dirt lot next to the unit, the structure provided a good view of A-5 as well as safe cover. Jim stood in the outer room of the pump shed built into the tower's first floor. Waiting for Pierson to return, he listened to the thrash of water as it cascaded above him. In the next room monstrous pumps roared and roiled water, forcing it into A-5's cooling lines against its will. A constant vibration carried through the cement floor.

A streak of sunlight shined through the cracks of the pump shed's outer walls like a flashlight beam in the night. Staring at the small explosive bundles laying on a workbench, Jim gently nudged one of them into the light. From their size and squared off construction, he assumed they contained C-4, possibly TNT. He wasn't sure, but thought that a bomb made with dynamite would probably be different in shape.

The shed's outer door flew open, momentarily flooding the room with sunlight and blinding Jim. As quickly as it opened, it closed.

Metal dug deep in Jake Pierson's stomach, preventing him from entering any further.

When Jim's eyes adjusted, he removed the shotgun's barrel from the former Navy man.

Closing his eyes a moment, Pierson drew a deep breath, thankful for Thurman's self-control. The shop foreman was about to speak when Sam Garrett's voice came on the radio.

"Is everyone all right?" Jim asked anxiously, cracking the door open to watch the A-5 unit as he talked.

"We're fine. Herschel bagged one in the computer room. We've been pinned down for a while. A merc is on the roof with one of the choppers, walking around checking the area."

The two men in the cooling tower's pump room looked at one another, glad to know their friends were alive.

"Jim, Herschel only had time to get the mainframe to keep repeating lock-down procedures. It'll safely override commands from the units and the Ops room, but he couldn't get control of A-5's cameras like he wanted." Fischer sounded disappointed.

Looking out the door, as Jim listened he observed several of A-5's cameras move erratically. The long camera boxes briefly pointed to the sky, panned left and right, then lowered and repeated the sequence. He glanced at Pierson. The foreman's proud smile told Jim who was responsible for the malfunctions.

"The cameras have been taken care of on this end," he said into his microphone. He continued, knowing Tommy and Joshua were monitoring. "Allen, find a truck and go the Admin building. Strike when you're ready and then move to the Ivory Tower. Tommy, hold tight. I'll be at your location in a few minutes."

Everyone acknowledged. The radio went silent again. Jim watched the cameras move. He looked at Pierson. "What's their status? Are they out for good?"

"I found the feed-in box and crossed a few wires. The video maybe garbled or still live, but there is no control of the movement."

"All right, we can work with that. Tommy and I will hit the control room. You move around to the HF storage vessels and locate any charges on them. If you can't disarm them, find some place they can blow with the least damage. We'll leave these here." Jim gestured to the explosives on the workbench.

Pierson nodded and lit a cigarette. "Want one?" he asked, blowing a thick cloud of smoke above his head.

Jim shook his head and looked out the door again.

"It's been a long time since I've worked with explosives. Last thing I need is jittery hands." Pierson took another deep drag and sighed at its calming effect. "You still planning to leave after all this is over?"

"Not much to hold me here." Jim kept his vigil on the unit.

"I know what you're going through. You'll survive. You've already made it past the toughest part."

The door eased closed and Jim turned to face Pierson. "Is your family dead too?" he asked softly.

"No, I'm dead to them—at least I am to my daughter."

Confused, Jim slightly shook his head.

Pierson smoked his cigarette a last time and let it fall. He squashed it with his boot and looked at Thurman, gaze tinged with regret.

"I was with a team pulling ops in Laos, looking for a POW camp when my wife ran off with our kid. Her letter caught up with me two months after she had emptied our house. Said our daughter needed a full-time father and she needed a full-time husband. Damn that hurt, but the real hurt came a year later when I learned she was living with some rich bastard in Colorado and had told our daughter that I was dead."

"I'm sorry, Jake. I never knew."

"At first I told myself it was for the best. You know, the crap I was involved with and especially running the chance of not returning from a mission." Pierson softly shook his head. "One day I woke up and realized how much I missed them. Hell, I began to hate the world and hate GOD because I was allowing my daughter to think I was dead. Then came the depression, the drinking...the thoughts of suicide."

Thurman remained silent. The hurt in Jake Pierson's eyes stirred the embers of Jim's memories. Only a week ago Jim had stood on that fine edge where life and death balanced between another ounce of trigger pull.

"But I managed to get my life squared away. If you can make it over the mountains, you can make it through the dark valleys." The former SEAL nodded to Jim. "I think you've already tackled your mountains," Pierson said with a protracted sigh.

Anguish rose and fell within Jim like rolling ocean waves.

"Go find your daughter, Jake. Explain everything to her. It's another mountain, but in the end it's worth the climb."

Pierson stared at the beam of sunlight shining through a crack in the shed's outer walls. Gradually, a warm smile formed on his lips. "I've been thinking about it."

"You've thought about it long enough. Do it."

"Right now?" Pierson glowed with a happiness he had not known in years.

Thurman laughed.

"Why don't we wrap up a couple of loose ends around here and you can leave tomorrow?" He glanced at his watch. "I better get my ass moving. Tommy probably thinks I forgot him."

"Hey, Jim…"

About to open the door, the Titan Oil security officer stopped and looked back.

"Steaks and beer are on me after this is over. It'll be my going-away party," Pierson remarked.

A thumb's up gesture rose into the air and sunlight bathed the room as Jim opened the door.

"So long, Jake."

Pierson watched the door close then glanced at the explosives on the workbench. As the machine shop foreman left the shed, he smiled. The cooling tower was destined for major reconstruction.

• • •

June 25, 12:22 p.m. A-5 Control Room

The gun barrel smashed into the operator's face with the speed of a cobra's strike, catching him off-guard and knocking him from the chair. Teeth broken out, blood dripping from his mouth, the man lay on the floor unconscious.

Murdock's hand shook from the blow. He raised the *Glock* .45 again but the operator remained down. A raging fury consumed the mercenary leader. Murdock spun and pounded a fist on the control desk as he looked at the monitors. *What did he do?* The cameras showed sky, ground, and turned so swiftly the screens blurred. He glared at the bloody operator slowly regaining consciousness.

Computer screens cleared and a fresh display of messages appeared. Murdock leaned forward and read them. Livid, he turned and aimed the semiautomatic at the terrified unit operator.

"Kotter?" Murdock asked, keying the transmit button on his radio. "What's the status of your computers?"

The man in the Admin Operations Room acknowledged in a tone of dismay.

"I lost all control. Something automatically took over. The screen keeps scrolling the same message, *Emergency Lock-Down Initiated.*"

While Kotter talked, Murdock read the same words on A-5's computer screen. Interference caused by the building's construction partially garbled Kotter's radio transmission.

Murdock's pistol never wavered from the operator's face.

Looking at the. 45's muzzle, it seemed large enough to place a fist into and never touch the sides. As the bleeding man stared at the cavernous opening, it belched fire. He never saw the bullet.

Kane rushed into the room.

Standing over the dead process operator, Murdock calmly returned the *Glock* to its holster. He glanced at Kane. "Send Nathan and Scofield outside to find Nicole. She's been gone too long. When they find her, tell them to check the charges again!"

Kane left at a run.

Murdock watched Kane through the large plate glass window as he relayed orders to Nathan in the hall. A scowl swathed Nathan's face. He rubbed his ears and strode away.

The thick-cushioned chair squeaked as Murdock took a seat before the computer board. He stared at the clock on the wall. Time was growing short. He touched his shirt and felt the outline of the remote control detonating device.

A simple click and every bomb will blow simultaneously, he thought. *The catalyst-cracking units, both of A-5's towering acid storage vessels, the two fully loaded tanker trucks and the grand finale—the butane spheres.*

Calmed from the technical problems, he removed a palm-sized box from his shirt and gently laid it next to him on the counter. At precisely 12:30 p.m., Murdock pressed a sequence of numbers into his cellular phone and listened to the clicks as it made the international connections. The board operator's chair was comfortable and he shifted his weight in it, enjoying the feel.

I like this. I'll have to buy some for Christmas gifts. He chuckled at the thought of squandering money. With the thirty million plus expenses he was receiving for disrupting OPEC's money pipeline and casting suspicion on the Middle East, he could afford to waste a dollar or two.

The ringing ceased. A pleasant voiced woman answered, her accent hardly detectable. "Zurich Bank of Commerce and Credit."

"I need verification on a transfer of funds," he stated, looking at the clock. He gave his personal identification code, account number, and password before sitting back to wait.

"Yes, sir. Our records show fifteen million was credited this morning. Would you like your account's total?"

"No, that won't be necessary. You've been most helpful." The mercenary leader disconnected the call and smiled. *Petroleos de Venezuela* had verified the refinery attack and transferred the second half on schedule. All that remained was for him to fulfill his agreement with the Venezuelan state-owned company. He would pull everyone back to the choppers, go airborne, and blow the place.

By tonight I'll be on a beach in Mexico.

Murdock looked at the corpse by his boots and laughed.

"I told you I was a businessman."

• • •

Standing at an office window, watching police cars come and go from the blockades, Peterson heard his name and keyed the radio. "Yes, sir?"

"Any new arrivals?"

Peterson looked to both ends of the public street. Nothing appeared to have changed since the last time Murdock had checked.

"Negative, sir. The police let more media through the barricades, but no sign of a strike force."

"Excellent. Be prepared to complete the mission on my command. It won't be much longer."

Peterson acknowledged Murdock's order and turned his head. Tonya stood listening from the door.

"I'm glad we're leaving soon. This place sounds like it's ready to go up before we want," she said.

CHAPTER ELEVEN

June 25, 12:35 p.m.

Thurman's vest stuck to him as if he had walked fully clothed through a shower. Sweat trickled down his forehead and temples, cutting crooked lines in the dirt on his face. He moved as swiftly as possible, wanting to be with Tommy before the assault on the Admin was launched. Reaching the high firewall encircling the sphere tank farm, he dragged an arm across his eyes to clear them of sweat and crawled to Tommy's side.

"Nice camouflage job." The machinist chuckled and gestured to Jim's face.

"Camo?" Thurman wiped his face and looked at his fingertips. Sweat had mixed with dirt to become a thin sheen of mud. "Very funny." He turned to look at the A-5 control room building. "Any activity?"

"Two came out and didn't appear very happy. I bet they miss their sweetheart." Tommy jerked a thumb toward the arrow-nailed woman twenty feet behind him. "They went to the right. Probably going to the north side of the unit."

Jim's eyes flared. "How long ago?"

"A couple of minutes at the most." Tommy didn't understand his anxiety.

"Jake—Jake, two mercs loose on the unit. Watch your ass." Jim yelled into his microphone.

Shifting onto his side, Tommy looked at him. "What's wrong?"

"Pierson is searching for charges over there. He's alone. I told him we were going into the control room."

They lay in the dirt, waiting for Pierson to acknowledge, hoping he would be all right. It was too late to change the plan and go to him. No response came.

Across the wide street a side door led into the building's interior. Jim stared at it. He knew the layout of the A-5 control room yet had no idea of how many mercenaries they would encounter. There could be no more waiting. The War Dogs had technically hampered the terrorists as much as possible. Only killing remained.

"You know, I sure don't remember that building being so big. Did it grow in the last hour?" Tommy asked as his trademark comical grin appeared.

Jim removed the rifle from his back and laid it carefully beside him in the dirt. *Won't do me any good in the building.*

"Yep, it grew," Tommy said, carrying his gaze from the building to Jim.

Taking hold of his pistol-gripped shotgun, Jim nodded.

"Well, *amigo*, we better go before it gets any bigger," he remarked with a halfhearted smile.

Tommy made one last visual survey of the area and crawled over the firewall. Clearing its crest, he jumped to his feet and ran across the street to A-5.

Jim crawled up the firewall. He halted abruptly, glanced at Tommy, then to the man carrying an AK-47 who suddenly walked into view seventy yards away. McLawchlin was almost to the wall of the A-5 building, moving as fast as his feet would carry him. The mercenary had not seen either of them.

"Run, Tommy!" Jim yelled into his radio microphone. "Bandit coming your way."

The mercenary walked between several tall pumps and piping, heading toward the control room door where Tommy stood gasping.

Dropping behind the firewall, Jim realized the terrorist would see Tommy within seconds, and Tommy didn't have any concealment. Looking across the street, Jim saw Tommy raise his sawed-off shotgun to waist level. Back pressed against the building's wall, the machinist didn't know whether to watch for the approaching terrorist, or watch the door.

Thurman grabbed his rifle and fell into a prone firing position.

"Where is he, Jimbo? Talk to me." The anxious words came in panting breaths on the radio.

"Your left," came Jim's whispering voice. "I lost him behind some piping. Watch that door by you in case someone comes out."

Jim lifted his head and looked over the scope of the bolt action *Remington* 30-06 rifle. His finger lay ready along the trigger guard. Sweat stung his eyes, burning them like hot coals. He ignored the torment. He couldn't afford to take his eyes off the area. The automatic weapon carrying terrorist had vanished. Jim knew he was skirting between the machinery, moving toward the control room, but where was he?

The sea of gray-painted equipment seemingly drowned the paramilitary dressed man. He appeared, rounding a corner, strides growing with each step.

Mouth dry, breathing heavily, Tommy licked his lips and struggled to remain calm. He craned his head back to check the door at the top of the steps that led into the A-5 control room.

• • •

Where is that woman? Eric Scofield thought. *No, Nicole knows better. Something's wrong.*

He started to call Murdock, but froze. The surprise of seeing an armed stranger near the side door made him forget the radio. Moving in a half crouch, Scofield raised his AK-47 and edged toward the shotgun wielding man fifty feet away. The mercenary glanced about the area. Not seeing anything out of the ordinary, he returned his attention to the unknown man.

That's it. Keep watching that door for a few more seconds and your mine, Scofield thought.

• • •

Jim lowered his eye behind the scope and brought the mercenary into view. There was no time to readjust the magnification and try a headshot. He had to shoot before the man killed Tommy.

The cross hairs filled with body mass. As fast as Jim was trying to pull off the shot, he was not sure of the strike zone. But it was the man's body and he could not wait. He had to shoot now.

The rifle's recoil kicked Jim's shoulder yet he never felt it. His right hand flew upward, striking the bolt, ejecting the spent cartridge, and slamming the bolt home again, reloading a fresh round. Immediately his eye adjusted to the scope and searched for the terrorist. This time, he decreased the magnification on the *Redfield* scope.

"Did you get him?" Tommy asked on the radio.

Jim saw blood splattered on the side of the A-5 building, but no mercenary.

"He's hit. Could you hear the shot?"

"Barely. The flares are too loud."

Jim exhaled in relief. There was still another terrorist on the unit. He looked through the scope again. Below and to the right of the blood on the wall, a leg extended from behind a large pump. "I see him, Tommy. Keep an eye on that door!"

The leg slowly withdrew from sight.

C'mon, you bastard. Show yourself, Jim thought, using the scope to search the vicinity of the pump.

Sweat scalded his eyes. He moved the rifle and aimed to the right of the pump. Between it and another piece of machinery was a narrow gap. If the wounded man wanted to escape, he would have to run past that opening. Jim knew he would only be able to see the terrorist in a brief glimpse.

The distance was fifty yards. No problems with a shot like that under normal conditions, but these were not normal conditions and time was being wasted. The terrorist might have radioed someone. Any moment more terrorists could pour out of the building. If the wounded man didn't show himself soon, Jim would be forced to go after him.

Tommy called again. Jim ignored him. His concentration was solely on the sparse opening between the pumps. Sweat fueled the blazing inferno in his eyes. Tears flowed over the rims as he forced them to remain open.

In South Texas, the brush is so thick that *senderos*, long, narrow paths are often cut to provide a lane of fire for deer hunters. The land is known for producing trophy bucks yet a hunter only has a brief second to shoot the deer before it crosses and takes refuge on the far side of the lane.

Not knowing why it came to mind, Jim remembered having taken such a shot when he and Tommy had hunted in Falfurrias, Texas. He adjusted the scope's magnification again and thought aloud, his whisper activating the radio microphone.

"*Muy Grande.*"

"He's big? Did you say the bastard is big? Dammit, Jim, quit talking Mexican," came across the radio.

Jim never replied. He kept the cross hairs centered in the gap between the machinery, and held pressure on the trigger.

A dark-splotched shirt moved into the cross hairs, appearing for a split-second.

The rifle bucked against Jim's hands. Immediately, he reloaded and sighted in on the mercenary. The shirt spun like a top. An AK-47 flew skyward, then crashed onto the concrete.

Eric Scofield fell over a pump and remained motionless.

Running to the terrorist, Tommy ensured he was dead while Jim crossed the road.

"He never warned anyone. First round went through his radio and gut shot him. Second one took his heart," Tommy explained, trying to slow his breathing from the return jog.

Jim listened as he watched the door near them.

"You and your *muy grande*. He wasn't that big. You need glasses," Tommy mumbled, about to walk around his friend.

"No, the *Muy Grande* contest in South Texas. The one every year for the biggest buck."

The machinist stopped and glared at Jim. "While I was here with my butt puckered, you were thinking about deer hunting?"

Jim started toward the steps leading up to the side door. He paused.

"All right. Next time I won't tell you what I was thinking."

"Next time? Funny, Jim…you're real fucking funny," Tommy said sarcastically.

• • •

Pierson heard Jim's radio warning and took cover under a tanker trailer at the HF loading dock. He leaned his shotgun against a wheel and the barrel's muzzle snagged a wire. The former SEAL froze. He gently moved the barrel. The wire was connected to an explosive charge set beneath the tanker trailer's framework.

A body crossed an alleyway. The sighting was brief yet enough to catch Pierson's attention. He left the shotgun and crawled out from beneath the truck. The surrounding equipment was too short to hide behind, but fifteen feet overhead were pipe racks and steel girders. He leaped atop a pump and climbed its protruding pipes.

The narrow steel beam wasn't much to balance on, but it elevated Pierson from a direct ground level view. He stretched himself along it and drew still at the terrorist's approach.

Searching between pumps and machinery, the man never bothered to look up. He walked a few steps, stopped, looked about him, and moved on. Gradually nearing the steel beam where Pierson laid, he halted beneath it and rubbed his ears.

"Nicole?" he yelled, scanning the area. "Nicole?"

Pierson watched the mercenary level an *H&K MP5* and sweep the area with its barrel.

He's getting nervous. Too nervous, Pierson thought.

Sliding a hand into a vest pocket, Pierson moved his fingers until they touched wood. His hand closed and withdrew slowly. Sweat dripped from Pierson's chin and dotted the concrete inches behind the terrorist. The man backed and stepped on the small splatters. Two more droplets fell and struck the mercenary's shoulder. They went unnoticed.

Being heard was the least of Pierson's worries. The whines of the surrounding pumps masked any noise he could make. What disturbed him, though, was keeping his prone balance on the narrow beam.

Palms slick, Pierson clenched the garrote's wooden handles and felt tension knotting the muscles in his body. He eased the long strand of piano wire clear of the beam and waited like a leopard above its prey. Another droplet of sweat fell from his chin and plopped on the terrorist's shoulder.

The former SEAL squeezed the handles and his knuckles grew white from the strain. Movement came, but not as he wanted. The terrorist halted and glanced at his shoulder as a droplet struck him. Raising his face, he saw two cold, unforgiving eyes staring at him.

Allowing his weight to carry him off the beam, Pierson made his descent. His knees slammed into the terrorist's shoulders and drove the startled man to the ground. He circled his hands about the terrorist's head and felt the wire snag on the chin as he sought the throat. The wire sliced through skin, popped free, and dug deep into the flesh below the Adam's Apple.

They smashed into the concrete floor with a harsh thud and rolled to one side. Fire spewed from the *H&K's* muzzle as the terrorist tried to shoot his attacker. Hot shell casings pelted Pierson's face and barely missed his eyes. The staccato of gunfire bellowed in Pierson's ears.

Flooded with adrenaline, Pierson tightened the garrote's noose. The firing stopped. The weapon clattered against pipes and pumps as it fell from the mercenary's hands. Fingers clawed at Pierson, then closed into fists and frantically reached back to smash the sides of his head. Jake Pierson never released his deadly hold.

Regaining balance, Pierson yelled through clenched teeth and savagely drew the garrote tighter. The terrorist thrashed about madly on the concrete as the wire cut through his skin and into his esophagus. Blood spewed into the air when the jugular vein severed. After a few convulsive jumps, the terrorist's body drew limp.

Hands cramped, fingers refusing to open more than a few inches, Pierson rose from the ground and let the man's weight pull the garrote from his hands. Heart pounding against his chest, Pierson stood breathing in powerful blasts. He knew better than to stand and admire his work. One last thing had to be done.

The garrote was buried deep in the throat. Pierson jerked the wire free and withdrew his survival knife. In one deft move he guaranteed the terrorist's death, then left.

• • •

June 25, 12:45 p.m., Admin Building

The fire escape ladder was the fastest means of reaching the roof. When the aging three-story building was renovated, the ladder had been left attached to the outside wall against the wishes of the architects. Now, as Joshua Allen climbed each rung, he was glad. He didn't know how they would have reached the roof otherwise.

Below him, Sam Garrett and Fred Braun kept pace as he climbed. Staying on the ground with Herschel, Bob Fischer provided protection until the team reached the top. Once the all clear was given they would climb and join them.

On the ladder, Joshua peeked over the roof's ledge then lowered himself below its rim. Holding up one finger, he silently told the others of the terrorists he had seen. He rose to the ledge again and waited for the lone terrorist to walk behind the helicopter.

"Wait until I call," Joshua whispered into his microphone.

Sam Garrett held a thumb up in confirmation. Allen never saw it. He had already slithered over the ledge and was moving toward the chopper.

As Garrett waited on the ladder, he wondered if anyone from the Ivory Tower would see them on the Admin building's rooftop. There were no alternatives though, just high risks.

Looking out over the flagship, Garrett thought about how bizarre the refinery appeared. Any other Monday, the refinery streets would be congested with vehicular and pedestrian traffic. Vendors; contractors; employees; all hustling about, wrapped in their own worlds. Today, though, no life stirred on the streets. The corpses along them testified to that sad fact.

Flare stacks still burned wildly but the relief valves had settled to intermittent howls. From the sounds Garrett hoped the dangerous pressure levels were gradually coming under control. The refinery was struggling to stabilize, struggling to survive.

Canting his head back to look up at the roof's ledge, Garrett saw gray and black smoke-filled clouds drifting past. He glanced northward and realized the daily afternoon summer storms were fast approaching. All he could hope for was that the showers held off until the team reached the Ivory Tower.

That's a lot to hope for... First, we have to live through a firefight in this building, he thought.

Garrett shook his head lightly at the foolishness of thinking about rain while mercenaries held hostages and intended to destroy the entire complex.

"Clear here, Sam. Bring everyone to the chopper."

Glancing at the men below him, Sam Garrett knew they had heard Joshua's transmission.

"Here we come," he radioed.

• • •

June 25, 12:50 p.m.

The corporate jet was forty minutes outside of Houston Intercontinental Airport when the pilot announced the turbulent weather they would encounter. His words fell on deaf ears. The Chairman of the Board stared out the window, lost in thought. On his lap laid a report faxed to him only minutes ago.

Across the aisle, Dave Simmons, the refinery manager, sat frustrated by his absence from Grainger City during such a crucial time. He knew he could not have prevented the attack, but at least could have been there to negotiate with the terrorists and possibly save lives. His vexations increased when Clarence Calder surfaced among his squalid thoughts.

Complaints had crossed Simmons' desk for months about the superintendent's ill regard for his own department, of the need for security, and in general, the arrogant bastard Calder had become. There were so many management brush fires to be extinguished in the refinery and remaining profitable for the shareholders had consumed Simmons' days. Calder had simply fallen through the cracks in the system, landing on that lingering list of *'things to look into when there is time.'* Unfortunately, the refinery's security department had fallen into those cracks as well, but physical security had also never been a priority issue in the petrochemical world.

"Dave…"

Simmons didn't hear his name called until the Chairman spoke again.

"I'm sorry, sir. I was thinking about the news report we read earlier."

"I understand," the Chairman replied calmly. He massaged his left temple as he lifted the faxed report from his lap. "Our analysts studied the film footage. We have at least thirty dead and wounded at the main entrance and adjacent parking lot. God knows how many more are inside the buildings and throughout the refinery."

Dave Simmons sat speechless, unable to comprehend the magnitude of tragedy in progress at Grainger City.

"Jesus Christ… the broadcasts keep showing those murdered security men laying out in the road." The Chairman remorsefully shook his head. "One of them looked as if he didn't have a head. " His eyes briefly shut. "What kind of animals would do this?" Lowering his gaze, he stared at the floor. "Were we such an easy target?" The Chairman spoke as if he were searching his soul for the answers to a thousand questions.

Simmons sat thinking, not liking his thoughts. He recalled once asking if there were any worries about a terrorist attack, and the security superintendent had laughed.

"Terrorism only happens overseas…in the middle east, not here," Calder had replied.

But it did, and when Clarence Calder began telling him how worthless the in-house security officers would be in such an event, Simmons should have alerted. The refinery manager realized too late the problem had always existed with Calder. Aggravation rose within the refinery manager at his failure to take note of Calder's repeated berating of his own people. With Simmons' every thought came a question and with every question, the same ugly answer.

Profit first. People last. Protecting them wasn't even on the radar. But Simmons was no longer concerned with profit. If every processing unit exploded, the death toll within the refinery could easily reach over two thousand.

Sitting back, the Chairman wearily closed his eyes and let his head sink into the soft headrest. Worry etched his face. The flight attendant approached, carrying a paper in her hand. She held it out to the Chairman and apologized for the interruption.

"Sir, we received this communication for you."

Thanking her, the Chairman solemnly read the paper before passing it across the aisle to Simmons.

"This 'Serpent and Sword' group wants the President to denounce Israel as criminals and publicly apologize for America's interference in middle-east affairs." The Chairman grew silent for a minute. "There's more. They want twenty billion dollars in aid to the Palestinians. If the financial transactions are not completed within two hours, the Serpent and Sword will detonate charges, destroy the refinery, and release hydrofluoric acid across the civilian population." Finishing, his gaze tediously rose to Simmons.

Simmons was speechless. His death toll calculations had just risen, and the downfall of Titan Oil had come.

• • •

June 25, 12:50 p.m., Admin Building

Herschel was the last man up the ladder. By the time he joined the others on the roof, they had a woman bound and gagged inside the seating area of the helicopter. A massive red discoloration across the right side of her face told him she had not surrendered peacefully.

"Keep watch," Allen ordered, motioning to the door leading down into the building. "I won't be long." His voice held an icy ring.

Fischer nodded and with Braun took defensive positions underneath the chopper, not wanting to be observed from the Ivory Tower.

"Go with them, Herschel." Garrett's tone implied more than he spoke. "You don't want to be here."

The young technician started to argue, but Joshua Allen's stare silenced him. He dejectedly crawled under the chopper and aimed his shotgun at the rooftop door as Fischer and Braun did.

Allen and Garret climbed into the helicopter and knelt beside their prisoner. Removing the radio, grenades, and pistol from her belt, Allen placed her radio in his vest pocket for safekeeping. Glancing at Garrett, he knew they had no time to waste on the interrogation. Drawing his *Kabar*, he held the ominous blade in front of her face. Neither Allen nor Garrett displayed remorse over what they were about to do.

"I'll ask questions. You answer by nodding. If you don't answer fast enough, I'll cut off parts of your body until you do—or die." Allen stared at her. His voice was flat and tranquil, leaving no doubt as to his earnestness.

Hate filled Jessica Carter's eyes.

"How many of your friends are inside? Nod once for each person."

She made no effort to answer. Joshua grabbed her left ear and sliced it off in one swoop.

Her eyes flared as pain exploded in her head and throughout her body. She screamed, but the thick gag in her mouth allowed only muffled moans. She twisted and tried to break free.

Joshua Allen slammed her back onto the floor of the helicopter.

"I asked you a question," he said calmly. No response.

The right ear was cut off and dropped onto her chest. When the spasms of anguish decreased, her glazed eyes opened. Tears flowed freely. A pleading look for mercy replaced her earlier hate-filled glare.

"How many?" Joshua wiped the knife clean on her breasts and let its edge brush over her nipples.

Looking at the menacing blade, she cried and began to nod.

"Three in this building?"

Jessica immediately confirmed the question by bobbing her head.

"Are all the hostages in the conference room?"

Her eyes shut and she nodded.

"Okay, how many are in that building?" he asked, motioning with the knife toward the Ivory Tower.

She hesitated, deciding if she should let them kill her or answer the question and possibly live. The decision came easy. When Allen brutally grabbed a breast and laid the blade across it, she feverishly nodded in answer.

"Four?"

Confirming nods came again.

"Now see how easy that was," Joshua said with a benevolent smile. "Here, maybe someone can sew these back on later." Picking up the two severed ears laying on her chest, Joshua shoved them into her shirt pocket. Turning his head, smile gone, he looked at Sam.

"I'll be along in a moment." Joshua's face was as hard as granite.

Climbing out of the helicopter, Garrett knelt and looked at Fischer. "She talked. Let's move." He walked away.

Herschel was the first one out and on his feet. Braun and Fischer trailed him to Garrett. Within seconds Allen arrived and calmly sheathed his knife.

The blood on Allen's hands caught Herschel's attention. He looked back and his stomach soared into his mouth. The woman laid with crimson holes for ears and her head was twisted in an abnormal position. She stared out the helicopter's door with a vacant gaze. Nausea forced Herschel to turn away. He glanced at Allen, then to the men about him. No one appeared disturbed. Braun's whispering voice carried to him.

"We live, they die. That's how you deal with terrorists."

Herschel sluggishly nodded and looked away.

"She said three are down there but we'll count on at least twice that many. Hostages are in the conference room," stated Garrett. "Tie the ropes onto the chopper. We'll go over both sides of the building and through the windows. Don't try to swing down and blow the glass as you go in. It's too thick. Hang off the side and shoot them first. When you have enough clearance, move in. If we're lucky, the bastards will leave the hostages unattended long enough for us to get inside."

Fischer gestured to Herschel as he lifted the rappelling rope off his shoulder. "He can stay here and keep watch on the roof door." The other men readily agreed.

"Best place would be under the chopper, Herschel. It's good cover and you can pick off anyone coming out the door."

"Wait a minute! I'm not scared. I'm going too," the technician protested.

"No one said you were scared. As soon as we clear the building, we'll come for you. Until we get through the windows, these ropes are our lifelines. If someone comes out that door and cuts the ropes... Well, I don't have wings attached to my ass." Joshua shook his head. "And I'm sure that ground would hurt after a three story fall."

A few chuckles and nods came. Herschel quietly accepted his assignment. There was no need for further discussion. In silence they secured the rappelling ropes onto the helicopter's landing skids and measured out lengths to the windows. Moving into position, the War Dogs tied knots and loose fitting, crude harnesses into the ropes, then eased them about their waists.

Sam Garrett inspected his shotgun and double-checked the pistol in his shoulder holster. He chose the conference room side of the building and hoped the thick windows would break before he ran out of ammunition. Across the roof, Sam observed Braun and Fischer standing with the butts of their short bush guns resting on their hips. They were examining themselves, not wanting anything to snag or fallout of a pocket. He turned to his left and saw Joshua holding the confiscated radio.

"I'm going to jam the transmit button so it remains keyed. They won't be able to call each other," Allen commented. "Are you ready? We'll both have to go through the same window, so blast that son of a bitch good."

Garrett nodded and glanced over his own equipment. When he lifted his head, everyone was watching him, waiting for a sign.

The clamor of relief valves screaming from pent-up pressures momentarily increased to deafening proportions.

Allen pointed to his ear, gesturing for all earplug buttons to be depressed, allowing simultaneous transmit and monitor capabilities. Hands rose and fell.

"Ready?" Joshua asked softly, adjusting his microphone.

Braun and Fischer held their thumbs up into the air.

Shoving a chipped piece of rooftop gravel into the transmit button of Jessica's radio, Joshua laid it on the rooftop.

Holding onto the rope, letting it slide slowly through his hand, Garrett descended over the side with Allen staying even. The two men on the opposite side of the building gradually disappeared below the rooftop's ledge.

"Going in!"

The words came through the radio earplugs, exploding in their brains with the force of a thunderbolt's crash. Adrenaline coursed their veins in raging torrents as the fiery eruption of automatic weapons blended with the chaotic din of the day.

Braun and Fischer raked the secretary's office window with bullets and shattered the glass. They swung through the gaping hole and onto the sill. Free of their harnesses, they jumped into the office and tripped over Brenda Avery's body.

Dutch Williams heard the gunfire as he patrolled the hall. Throwing himself against a wall, he slid along it toward the room and swung into the doorway. He fired a long burst at the window, expecting to cut down the invaders. No one was there. Stunned, he scanned the room. Movement caught his eye, but it was too late. From the floor, Braun and Fischer raised their bush guns and returned fire.

Dutch's trigger finger never released its hold until life drained from him. Bullets cut a line across the ceiling as he crashed backward. Dusts fell from the bullet holes in the ceiling tiles and mixed with the gun smoke to make a cloud across the office.

• • •

Joshua mentally counted off four seconds and nodded. Garrett saw the signal and swung the barrel of his twelve gauge toward the conference room window. He lowered his feet to angle himself better, squinted in anticipation of flying glass, and prayed the rough-made harness would hold him while he worked the shotgun. Eyes narrowed to mere slits, Joshua's grip tightened on his rappelling rope as he squeezed the trigger of his bush gun.

The first three blasts of Garrett's shotgun pulverized the window but the following rounds, fired point blank, made it blow apart. Slivers and fragments of flying glass repeatedly stabbed the dangling men, cutting their faces, making them bleed freely. Fire spewed from Garrett's barrel in one long stream as the weapon fought against his hand. The shotgun steadily whittled an entrance.

When the first shots rang out from the secretary's office, Martin turned his back on the hostages in the room to look down the hall. The shotgun blasts at the conference room window made him spin back and take aim. His first instinct was to shoot the hostages, but he hesitated too long. They were already yelling and crawling for cover beneath the thick wood table.

Calder screamed and clamped his hands over his ears. Crying, he tried to stand and beg for mercy. Danny Barton reached out, grabbed him by the belt and yanked him back to the floor with everyone else.

As Martin twisted in place, firing bullets down the length of the conference table's top, the window succumbed to the shotgun. The first man through was Joshua.

Martin's bullets dug deep into the rich wood, splintering the table's polished top, spraying the air with needle thin wooden slivers. Except for striking one another with elbows, knees, and heads as they dove for protection, the hostages remained unharmed.

Firing from hip level, Joshua cut a line across the doorway where Martin stood shooting. The terrorist's body slammed against the doorframe and bounced back. His rifle rose in Allen's direction. Bush gun empty, Joshua Allen was reloading when Garrett yelled and shoved him hard from behind.

Kotter had entered the room through the concealed operations door, aiming a rifle at Joshua. As he pulled the trigger, a bullet struck the weapon, knocking it from his hands. Two more bullets hit him dead center of the throat. Allen spun to find Sam Garrett standing with a semiautomatic pistol trained on the wounded mercenary.

Sam raced to the dying mercenary and double-tapped Kotter to ensure death.

Danny pushed a division manager aside and crawled out from under the table. Not hearing any further action, he poked his head up to see if the firefight was over. He found himself face-to-face with the muzzle of Allen's CAR-16.

Recognizing him, Allen grabbed a handful of shirt collar and pulled him to his feet.

"How many of them are there?"

"Four…four," the young public affairs man tried to say. The anguish from his broken nose and bruised jaw slowed his speech. Holding four fingers up for Allen to see, he found himself beginning to shake uncontrollably.

"You're safe now, son. Get their weapons and don't leave the building. If one of these bastards gives you any lip, shoot them," Allen ordered, gesturing to the managers. He patted Danny on the shoulder to strengthen the man's confidence.

The division managers heard him as they gradually came out from underneath the table. They nodded in acceptance of the command.

Rushing through the door, ready to fight, Braun and Fischer scanned the conference room, searching for Garrett and Allen. Each man smiled in relief when they observed everyone alive.

Sam Garrett reloaded his shotgun. He had not realized he was empty until he entered and saw the terrorist about to kill Allen. Without thinking, he had drawn and fired the pistol. Hitting the rifle was not intentional. His aim had been at the man's body, but the excitement of the moment made him jerk the trigger, missing his original target.

"You're shot. " Braun touched Allen's bleeding arm.

"Hell, I'd be graveyard dead if it wasn't for Sam," he commented, lifting the arm to examine the wound. The bullet had grazed the length of his forearm, bleeding enough to make the wound appear far worse than it was. Seeing small drips of blood over Garrett's face, Allen knew the shattering glass had cut them both. He refused to accept the tingling pain across his cheeks.

"Everyone reload and let's get moving," Garrett commanded, starting for the door. "Braun, get Herschel and watch out that he doesn't shoot you!" The team laughed and walked to the door. Allen paused and repeated his earlier instructions to Danny.

Calder's bravery returned when he believed there was no further danger from the terrorists. Rising from beneath the table, he looked at Allen and arrogantly flipped a hand in Danny's direction.

"I don't know who you are, but I don't take orders from him." Calder's hand dropped and with a contemptuous expression, he began to leave.

A pile-driving fist struck Calder square in the face, taking him completely off his feet. He was unconscious by the time he hit the carpeted floor.

"That's from Jim," Allen snarled.

Even though it hurt to move his jaw muscles, Danny could not resist smiling.

CHAPTER TWELVE

June 25, 1:05 p.m.

Dan Draeger swept the tall refinery office buildings with his binoculars. Even through all the chaotic noises, he was sure he had heard the report of automatic gunfire. Being forced to remain further down the street, and with the roar from the burning flares howling in his ears, he wasn't sure of what he heard anymore.

"Chief, did your men go in there?" shouted Special Agent Hayes, raising his own binoculars. The youthful appearing man strained to see any activity. None was found.

Draeger knew he wasn't going crazy now. Even the baby-faced FBI agent had heard shots fired. Irritated by Hayes' tone of voice, Draeger glared at him, wanting to bark back. He was rapidly growing tired of listening to the agent spout orders as if he were the saving grace of this entire situation.

Boy, I've got more time in police work looking for a place to park my patrol car than you have years of age, the Chief thought.

"I specifically ordered you to not try a rescue attempt. This is a job for *professionals*. The Bureau's Hostage Rescue Team is coming," Hayes said, letting the binoculars drop to his chest by their straps.

Draeger snapped when he heard the venomous insult directed at his officers. The maelstrom of problems he faced tore away all self-control. The

Chief wheeled on Hayes with fury, jerking the FBI agent's shirt with both hands, pulling him so close their faces were mere inches apart.

"You wouldn't make a good pimple on a rookie's ass, so don't fuck with me, and don't fuck with my men. We're here to do whatever is necessary, but we won't eat shit from you in the process," Draeger said in a loathing voice.

A shockwave of fear rushed through the agent. The Chief released his hold and let the ashen-faced man fall back. Turning, Hayes found three stern-faced police officers standing behind him with arms crossed over chests. Dark sunglasses hid their eyes but he could feel their piercing stares.

Draeger lit a cigarette and stormed away, trying to calm. Deciding he had walked far enough, he leaned against a squad car and stared at the Ivory Tower. The mental picture of three men being shot in the back and falling six stories kept replaying in his mind.

"Are you Chief Draeger?" a soft voice asked.

The Chief of Police didn't move. He kept gazing at the tall building. Taking one last hard drag off the cigarette, he let it drop to the ground and tiredly stepped on it.

"That's me," he said. When his head lifted, he was surprised to find a beautiful, dark haired woman with ocean blue eyes standing beside him. Unintentionally, he stared at her for several seconds.

The black jumpsuit with FEDERAL AGENT sewn across a front pocket seemed out of place on her for some reason. He wasn't sure why. Maybe it was her attractiveness that struck him odd. Seeing federal agents who looked like models, especially on a scene like this, simply didn't fit into what he expected, if he even knew what to expect anymore.

When the woman put her black baseball cap on, he looked at its embroidered governmental agency emblem—National Security Council. His gaze lowered to her face, but she slid sunglasses on and turned her head. A thin wire ran from an earplug to a radio on her hip.

An identification wallet rose for him to see.

"I'm Agent Burrows with the NSC. I'm here strictly to assess the situation due to foreign operatives possibly being involved in the attack. I won't interfere with your command unless I'm directed to by my superiors." She closed the wallet and swiftly put the ID away.

The Chief glanced at the semiautomatic in her shoulder holster and raised his gaze to her face.

"Well, Agent Burrows, you can assess all you want. I don't know who you are reporting this to, but I already have enough federal agents spouting orders around here. You might coordinate with them and see if y'all can really screw things up." He shook his head and pulled another cigarette out of his shirt pocket. As he lit it, he stared at the woman.

Another damn fed. That's all I need.

Alex grinned. She assumed he referred to the FBI. Logically, they would be the first federal agency the police contacted, and they had a way of coming in and immediately rubbing everyone wrong.

A blast of cigarette smoke shot skyward. Draeger scratched his head and let his gaze carry to the refinery.

"Chief?"

He turned to face the woman.

"Has the FBI already told everyone how they are running the show?"

He answered with a nod.

"If I need information I can trust, I'll come to you," she remarked. A wry smile appeared at the edge of her mouth, and then vanished.

Draeger watched her walk away. He flicked his cigarette through the air and smiled.

I'll be damned... A fed who doesn't look down their nose at cops.

• • •

June 25, 1:07 p.m.

Finding the bombs under the acid-filled tanker trucks had been sheer luck, but removing them was tricky. Whoever had set the charges, knew their business. The additional wires told Jake tamper switches were added, rigged to detonate if the bundles were pulled or fell from their positions. His hands lightly shook. He forced himself to calm before working further.

"I'm getting too old for this crap," he grumbled. Taking a deep breath, he groaned and reached under the fender well. The first retaining wire clipped easy, but freeing the second made sweat trail from Jake's brow. He eased the small package to the ground and laid it beside the first explosive device he had found.

Resting a moment, he wiped his face and crawled out from beneath the truck. He stood and studied the surrounding area. *Too congested. Too much to blow and go wrong.*

Palms slick with perspiration, Jake carried the explosives down the street and placed them out in the open. Running back to the unit, he searched the acid storage vessels.

"Where would…" Pierson's gaze came to rest on a larger than normal bomb attached underneath a valve. Looking higher, he observed another explosive device taped to an acid feed line jutting out from the giant structure.

"Lord have mercy," Jake mumbled, moving toward the one hundred fifty feet tall vessel. "Didn't anyone tell these bastards that bombs work just fine at ground level?"

He shook his head and began to climb the ladder on the side of the vessel.

• • •

June 25, 1:07 p.m.

The building was quiet. Too quiet. Thurman anticipated hearing men yell, dictating orders, anything but silence. It bothered him.

Creeping in duck walk fashion along the half wall of concrete and glass windows, he stopped at a door. The sign declared it to be A-5's training classroom. He listened. Still nothing.

His heart raced as the tension in him mounted. He started to move on, but someone coughed and he froze. Glancing behind him, he realized Tommy had gone down an adjacent hallway leading into the unit's on-site laboratory. The cough came again. This time followed by a cruel smack. A muffled cry rose, then silence returned.

The door was ajar. Thurman eased it open a fraction more to look. A slender man dressed in military clothing stood staring at his hostages, an AK-47 held casually in his left hand. Three older men and a young brunette knelt, hands behind backs, gagged with torn pieces of cloth. In the men's eyes could be seen the terror they had evidently been subjected to. The woman gazed at the floor, lost in a private world of humiliation.

The men had been severely beaten. That was easy enough to tell, but the woman knelt on the floor, shirt beside her on the floor, small breasts peeking from beneath the cut bra that hung open on her. She had received a different torture.

Jim's blood grew hot. He withdrew his *Kabar* and readied himself to attack.

The terrorist moved proudly down the line of his prisoners, halting long enough to taunt them with a raised hand before walking on again. At the woman, he paused and lifted her chin with his fingertips. He stared at the smooth skin of her face. The anger in her eyes brought a faint smile to his lips.

Jim knew he would enjoy killing this one.

Intrigued by the softness of her skin, Doug Jordan ran his fingers along her throat and onto her chest. She trembled as he slid a hand over a breast and toyed with her nipple. He pinched it lightly and rolled it in his fingertips, smiling all the while at her grimace. The brunette's eyes scrunched closed.

Jordan laughed, released his hold, and stepped back in delight. Lightly shaking his head, he glanced at the three men to see their reaction, but they remained with heads bowed. The mercenary listened to one of the gagged hostages mumbling a prayer, then he returned his attention to the woman.

"Real shame a nice piece of ass like you has to go to waste. But, when we leave, I have to shoot you." Jordan paused and looked across the room at an older hostage who appeared as if he should have retired long ago.

"Hey, pop, ever wonder if she spits or swallows?" His vile laughter rose then fell to silence. He stepped to within inches of the brunette's face and rubbed his groin. "Let's find out."

The mercenary swung the rifle's strap over his shoulder and settled the weapon well onto his back. The woman lowered her head, but Jordan grabbed a handful of hair and yanked her face upright.

"Now, sweetheart, is that anyway to act? You be a good girl and take care of business right, and when the time comes to kill you, I'll make it quick." He released her hair and lowered his hands to his trousers.

Jim stared at the mercenary's back and waited until assured the man's hands were busy. He eased the door open more and hurled the knife across the room. The steel blade became a blur, then buried itself deep into the man's back with a dull thud. Jim burst into the room while the terrorist futilely grasped for the knife. He wrapped an arm around the mercenary's throat and viciously wrenched the *Kabar* free. Bending the man back, Jim brought the knife around and drove it to the hilt into the squirming terrorist. In the struggle, Thurman's radio worked its way out of his vest pocket and fell.

Anger flowed through Thurman's veins and fueled the fiery inferno within him. Teeth clenched, knuckles white, Jim Thurman savagely stabbed and ripped the blade through flesh and cloth. One last convulsive jump and the mercenary went limp to the floor.

Jim saw the wide-eyed expression of the hostages and realized too late they were trying to warn him. A rifle butt struck him hard between the shoulders at the base of his skull. Pain shot along his spine and exploded in his head. The room spun and he fought the blackness engulfing him. As he fell into the corpse's spreading pool of blood, he tried to swing the barrel of his automatic shotgun around to fire. A booted foot kicked it away and a rifle butt smashed into him again.

Breathing hard, Kane Thompson raised his rifle, ready to drive it into the big man again. But Jim was out cold.

The brunette lowered her gaze and saw the radio by her leg. She repositioned her body over it by pretending to fall. When she raised herself again, the radio was gone.

Kane caught movement with his peripheral vision and spun, bringing his *Kalashnikov* to bear on the hostages. Eyes closed, faces scrunched, they waited to be shot. Nothing happened. The passing seconds seemingly became hours.

A dull scraping carried through the air. The woman opened her eyes in time to see the unconscious giant being dragged from the room.

· · ·

The radio transmitted sharp blasts and remained keyed, jamming the frequency. Holding the handset to his ear, Bruce Peterson tried to discern what the noise actually was.

Running out into the Ivory Tower's sixth story hall, Trey Richards excitedly shouted for Peterson to come to the telephone and computer room. Zachary Caan stuck his head out from the office where he held the hostages and yelled to Tonya, wanting to know what was occurring. As Peterson raced by Tonya, he ordered her to watch the police cars in the street.

"What's wrong?" Peterson asked, trying to slow his panting breaths.

Trey Richards set the telephone receiver down, visibly disturbed.

"Our radios are useless."

"Yeah, sounds like static or someone has their radio keyed and doesn't know it."

"That's not all. I can't get Kotter or anyone in the other building to answer the damn phone. We've lost control of the computers and…" His voice died away.

"And what?" Anxiety mounted in Peterson.

" Murdock called from A-5. Said a half-dressed man in military clothes killed Jordan, but they caught him."

"Half-dressed? What the hell does that mean?" Peterson stared down the hall. Doug Jordan's death meant nothing. He never liked the bastard anyway, but Peterson's thoughts came aloud. "Tactical teams don't make an assault half-dressed. They wear so much equipment they can barely move."

"Murdock said he's a big son of a bitch," Richards stated with a hearty nod. "No shirt. He only wore a bulletproof tactical vest and was carrying a drummed shotgun."

Peterson stood silent for a moment before laughing. "Sounds like that guy's been watching too many movies." His gaze grew cold as he looked at Richards. "Don't worry. If Murdock has him, it won't be long before we know his entire life's story." He grinned and left the room at a brisk pace.

"Tonya?"

"Here," she yelled, stepping out of an office.

"Tell Zachary to kill the hostages," Peterson ordered. "We don't have time to be watching over them."

"Counterstrike?"

Peterson nodded. "Something's going down, but we don't know what. Murdock caught some guy with a drummed shotgun and we've lost communications with Dutch and the others."

Tonya brushed a long strand of black hair from her face as she glanced down the hall. "Are we pulling out? I can stand guard while Richards readies the chopper."

"No, not yet. Stay alert. Murdock will call when he's ready for extraction. Knowing him, he'll time it down to the last second. Kill the hostages and wait for further orders."

A glimpse of a smile flashed across Tonya's face.

• • •

Climbing up the elevator shaft ladder wasn't Herschel's idea of the best way to get to the sixth floor. Fischer had insisted it was the safest route, though, and before Herschel could open his mouth, the team agreed.

The computer technician refused to look down into the black pit. Even though he knew there was a bottom, the shaft appeared to drop away forever into the darkest regions of the underworld. Pausing to look at the men above him, Herschel realized he had at least fifty feet more to climb.

A voice on his radio's earpiece said Braun was crawling onto the sixth floor's largest steel beam. Herschel continued up the ladder, breathing a protracted breath and silent thanks that their climb was nearing its end.

The wide steel girder was a main structural beam for the Ivory Tower. A narrow corridor ran its length and housed electrical wiring, computers cables, and plumbing. Two feet below it hung the acoustical ceiling tiles of offices and hallways. Dim light from recessed light fixtures painted the corridor in an odd glow, and the musty odor of insulation filled the air. The warriors shuffled along the girder like rats in the dark, pausing only to listen and get their bearings.

A woman's muffled voice carried through the ceiling panels yet was audible enough to understand.

"Peterson said kill the hostages. We're leaving soon."

Fischer looked at Braun, wondering if he had heard the woman. Braun nodded. Garrett and Allen did the same. Herschel tried to but the movement only came in a jerky motion.

They knew their attack couldn't be delayed. Each passing second meant the difference between a hostage living or dying. There were no options. They had to drop through the ceiling panels and hope for the best.

"You don't have to go. What do you want to do?" Allen asked, whispering in Herschel's ear.

Unable to form words, the computer tech gestured to the acoustical panels.

"All right, don't shoot the hostages—or us."

Herschel frowned. Allen's granite expression told him there was no humor involved.

Spreading out double-arms length wide until fingertips touched fingertips, the five men stopped and drew deep breaths. One by one they turned to look at Garrett.

The former Marine sniper held three fingers up for them to see. His hand closed into a fist and along the beam, each man nodded.

The first finger rose. Sweat trailed down the sides of Herschel's face. The second finger slowly unfolded. Joshua Allen's grip tightened on his bush gun. The final finger came into view and the team stepped off of the beam.

Ceiling panels exploded into large chunks and chalky clouds choked the air as the War Dogs plummeted toward the floor. The crashing thunder bellowed through the silent halls.

Garrett dropped four feet and came to a teeth-jarring halt. He had landed atop a tall file cabinet in a vacant office. Kicking and smashing the panels, he fought to free himself.

Plowing completely through, Braun landed with one boot on a desk, the other on the seat of a chair. The chair rolled and his legs immediately split into a *V*. He fell and landed on his side, ribs striking the rim of a metal trashcan. His bulletproof vest cushioned the fall yet he felt a sharp pain in his side.

Tonya had already killed four people by the time Fischer came through the ceiling above her. His boots struck her shoulders and his weight drove her to the floor. The barrel of her Uzi swung upward, spewing fire, blasting out pieces of the ceiling above the remaining hostages.

Stunned by an armed man falling from the ceiling onto Tonya, Zachary could only stand and stare. Then the ceiling tiles along the hallway to his right blew apart.

Joshua Allen crashed to the floor with dust flying and chunks of acoustical ceiling panel cascading about him. Two feet further down the hall, Herschel fell through in a rain of panel fragments and chalky clouds. The computer tech hit the floor, lost his balance and collided into a wall. Upon impact he accidentally squeezed his shotgun's trigger. The weapon roared, streamed fire, and cut a gaping hole in the ceiling above Zachary Caan.

The mercenary's senses returned. He opened fire on Fischer even though he was atop Tonya. Striking Fischer in the arm and leg, Zachary looked at Allen lying out in the hall floor. He turned to kill him and fired, spraying bullets in a jagged line across the wall.

Small glass panes along the side of a door shattered. Ejected casings flew into the air in a steady stream, stirring the haze that hung in the hallway.

Allen swung his bush gun around, but realized too late he couldn't move fast enough. He caught two bullets in the shoulder before Fred Braun appeared and unloaded a full magazine into the mercenary.

Zachary Caan's body did a dance of death, bathing Joshua with a spray of blood. As he fell, his arms spread and a grenade dropped into the hall four feet from Joshua. Its spoon *clinked* and popped free. It was live.

"Grenade!" Before Joshua could move, a black vest passed over him. All he could see were the skinny, outstretched arms of a diving man.

"Herschel, no!" Joshua yelled, reaching out as if to pull the young man back.

The computer technician landed atop the rolling metal ball with a harsh thud. His head was angled back enough to allow him to see Joshua. Face pale as snow, he closed his eyes a second before the grenade detonated.

Herschel's body violently heaved. The explosion was loud yet muffled. The flooring beneath Herschel opened and swallowed his mangled body.

Madly kicking and hitting Fischer, Tonya fought to be free of his weight atop her. Her boot caught his leg wound. An elbow smashed his bleeding arm. He fell beside her on the floor. Breaking loose, she reached for the Uzi as she tried to stand.

The gleaming, thick *Kukri* blade swept through the air.

The curved knife sliced through her arm, cleanly severing it below the elbow. Mouth agape, eyes flared, she gasped in furious throes. She looked at the forearm on the carpet as if unable to comprehend it was a part of her body. When her gaze rose, she met Sam Garrett's emotionless stare.

A cannon-like barrel dug deep into Tonya and shoved her against a wall. Garrett stood with the massive curved knife in his right hand, his left pressing a shotgun into her stomach. His expression never changed nor did he speak a word as he pulled the trigger.

The din of gunfire and grenade explosion had masked the hostages' screams. When Garrett turned, he observed shock and terror taking its toll. One man vomited as he stared at the gory corpses, while another held his mouth and fought the sickening sensation swirling within him. A young woman crouched in the corner released her bladder from the horror of the battle. An older woman, blood trickling down her forehead, sat hugging and assuring a terrified, pregnant woman of their safety.

Ordering the hostages to remain in the room, Garrett helped Fischer to his feet. They walked to the crater in the hall and stared down at the computer technician's twisted corpse lying on the building's floor below them.

"Damn you, Herschel," Joshua softly said, shaking his head. But there was no anger in his voice. Only the realization that he had grown to like the skinny kid against his will. "We can't get to him. He's too far down there."

"We don't have any choice but to leave him," Braun said. "We've got to keep moving. There's more mercs around here."

"Wrap your wounds. Braun's right," Garrett commented, reloading his shotgun. He took up a defensive position and stood guard while they quickly bandaged themselves. Nothing more was said among them, and when finished, they dispersed throughout the sixth floor.

Fischer's wounds were the worst. His leg dragged behind as he walked, leaving a light trail of blood on the carpet. A diagonal gash on his arm bled freely but did not slow him.

Braun searched each office he passed, leaning slightly to one side to ease the pain in his ribs.

Holding his bush gun in the hand opposite his wounded shoulder, Allen edged along the hallway, watching the doorways ahead. They knew there were at least two more terrorists loose on the floor. Now all they had to do was find them.

The roar of a shotgun is loud but when the weapon is feverishly pumped, the deafening blasts sounds like an army in battle. When each man heard the shotgun's eruption, they raced toward the lone war. The hammering explosions ended and the halls grew eerily silent.

Allen was the first to find Sam Garrett and the two decimated mercenaries. The room looked like five tornadoes had whirled through and splattered the walls with fresh red paint. Sam's stomach was torn wide. His vest had caught the majority of bullets yet had not stopped all.

A choking cough told Joshua that Garrett was still alive. Sliding down the door, he sat and cradled Sam's head in his arm. Brushing dirt, sweat, and filth from the man's face, Joshua held onto him, refusing to accept his friend's pending death.

"What's the score?" Garrett asked, voice fading.

Tears fell from Joshua's cheeks onto the dying man's head.

"We're kicking ass and taking dog tags, old timer."

Sam Garrett tried to smile. The effort was too much. He looked up into Joshua's eyes.

"I need to rest a moment before we move out again," he said faintly. His face contorted. "I need to rest..." Garrett's eyes squeezed shut hard and his body drew rigid. He went limp in Allen's arms.

"Get some rest, brother," Allen whispered as he wept.

Braun and Fischer walked from the room.

"Stay with him," Fischer said softly, motioning to Joshua Allen. "I need to clear a stairwell and get the hostages out of here."

Fischer waited for Braun's nod and then left. Joshua's tormented cry forced him to pause in the hall and take a deep breath. He understood the hurt from losing friends all too well.

• • •

June 25, 1:15 p.m.

Jake Pierson moved cautiously, knowing if he tripped and dropped the bombs, few pieces of him would be left to find. Half running, half walking from A-5, all he wanted was a place they could detonate and cause the least harm.

Angling across the cooling tower lot to the wide-open flare yard, he set the charges at the base of the monstrous burning flare stack. Their explosions would destroy the main pipelines carrying products to be vented and burned by the flare, but he had little choice. Everywhere he glanced were storage tanks and piping filled to capacity with oil and finished gasoline products.

He chose the least disaster, knowing when the bombs blew, pressurized lines would rupture in a hellish display, making the flare yard resemble a giant blown-out oil well. The mammoth burning clouds of hydrocarbons would soar into the sky, fast and furious, making people for miles believe the refinery was obliterated. Yet in time, once the initial releases of pressures were made, the fireballs would settle and eventually allow themselves to be mastered.

Jake laid the explosive charges on the ground and fled. His luck had already been pushed to the limit. The bombs could detonate at anytime.

Luck doesn't last forever, he thought.

• • •

June 25, 1:40 p.m.

Each beat of Jim's heart reverberated in his head with the strength of a crashing Tibetan gong. His left eyelid, discolored and swollen, refused to open. Out of his right the world appeared a blur. He could see the outline of a man, but the moving object puzzled him. The blur came into focus. A mercenary stood examining the short, pistol-gripped, drummed shotgun.

An air of authority hung about the man. By his hard-set jaw, squared shoulders and straight stance, Jim believed him to be the leader.

Maybe forty or more, Jim thought, looking at the raven black hair pulled into a tight tail. His clothing, although military by style, fit him well and displayed an athletic frame. The mercenary's attention remained on the automatic shotgun in his hands. He nodded in approval and laid the weapon on a desk.

Jim tried to move. Straps bound him to a chair preventing freedom of legs and arms. He lowered his chin and saw that he had been stripped of his vest.

Kneeling, sorting through equipment spread out on the floor, Kane Thompson threw the bulletproof tactical vest across the room.

"Baaah!" he yelled, furious at not finding a radio or any type of personal identification. "If he's here, there are more. I don't like it, Adam." Kane glanced at the bound man and carried his gaze to Murdock. "Our mission is complete. Let's call a chopper and push the fucking button."

"We're still in control. Calm yourself. We want our friends, the news reporters, to fully spread the terror of what is to come," Murdock said. Turning to the prisoner, a sadistic stare filled the mercenary's eyes.

"Murdock?" Jim's voice was raspy and strained.

"You know me? Excellent, excellent," Murdock remarked, pleased with his notoriety. White teeth flashed then disappeared behind a thin-lipped line. "But I do not know you and that disturbs me. I'm not worried though. You'll tell me what I want to know."

He raised Jim's *Kabar* to face level and turned the knife, admiring its sharp edge and point. The motion stopped. Murdock's eyes shifted to the battered man. "You will not die... only wish you had."

The knife's tip touched the right side of Jim's bare chest. Skin gave way to the pressure Murdock applied. A single tear of blood developed from the puncture.

Murdock watched his hostage, wanting a sign of pain. He saw the muscled abdomen contract. The prisoner stared back, depriving him pleasure. The tip dug deeper, traveling across the chest, leaving a straight trail of blood to begin draining.

Thurman's body shook. The pain burned as hot as a branding iron. Jaws clenched, he fought the urge to scream.

Murdock's lips quivered, wanting to smile at the anguish he had instilled. He looked at his prisoner's scarred chest and spoke in a voice barely above a whisper.

"You and I are brothers to pain. We've shared the same mistress of suffering, but now her kiss will be fatal for you."

The agony within Jim decreased. His senses calmed. Murdock took another swipe, cutting his prisoner again, only deeper.

Kane walked to Jim, hands curled into knotted balls. "Who do you work for? How many men are with you?"

The questions came faster. Fists smashed into Jim's face. Sharp steel pierced and slashed his flesh. An unending barrage of battering to the body began.

A human can endure far more torture than one believes, but a point is reached when the mind retracts, safeguarding the soul, leaving ravaged flesh and bone to mortal demise.

For Jim Thurman, that plateau came when his body no longer reacted to the devastating blows. Fantasy and reality intertwined. He entered a plain of visions, all fleeting, unveiling his life and approaching death. Words mingled between flashing images, swirling in a vortex of hallucinations.

Charon, the boatman of the River Styx, appeared in a flowing black cloak, crying out in derision. Jungle branches became tentacles with life. Susan, his wife, stood beckoning him with outstretched arms, their son, James, standing by her side. Hands entered Jim's abdomen, pushing his intestines back into place. James cried in fear, seeking his father's comfort, and cold eyes stared at Thurman while fists mercilessly hammered his body.

"Two six one eight two seven three—," Jim mumbled, reciting his former Marine Corps military service number. He spun in time, recalling what he had been told prisoners of war were permitted to say to their captors. "Thurman, Sergeant, two six one eight—"

The words grew unintelligible. His head flopped to one side then rolled, chin dropping to chest. The dark of a moonless night enveloped Thurman.

Kane gingerly touched his sore knuckles. His hands hurt and his arms needed rest.

The prisoner's answers made no sense, infuriating Murdock more. But fury turned to stubbornness and the fanatical leader became adamant about having the prisoner confess anything.

Wrapping his fingers in Thurman's hair, Kane viciously jerked the head back and looked at the battered face. He released his hold and watched the prisoner's head fall forward.

"We're wasting time with him," Kane remarked.

Murdock sliced through the straps binding Thurman. He kicked him out of the chair, unable to remove his eyes from the unconscious captive. The barrel of Kane's rifle swung toward Jim's chest.

"No, I will kill him!" Murdock yelled.

Lowering the rifle, Kane waited for the execution but it didn't come. Instead, Murdock stood staring at their prisoner as if deciding upon an alternate action.

Kane turned his head and looked away. He realized Murdock had lost sight of their mission because the prisoner had failed to break.

Sprawled on the floor, Jim knew he was about to die. His mind had crossed over the threshold of agony, numbing his body. He felt himself trying to black out whenever spasms of pain returned. The knife cuts bled freely, swathing his chest in glistening red. A severe bolt of misery shot between his temples when he tried to move his left arm and hand. His fingers refused to obey his mind's commands. The arm was broken. Lying still, he used the momentary reprieve from the beatings to regain strength and control his mind.

Murdock stood with hands on hips, gazing at the floor. His blue eyes glowed with the intensity of his thoughts. With each strike to the defiant man's face, Murdock's determination to crush his willpower had increased. This bloody pulp represented everything Murdock hated.

• • •

June 25, 1:40 p.m.

A morose atmosphere immersed each adviser as they walked through the door of the Oval Office.

Elbow propped on desk, thumb beneath chin and forefinger lightly touching his lips, the President sat watching a television. Never bothering to see who entered, the Commander-in-Chief's attention remained riveted to the spectacle of murdered people. Halfway through the newscast, he gestured for an aide to turn it off.

Facing the television, the President removed his glasses and carefully laid them on the desk. He rubbed his eyes and put the glasses back on. The high-backed, black leather chair spun to the waiting men. His distressed look relayed the magnitude of the problem confronting them.

"Gentlemen, by now you all know about the assault on the refinery in Texas," he said in a low, sedate tone. The President's gaze swept the room, evaluating their reactions. "If I do not make specific announcements in three hours, they intend to wipe it off the map."

"Mr. President." David Mathis, Secretary of State, slid forward to sit on the edge of his chair. "Our official policy is to not negotiate with terrorists—foreign or domestic. I fully understand this situation's critical nature, but we cannot have you go on national television in response to the attack. If you do, it opens the door for every fanatic in the world to hold America hostage. The implications alone are—"

The President raised a hand, interrupting him. A sorrowful look painted his eyes. "I know all about our official policy, but there are a few more facts you should know." He glanced to his right where Jeff McCall sat quietly.

Adjusting his tie, the Secretary of State eased back into his chair to listen.

Pausing, the President scanned his league of advisers. "That single refinery supplies the largest daily percentage of gasoline to our nation. If it is destroyed we will have a shortage like none before. That's the good news compared to everything else I've been briefed on this morning."

Confusion visibly crossed their faces.

"A total explosion of that refinery alone would reach out for miles, leveling everything in the force's path. That is not taking into consideration the chemical plants and other refineries surrounding it that will possibly detonate in a chained reaction." The President stopped, wearily drew a breath and lifted a briefing report from his desk. He read it aloud.

"Coupled with the explosive force of reactors, butane, and large quantities of on-site petroleum products, the amount of hydrofluoric acid stored and used at the Titan Oil refinery may raise the death count to an estimated two million people if a total release occurs." The President slowly laid the report back onto his desk.

Groans carried throughout the crowded room. The Secretary of State grimaced.

"Our citizens are in harm's way and our economy is being threatened..." The President's voice trailed to silence. His face flushed with anger. "...then I learn my CIA Director may have had prior knowledge of the whole damned thing." He rose from his chair and slammed a fist on the desk's top. "Tell me, gentlemen, when this is all over, and people are burying their loved ones, how do you think America is going to feel when we tell them Bill Haverty hid the information from us and, because it is official policy, I did not intervene when the bastards were releasing acid on the country!" The veins in his neck protruded as he spoke.

A heavy silence fell across the room.

"I don't care what it takes, but I want everybody and everything we have for fighting terrorism to get down there now. Surely, we have operational plans ready for such a contingency," the President ordered. He scanned the faces in the room. "Don't we?" He tapped his knuckles on the desk and shook his head in exasperation. "You have one hour then be back here ready to tell me what we can do. Time is running out, gentlemen. Don't waste it standing here gawking at one another."

Men rushed from the room in a mad flurry.

"Jeff."

"Yes, Mr. President?"

The Commander-in-Chief motioned to a chair. Jeff McCall walked to it, setting his briefcase next to him as he took a seat.

The Secretary of State was the last man to leave. The door closed quietly behind him.

Selecting the button marked CIA on his phone module, the President listened to the telephone ring. He grew impatient knowing someone was there. At last the ringing ceased and a man answered.

"Bill, I want your resignation within the hour."

"Yes, Mr. President," replied the Director of the Central Intelligence Agency. His voice was soft and respectful, like a child who was being admonished for some violation of a parental rule.

"And Bill, as far as I'm concerned, you're no different from those fanatics."

• • •

Haverty gave no reply. The line stayed open. His mouth tasted dry as a desert. He tried to swallow the lump stuck in his throat.

The silence over the phone grew heavier with each passing second. Finally, a *click* came and the line went dead.

A distant stare consumed Haverty's eyes. He sat with the telephone receiver pressed to his ear. Gradually, his hand pulled away and his forearm crashed downward with the weight of a towering tree falling to a lumberjack's axe.

The receiver bounced in his half-open hand, kept from dropping to the floor by curled fingers. Balanced precariously on fingertips, it hung in the air for several minutes before he regained enough composure to set it back on the phone.

The President called me a fanatic, he thought.

His gaze dejectedly traveled across the office to a plaque-filled wall. Framed photographs of him receiving awards throughout his career were hung row after row. Along the window, mementoes from special missions behind enemy lines covered the tops of tables. Shifting his gaze to a bookcase in the corner, he stared at the white stars on a folded American flag. The memory of the President, the same President who had just called him a fanatic, giving him "Old Glory" for patriotic service to the nation, flashed before his eyes.

The President called me a fanatic. The words echoed in his mind. *He doesn't understand. There are times when sacrifices must be made for the good of the country. I had to keep that report quiet. Yes, a few people would die, but it would've opened the public's eyes. We need stronger security measures. The people need the CIA. Too many already believe the Agency's power should be reduced—that the FBI should have full reign. But to call me a fanatic after all I've done.*

Public ridicule and scorn—Newspapers declaring my actions a violation of civilized societies' laws—Demands for an investigation—Me being placed on trial like a common criminal—The Agency coming under attack by spineless liberals. The thoughts spun in his head until they were whirlwinds.

Mindlessly opening a lower side-drawer of the desk, his fingers found the small, unmarked, plastic prescription bottle at the back. Removing its lid, he tilted the bottle forward and watched as an aspirin size pill rolled out on to the desktop. He mechanically put the bottle away and shut the drawer, dazed, staring all the while at the white pill. There were no doubts as to its effectiveness. Once in a human's body, no autopsy known could detect the slightest trace of the drug. A death certificate would simply state CARDIAC ARREST or whatever catchall term a physician chose to use for the corpse's heart failure.

"Yes, Mr. President, you'll have my resignation within the hour," Bill Haverty said despondently. Leaning back in his chair, he placed the pill on his tongue and swallowed. His eyes closed as he relaxed.

My President called me a…

His fingers shook in an electrifying tremble before drawing still. As the twitching ceased, Haverty's head rolled and fell downward to his chest. A fine thread of saliva ran from his bottom lip to his shirt.

CHAPTER THIRTEEN

June 25, 1:45 p.m.

Circling back to locate Jim, Tommy discovered the hostages in the A-5 classroom. When he saw the corpse on the floor, he knew he wasn't far behind him.

"Did a big guy wearing a tactical vest and no shirt kill that man?" the machinist asked, motioning to the terrorist as he freed the hostages. Tommy grabbed the shirt from the table and laid it over the brunette's shoulder.

She removed the cloth gag from her mouth and reached between her legs.

"Here." In her hand was Jim's radio. "This fell out of his pocket when he killed that bastard." Pointing to the corpse, she slipped the shirt on as she spoke. "They have your friend. They hit him with a rifle and dragged him out of here."

Everything made sense now. Tommy's anxiety increased. "I've got to go. Lock yourselves in the lab room." He eased the door open to leave.

The woman stopped him and pointed down the hall. "He's probably in the control room. That's where their leader is."

Tommy McLawchlin nodded as he stepped out into the hall.

• • •

The rubber soled boots squeaked on the waxed floor. Tommy tried to walk lighter, placing each foot down carefully. Nothing helped. The quiet hall magnified the irritating noise.

Kneeling, back against the wall, he paused, believing himself lost in the maze of halls and doors. This was new terrain. He had never been to a control room before. Thinking back, he couldn't remember going to very many places in the refinery other than the machine shop.

The squeaks grew louder and closer together as he hurried to the end of the hall. Reaching a door, he eased it open. Another hall. Frustration set in. He had to find Jim. Glancing back and not seeing anyone, he moved into the new hall.

Tommy tilted his head and looked up at the large glass panes above the half wall of cinder blocks. An unsettling feeling told him this was the control room. Ten feet ahead, a door led in. Sweat beaded his face and his palms grew sticky.

He rose enough to look through the window and observed a terrorist kicking Jim. At first he wasn't sure if it was Jim or not, or if he was alive. The man was badly beaten, drenched in blood, but the muscled body confirmed his identity.

Tommy watched the two militants argue in the room. The one that held an AK-47 spun in anger toward the door. Tommy dropped, but not fast enough.

The terrorist saw him and their gazes had locked for a split-second.

They'll kill Jim!

Tommy rose, bringing himself into full view. Swinging his shotgun up to waist level, he aimed at the plate glass window. The sight of his tortured friend on the floor sent him into a blind rage.

"You mother fuc—" The deafening roar of his fire breathing weapon masked the battle cry. A pounding recoil fought his hands, trying to free the shotgun from his iron grip.

Feverishly pumping rounds, empty casings flew out, thrown hard by the forceful ejection. Number-four buckshot pellets shattered the wide glass pane into hundreds of pieces, and traveled on, striking Kane Thompson's chest and face. Fragments of the window blew into the room like shrapnel, burying into the terrorist. Not giving him time to recover, Tommy raised the weapon and took direct aim. Hardened lead pellets thrust Kane back onto the massive computer control panel. His rifle flew into the air.

Kane's arms spread, hands grasping for a hold. Speckled with bleeding holes, he slid down the face of the computer bank onto the counter top. His flailing hand struck the explosives' remote control lying beside a computer keyboard. The cigarette pack-sized box flew out into the room, landing on the floor near the bleeding prisoner.

Jim's mind registered the battle, the shotgun blasts, and the rain of window glass.

Tommy.

Opening his good eye, the half-dead man saw Murdock bend toward him, fingers spread, reaching for the remote control. Instantly, Jim recognized it and its importance.

Kane's arm now draped the stock of his AK-47, fingers within inches of the trigger.

Tommy couldn't gamble on Kane's death. He shot him again and swung the shotgun barrel to the right like a skeet shooter, firing at the remaining terrorist. He missed. The man had dropped low to the floor.

Jim's body quaked from pain each time he tried to move. A sea of agony swept over him in crashing waves, growing stronger each second yet he had no choice. Murdock's fingers were clawing the floor for the control box. The bombs could be detonated.

Jim's drummed shotgun sat on the edge of a desk, an arm's length away from him. He rolled onto his broken arm and reached for the shotgun. His hand slapped the weapon, fingers jabbing metal, searching for something to grab. He felt the grip and his fingers wrapped about it.

Murdock stood, hands rising to chest level. One held the remote control. The other pointed a pistol at Jim's chest.

In the excitement, Tommy lost count of how many rounds he had fired. Aiming at the terrorist, he squeezed the trigger and heard the heart-sinking *click* of an empty chamber.

Murdock heard it too and grinned, readying himself to shoot the tortured prisoner. Holding the remote out for Jim to see, his thumb moved to depress the detonation button.

Thurman savagely cried out and swung the drummed, automatic shotgun around with every ounce of strength his battered body had. The scream was a blend of excruciating pain and insanity. Without hesitation, he pointed it at Murdock and squeezed the trigger. The shotgun roared, its recoil fighting Jim. *Flechette* rounds came out of the barrel so furiously that their fiery flames spewed in one, long tumultuous explosion.

Reflex made Murdock pull the pistol's trigger. A bullet plowed into Jim's stomach, driving deep, but it didn't stop him from emptying the shotgun's drum.

The terrorist's body catapulted off the ground, shredding into pieces as twenty shotgun blasts struck him point blank. With each *flechette* shell fired, Murdock's body grew more mutilated from the small nails. The last five shells in the drum were a mixture of number four buckshot and rifled slugs. What the *flechette* rounds didn't destroy, these did in grisly fashion.

Recoil hammered Jim's weakened body. He held on, refusing to release the trigger. When the last round fired, he still pulled the trigger, wanting more. Finally, his arm crashed to the floor bringing with it the smoking shotgun.

All shooting stopped. Tommy rose from cover behind the half-wall, pistol drawn, prepared to fire. A nerve-wracking silence hung in the blood painted room. Gun smoke drifted in a hazy cloud, leaving a pungent smell. Slipping, falling on human gore spread over the floor, he crawled to his friend.

Four feet away, Murdock's severed hand clutched the remote control. Between the curled fingers a light could be seen blinking in awkward rhythm.

Tommy saw it as he shouted into his radio microphone for help. Seeing Jim's chest barely move, he knew the man bordered on death.

The light ceased to blink and remained on. Within the same second, explosions rocked the building. A control room wall imploded, and the world appeared to be drawing to a fiery end.

• • •

June 25, 2:00 p.m.

The explosions came almost as one within the refinery. A massive shockwave raced through the ground, toward the city. The concussion swept outward from the explosions, smashing, breaking, and destroying with the force of an erupting volcano.

"Mother of God," the reporter screamed, feeling a powerful tremor in the ground. He spun and looked at the refinery. His head kept tilting back as he looked at the sky.

Three phenomenal black and orange, mushrooming clouds of fire rocketed into the sky, roaring like giant, wounded beasts. Their accompanying chain of colossal explosions sent ripped pieces of steel, wood, and rocks sucked from the ground, soaring through the air. Windows in refinery buildings and throughout the city shattered from the unified concussions. Flying dirt created a fog-like effect at ground level, spreading and rising, following the blazing clouds.

The newscast was live and for a brief moment viewers observed what appeared to be the end of the world. Fleeing for their lives, the media scattered, abandoning their camera equipment mounted on tripods. Debris rained down, striking people as they fled, filling them with a terror they had never known. Black to orange, then gray intermixed with red; the rapidly climbing, swirling clouds changed colors in an eerie spectacle. Secondary explosions followed, and the ground trembled again.

As fireballs belched from deep inside the refinery complex, jagged chunks of steel and pieces of machinery fell on Derrick Road at the main gate. Reporters with their cameramen returned to their former positions at the public street, braving the hail of debris to film Hell's inferno. Two reporters and their cameramen were smashed beneath a twisted chunk of metal that had once been a large motor. Several reporters and cameramen at the public street were crushed by a long stretch of steel pipe. Some debris still burned and gave the appearance of a fiery meteor shower bombarding the area.

A visibly shaken reporter narrated his personal observation as he pointed to the fires in the refinery. The fear in his voice alone emphasized the catastrophe.

"No one can live through that. No one..."

· · ·

Alex stayed back from the jabbering throng of city officials surrounding the Chief and FBI agents. She especially shied away from the news hungry crews filming at every turn.

The public street had transformed into a comical parking lot. Squad cars, emergency vans, and ambulances all sat angled in opposing directions not wanting to be blocked in by another. More vehicles arrived by the minute, parking between their gaps, congesting the area.

Standing next to a public utility truck at the edge of the sea of vehicles, Alex switched between radio channels, relaying information to the SEAL team as she monitored Jim's men. It was during one of those switches she heard the tail end of a screaming radio request for help, but the explosions had come, drowning out everything the man said except one word—*Jim.*

Fifteen feet away, a chunk of burning steel fell from the sky and sliced through the roof of a squad car. Chunks of concrete rained down like hailstones over the running crowd.

Taking shelter beneath the truck, she anxiously turned the radio volume up, listening with bated breath. The radio remained silent. Her mind jumbled with conflicting thoughts, wondering if Dark Angel should be ordered in now. The earlier radio traffic was sketchy, only enough to piece parts of the puzzle together. Some terrorists were neutralized, the total, though, was unknown. Jim's team had sustained casualties and from the last frantic call for help, she believed he was one. They had effectively crippled Murdock's plans, but to what extent? And what did the explosions signify? Had the tide turned in favor of Murdock? There were more questions than answers.

The hailstorm of debris gradually halted. She crawled out from beneath the truck and scanned the refinery. The rising fireballs had grown, consuming the sky above the oil complex with apocalyptic appearing clouds of swirling smoke.

Alex stared at the ascending mass, curious why it held her interest. Thoughts raced through her mind, wild guesses at best, lighting hope within her. *The fires were remaining in the center of the refinery. If Murdock had caused them, we would have all died with the first explosion. Jim's men must have altered his plan somehow.*

She gambled on the chance and switched channels on the radio. It was time for Dark Angel.

• • •

227

June 25, 2:10 p.m.

The effects of the flare yard explosion were visible at every turn, but the raging inferno continuously blanketed the land in a scorching heat for blocks. What had formerly been large tin buildings for storage now looked like flattened, mangled steel pretzels, their framework bent in ruin, their contents melted or swept away in the blasts. Brick buildings suffered one of two ways; they stood half demolished, or lay spread across the landscape, crudely paving it like misplaced cobblestones.

Using partial standing walls as protection from the intense fire, the men steadily walked toward the inferno, toward A-5. Tommy had screamed for help. He needed them.

Braun walked point with Allen in the middle and Fischer bringing up the rear. Garrett's body lifelessly draped Allen's arms. Finding an abandoned truck, Braun drove while the others held their friend.

Dirt swirled, stirred by the force of continuous explosions. As thick cloudbanks of dust rolled over them hiding the road from sight, the truck was forced to slow.

A tire went flat, punctured by unseen debris. Braun never slowed, plowing a path as he drove. The front of the truck lifted then dropped to an abrupt halt. A second tire blew out with a loud report. Braun tried to drive on. The vehicle wouldn't budge. They were stuck and unable to see what caused it.

Braun turned the ignition off. No one spoke. A-5 was close, but where? The dirt clouds played havoc with their senses of direction, creating a fog that confused them as if they were blindfolded.

Allen leaned forward, his gaze focused on the windshield.

Droplets of rain spattered the glass. The pace of the rain increased until a torrential downpour bombarded the truck. Without warning day turned into night. The black smoke of the refinery fires wove itself into the wide mass of thunderclouds and blocked the sun.

"Damn, damn!" Braun yelled, striking the steering wheel with his hand. He gripped it with both hands and angrily tried to rip it from the steering column. He shouted in fury, but as the fit of madness passed, his rage settled.

Joshua understood. He felt the same frustration and waited a moment before speaking.

"There's too much debris in the road anyway. We'll walk the rest of the way. We started as a team and we'll finish as one."

Turning his head, Braun looked at the lifeless body Joshua Allen held. His eyes softened and he nodded. "Let's go."

The cold rainwater was a shock to their bodies as it drenched their vests and clothes, soaking through to skin. Heads craned back, allowing nature to cleanse their faces, each man stood with eyes closed, thankful to still be alive. The hurt from their wounds diminished as the rain renewed their strength.

Tightening the bandages on his leg and arm, Bob Fischer prepared himself for the walk ahead. Fred Braun fought to ignore the piercing pain in his side. It was growing increasingly difficult to deny its presence. Every movement of his ribs created some degree of anguish.

The bleeding wounds in Joshua Allen's shoulder throbbed. Sweat broke out over his face and chest as blinding pain shot through him. He refused to let Braun carry his friend and tied a makeshift sling about his waist to hold Garrett's legs. The determination to not leave Sam behind gave Joshua the strength needed to carry his friend's upper torso with his one good arm.

Their journey continued in a pelting rain.

"Over there," Fischer shouted, pointing ahead as he dragged his leg in a crippled walk.

The intensity of the thunderstorm slackened. The crumbled wall of the A-5 control room came into view. Charred wood littered the landscape, the only remnants of the three-story cooling tower. Across from the leveled cooling tower, a burning chasm in the earth roared wildly where only hours before had been the flare yard. Deeper into the refinery, flames leaped into the sky with broiling black smoke from burning oil storage tanks.

Raging bonfires dotted the terrain, fueled by underground pockets of leaked oil and years of oil spilt on the ground that had been heavily covered with fresh dirt. The wind shifted. Smoke from the blackish orange fires floated northward across the refinery sky toward the main gate entrance. Heat off the crater's fire was tempered by the rain and cool wind, and warmed their wet bodies as they walked to the half-destroyed A-5 building.

Deciding to enter through the unscathed entrance, Braun took the lead. Fischer stayed close to Allen, providing protection in case they were attacked.

Braun drew to a halt as he rounded the corner of the building. Three men and a woman stood in a circle, staring at their feet.

Having seen Braun's bush gun rise, Fischer moved in front of Allen, bringing his own weapon to the ready. All he could do was wait.

The woman looked up and saw Braun. She touched the arm of the man next to her and gestured. Heads lifted. Seeing the armed man, they stepped back to allow him to enter their circle.

Braun's weapon lowered as if its weight had become too much to bear. He stood in the rain, gazing at the ground. Finally, he mustered the strength to turn and signal Fischer and Allen.

They heard him before they saw what he was looking at.

"The cost of this war just went up again," Braun said, breathing wearily as he stared out to the horizon. The storm made it difficult to tell whether the water running down his cheeks was rain, or tears.

Face down in the mud, ten feet from the control room door, Jake Pierson lay with a broken piece of pipe protruding from his back. The rain carried his blood over the ground in three separate streams until it flowed into the shallow ditch along the refinery street.

• • •

June 25, 2:15 p.m.

The police maintained their blockades, watching, wondering what was happening within the fenced confines. They had no opportunity to get rain gear before the thunderstorm blew in. The showers came upon them faster than expected, catching everyone out in the open. When the chain of explosions occurred, the rainstorm was immediately forgotten. Now they were happy to be standing in the pouring rain, alive, having thought themselves doomed in the first monstrous blast and bombardment of debris.

Chief Draeger paced the barricades, pausing briefly to talk with his men before continuing on. Glancing skyward, he knew the afternoon storm would soon pass, but he did not know if it would be to their benefit or not. The rain helped contain the spread of fiery holocaust within the refinery.

Turning his back to the tempest, he lit a cigarette and tried to keep it dry. Barely managing to take a drag before raindrops fell onto it, he cursed and threw it away.

"Sir, we have people coming out."

Draeger spun, gaze searching where his officer pointed. Scores of reporters and camera crews rushed forward to interview the people fleeing through the refinery's main gate.

"I want five men to escort those people out of there. Get paramedics up here to start checking them, and for God's sake, don't let those goddamned reporters badger the hostages," he shouted, running to the blockade line to observe.

"Tac One," he radioed, "I'm sending five men to bring hostages out. Give them cover-fire if necessary. If you spot a terrorist ready to shoot, kill him."

The sniper team acknowledged from their camouflaged positions, keeping watch on the surrounding area and rooftops of the two refinery buildings.

Overhearing Draeger, Special Agent Hayes was about to interrupt him, but the intensity in the Chief's eyes made the government man decide otherwise.

The raging inferno and swirling clouds of black smoke rising out of the refinery provided a dramatic backdrop for the cameras. Hostages dashed to freedom while reporters raced one another to capture an interview.

"Dan, we have people coming out now," said Al Wilson, the *NBC* network news correspondent on the scene. He stumbled and fell, trying to talk to the anchorman at the station and be filmed at the same time. The sound garbled. The film footage went awry.

Looking through his lens as he followed Wilson, the cameraman tripped over the correspondent and went down too. Undaunted in their determination, they recovered and straightaway joined the race again.

The freed hostages never slowed as they raced past the bodies of the security officers. Reporters yelled questions and received few answers. Blocking the newsmen, policemen directed the fleeing people toward Chief Draeger's location.

Calder followed the division managers to freedom. He stared at the burning cars along the wrought iron fence and at the wreckage of a vehicle climbed atop the crushed gate. Observing the three blood-drenched uniformed bodies in the street, he snapped his head away, refusing to look. Having closed his eyes to halt the nausea rising up his throat, when he opened them again, the demolished gate office was before him. He slowed to a staggering shuffle, gaze racing over the building as he went past.

The Superintendent of Security walked with his head hung low to the police blockade set back on the public street. Men and women cried, holding one another in consolation, thankful their brutal experience was over at last. Raising his head, Calder saw Dave Simmons standing beside the

232

Chairman of the Board. Before Calder had an opportunity to speak, Dave Simmons stepped forward.

"If you ever set foot on Titan Oil property again, I'll have you arrested," the refinery manager said, so furious his words came out in a low, gravelly voice.

Calder's face sunk in sheepish manner. He left in silence. Having taken only a few steps, his path was blocked. The Security Superintendent lifted his head and looked into the austere face of Sergeant Maddox, one of the Security supervisors who had luckily been off-duty when the attack came. Calder tried to side step around the mountain-born Tennessee man, but grew paralyzed when Maddox's icy voice cut the air.

"The terrorists didn't kill Jim and the others...you did."

The lump in the superintendent's throat grew, choking him more each second. He tried to walk away, but his legs had grown rubbery and refused to move. There was no love loss between the two men. They had argued many times and Calder had made Maddox's work life miserable until the sergeant finally submitted his retirement papers last week. Now, Calder remembered Maddox's words from months ago.

"If any of our officers ever get hurt, I'll come looking for you. Don't try to hide. It won't do no good. I'll find you."

• • •

Returning to their designated positions in the street, camera crews zoomed in on the freed people as they cried and related the horrors of the past hours to the police.

"Dan, as you can see, the trauma of this ordeal is horrific," Wilson stated, staring somberly into the camera. "I've been told that the sixth floor of the building behind me, and the third floor of this shorter building, is filled with murdered Titan Oil employees."

Wilson pressed his earplug, attempting to better hear the anchorman's questions from the news station.

"That's correct, Dan. We've learned a highly professional team of armed men are solely responsible for freeing the hostages, and, as best we can tell, have killed the terrorists. One of the hostages said the unknown team left immediately, moving deeper into the refinery. At this time, we're trying to confirm what agency the counterterrorist group is from. We saw no one arrive but this refinery is so massive in size they could have entered through a rear gate." Pausing, Al Wilson's eyes squinted as the sun gradually broke through the clouds in patches. The rain slowed to a drizzle then stopped.

Sunlight spread across the landscape, painting the broiling black clouds rising from the refinery's interior. Rays of light caught the black, red, and yellow streaks of fire snaking upward within the smoke. Smoke continued to move about the buildings like a fog covering the land.

"Dan, the explosions you witnessed earlier were so powerful that we were almost thrown to the ground. Evidently, they were not from the A-5 unit we were so worried about." The reporter flashed a smile of thankfulness, but quickly returned to the grave look he believed the audience wanted to see.

Wilson looked around, hearing a rustle of excitement from the crowd of former hostages. The people had fallen in behind Draeger and his officers as they walked from the police cars toward the refinery.

"It's them," the cameraman said, voice faintly audible. He turned to film Derrick Road.

The correspondent temporarily forgot he was still live on national television. His head swiveled, eyes searching, confused by his cameraman's excitement.

Exasperated with keeping his voice low, the cameraman focused the lens on the wide gate next to the demolished building. "It's them!" he yelled, pointing to the men at the main gate.

Chief Draeger slowed his steps and gradually came to a halt. When he stopped, so did his officers and the crowd. All eyes were locked upon the sight. The freed people cheered and exchanged encouragements with each other. Their liberators were walking out. But the smiles and happy mood began to vanish as the reality of what they were looking at set in.

A menacing cloud of smoke floated along Derrick Road, hugging the ground as it drifted on the wind. Sunlight transformed the black cloud to light gray, outlining moving shadows within it.

The smoke gently swirled, parting as the breeze cut a path to allow seven men partially dressed in tactical clothing to solemnly pass through. Of the seven, three bodies were being carried.

A necklace gently swung in small circles as it hung from the limp fingers of Jim's half-closed hand. The small, gold cross on the chain reflected the sunlight that struck it.

CHAPTER FOURTEEN

June 25, 2:40 p.m.

A dark jacket with FEDERAL AGENT across its back whisked past the Chief of Police. He had forgotten about the woman. She had disappeared after they met. Her words were fleeting, confusing as she ran. He watched and realized she was talking into her radio.

Ten steps ahead of Draeger, she spun and looked at him with an air of authority.

"Keep your people back, Chief. Those are my men," she yelled.

Draeger stood stunned by her command, shocked that she had known a counterterrorist team was in the refinery. He looked beyond her at the armed men walking out of the swirling smoke. By the time his gaze shifted back to the woman, she was gone, sprinting toward them again. He shouted for her to wait. His words were drowned out by the screaming turbines of three midnight black helicopters swooping past overhead.

"What the hell?" His face rose to the sky. The helicopters split formation, two lowering to the ground in front of the wide refinery entrance while the third circled. Draeger's momentary shock wore off.

"All units, hold your positions. Don't shoot. I repeat, don't shoot," he shouted into his radio.

The roar of turbines and rotors slashing the air increased the din of noise already assaulting everyone's ears. The smoke rolling out of the refinery was caught up by the whirling rotors and spread in macabre fashion across the landscape. A gusting wind born from the helicopters flung loose grass and trash at the police blockade and media. Arms rose in protection against the onslaught of flying debris. The crowds of former hostages were forced back by the wind, preventing them from thanking their liberators.

Draeger watched the helicopter overhead fly an offensive pattern. He had never seen an Apache gunship this close. Photographs in magazines, a brief glimpse on the evening news of one in some foreign country, but in person, he realized how awesome and fierce they truly were. It fascinated him how the aerial maneuvers declared a readiness to engage in combat—an engagement he wanted no part of considering the armament the Apache carried. Ensuring his men's safety, he radioed again, ordering them to standby *and definitely not shoot.*

• • •

Tommy didn't know what else to do except head for the Gate House. They couldn't wait for ambulances to enter the refinery. The authorities did not know the terrorists were dead, and with the ongoing chain of explosions, the police would hold everyone back. The other men had agreed with him. Nothing more could be done for Sam Garrett and Jake Pierson. Jim was alive, though, barely, and if he did not receive immediate medical attention, he would soon join the ranks of their dead comrades.

Walking out of the fog-like smoke bank, the outline of news vehicles and a swarming crowd of reporters took shape. That wasn't what they wanted. The men stopped, standing in the middle of the gate entrance, searching the area for ambulances.

Joshua Allen had gone as far as he could. Sam's limp body had become too much to carry. Excruciating pain from the shoulder wounds made him almost black out. He felt his knees buckling and knelt to the pavement, fighting off the darkness that tried to drown him.

Tommy, exhausted and drenched in sweat from carrying Jim's heavy weight, managed to retain enough strength to remain standing. His eyes scanned the landscape. Anxiety built within him. *Where the hell is an ambulance?* Each second that passed meant precious life was draining from Jim.

Dragging his leg as he walked, Fischer moved next to Braun and helped him lay Jake Pierson's body on the ground.

The exhausted team heard the choppers before they saw them, then the screaming machines were upon them, one circling the perimeter while two came in for a landing, hard and fast onto Derrick Road between the public street and the gate entrance.

Faces smeared with camouflage, weapons held at the ready, men dressed in coal black tactical uniforms hung out the sides. They were ready to jump onto the ground as soon as it neared. The midnight black helicopters had no insignias or identifying markings. The men's uniforms gave no display of patches or nationality.

Nerves ragged from the day's events, the surviving men of the War Dogs looked at the descending helicopters and assumed they were arriving to aid Murdock. The end had come.

Fischer's knife blade flashed, cutting the sling holding Sam's body to Joshua. Tommy laid Jim down and covered him with Sam Garrett and Jake Pierson's dead bodies for protection against the imminent gun-battle. He swung and dropped to his knees, placing himself between Jim and the helicopters. Fischer, Allen, and Braun formed a defensive half-circle with him, weapons raised, knife sheaths unsnapped, prepared to make their last stand at all cost.

Wind gusts drove the smoke away, leaving them in plain view, out in the open at the gate entrance. The roar of turbines washed over them.

The ground was less than two feet away when ten heavily armed men leapt from the helicopters. Crouched low, they fanned out in different directions with weapons raised. Their leader gave hand signals to direct their actions.

Mentally and physically drained, bleeding from their wounds, the refinery's protectors silently announced they would not be taken prisoner nor peacefully succumb to a larger force. Stone-faced, jaws set hard, eyes narrowed into mere slits, they now welcomed death.

Tommy's fingers tightened on the pump shotgun. Fischer held his rifle in one hand and Garrett's shotgun in the other. Braun and Allen filled their hands with semiautomatics. The barrel of Tommy's pump shotgun started its path downward to aim. Each man knew the time had come. But the woman's voice that came across their radio channel shocked them, keeping them from shooting.

"They're here to help you!"

The leader of the Dark Angel SEAL team ran at Tommy, weapon lowered, hand raised in peaceful gesture. His men swept forward, enveloping the kneeling group of weary warriors, automatic weapons sweeping the buildings and landscape about them.

Braun touched Fischer's arm, motioning him to wait. Tommy's head whipped around, looking for the person who had made the radio call. Allen pointed to their front right.

Thirty yards away, a woman wearing a black nylon jacket with yellow lettering across the chest raced toward them, radio in one hand, a semiautomatic in the other. The radio covered her mouth. The thrashing wash from the helicopter's rotors blew the baseball cap off her head, unleashing her air into the wind. She never slowed her pace.

"They're a SEAL team. Let them help you!"

Tommy glanced at his friends, curious if they had also heard the transmission. They had and were already lowering their weapons. Tommy nodded in her direction and laid the shotgun across his leg.

The SEAL leader talked into his mouthpiece and the team descended upon the exhausted group. Medically trained members immediately started working on Jim as he was being carried to a waiting helicopter. When Fischer and Allen were lifted to their feet, they refused to move without taking Garrett and Pierson.

A brawny SEAL leaned close to Allen. "Mister, we don't leave our own behind and we sure as hell aren't going to leave them," he shouted. A proud smile broke over his camouflage painted face.

Climbing into the helicopter, Tommy did not know where they were going but knew Jim would receive help. He moved to the far side, allowing room for Jim to be laid beside him. Two SEALs swiftly went into action on the dying man. They administered shots, began intravenous feeds and applied pressure bandages to the stomach wound while their team boarded to lift off.

Braun, Fischer, and Allen climbed into the second helicopter. No sooner had they sat than SEALs began treating their wounds. Garrett and Pierson's bodies lay next to them. Joshua reached out and laid a hand on his deceased friend's chest.

Tommy watched the Dark Angel leader jump in. He raised a thumb into the air and the helicopters' engines growled louder. The ground began to fall away.

Tommy leaned back, resting his head against the wall of the helicopter. His eyelids wearily sagged, thoughts rambling. Nothing more could be done now except wait until they landed. Jim was being treated. They had miraculously survived with only two losses.

No, three, he thought. *Herschel was a part of the team.*

Opening his eyes, Tommy looked at his badly beaten and wounded friend.

Hopefully, no more than three.

Frantic movement at the bay door drew his attention. The unknown woman hung half in and out of the helicopter. She had jumped onto the skid as they were about to go airborne. He glanced at the ground. The people below were swiftly becoming dots on the land.

The SEAL team leader held onto her arm, preventing her from falling out. Grimacing from the strength he exerted, he pulled her into safety with one arm.

• • •

Alex felt her heart tear apart when she saw Jim's condition. He was unconscious, face swollen, bleeding, severely beaten. The bandages about his stomach showed spreading crimson blotches where blood was already soaking through. Kneeling beside him, she took his hand in hers and looked at the Navy corpsman examining him, wanting assurance Jim would live. But none came. The corpsman kept working.

Desperation flooded her, making her stomach churn. Jim balanced on that thin line between life and death. He slowly opened his good eye and looked about him. Alex's heart soared. The movement stopped and he displayed a distant stare. Jim looked at her. A cheek moved so slightly that it was almost imperceptible. He tried to speak. The roar of the helicopter's turbines drowned his words.

Alex leaned forward and kissed his forehead. She placed her mouth next to his ear.

"I love you," she said. When she straightened, tears rimmed her eyes.

Warmth flooded her soul when she saw his lips move.

Thurman's fingers tightened about her hand. His gold cross swung from their grip.

EPILOGUE

The refinery became a madhouse of federal agents clamoring over it, often times interfering and arguing with one another over their jurisdictions.

Seven SWAT teams were assigned to search the entire complex from buildings to debris piles for any remaining, live terrorists. Only the dead were found.

Explosive Ordnance Teams followed close behind, combing the buildings and process units for explosive devices. A live hand grenade was found beneath a body in the Ivory Tower's elevator. Miraculously, the spoon was caught in the corpse's clothing and failed to spring free when the deceased was moved. Three bombs were discovered on process units still attached to extremely flammable product lines. On each device, though, bomb techs noted the proper wires were pulled free that rendered them safe.

Emergency responders were allowed to enter the facility to control the fires and complete the tasks of finding wounded people and removing the dead from the refinery. Federal agents and Titan Oil personnel accompanied the recovery teams in order to identify each and account for the terrorists. While some of the dead were easily identified, others were burnt beyond recognition or completely dismembered from the explosions. The number of injured from climbing fences to escape, or wounded by flying debris and bullets changed daily. By the third day it had climbed to over a thousand with no end in sight. But the death toll held steady at one hundred seventy-five. The authorities all agreed that the number would have been far more if the initial emergency evacuation orders had not been given.

For over a week after the attack Grainger City's summer sky remained heavily clouded with pillars of black smoke while the bonfire in the refinery's flare yard was allowed to safely burn itself out. Fire fighters from every oil corporation arrived to assist in extinguishing the multitude of storage tank and lesser fires, but as an additional precaution, kept a constant umbrella of water spray on the butane spheres and HF storage vessels to protect them against the intense heat cast from the flare yard. When all fires were brought under control and the refinery's operation was declared stable, Titan Oil's flagship was shut down for intensive corporate and federal inspections. This was the first time in the history of the refinery that anyone could remember it being down.

To the amazement of corporate management and relief of federal government officials, the refinery overall had endured the terrorist attack far better than they ever anticipated. The flare yard that had once been a central point for the majority of processing units to discharge and burn off gasses resembled a massive burning crater created by a meteor.

Throughout the refinery every process unit had sustained damages and some level of fires, but none to the degree of devastation as A-5's control room and its water-cooling tower. Investigators remained baffled as to why the unit's monstrous HF storage tanks were untouched when the terrorists had threatened to destroy them and release their contents.

Minor warehouses and smaller metal storage buildings lay throughout the complex like piles of burnt, twisted metal pretzels. On the process units, contractor office trailers were found flattened, or shredded and charred to their frames by the explosions. The Gate House and its surrounding fence would be rebuilt, but the Admin building and Ivory Tower had to first be cleaned of blood before any evaluation of repairs could begin.

Titan Oil had teetered on the brink of financial bankruptcy, but survived. It always seemed to survive.

Throwing refinery and contract construction crews into an intensive around-the-clock cleanup and repair, the corporation began the monumental task of rebuilding its flagship. The magnitude of the feat was unprecedented throughout the petrochemical industry. Every employee became important, not simply those at the top of Titan Oil.

• • •

The Chairman of the Board remained in Grainger City for three months to conduct a personal investigation of the events surrounding Murdock's assault. During that time, he and Danny Barton, the refinery's young public affairs spokesman, fended all media attacks through exhaustive hours of question and answer sessions and Town Hall meetings.

In an extraordinary tactic appalled by several of its fellow oil giants, the Chairman and his flagship's spokesman stood unflinching before the glare of camera lights, irate citizens, and hounding reporters to speak the truth. To save the corporation, there was no other option but the harsh truth. Titan Oil had placed more emphasis on profit than its personnel and site security, and failed to address a long list of maintenance and employee problems. A security officer and a handful of unknown men were solely responsible for taking all protective measures against the mercenaries. And to the best of the Chairman's knowledge and sorrow, it was believed several members of that team had died in addition to the one hundred seventy-five Titan Oil employees and contractors.

The costs to Titan Oil for the loss of lives, reconstruction of the refinery, and civil lawsuits were in the billions of dollars. The end costs to its reputation proved to be far more.

• • •

Despondent over not being able to find a massive whitewash in this newly established platform of oil corporation honesty, the media focused on Clarence Calder's history of inept supervision of refinery security. He received the bulk of blame for the deaths that occurred, then the press turned on the President of the United States, attacking his CIA's administration with the ferocity of a pack of wolves.

The former Security Superintendent of Titan Oil's flagship refinery, read and heard his name daily far more than he wished in television broadcasts, newspapers, and magazines. He was ridiculed by the media and remained locked in his home, a prisoner of his own making, afraid to leave for fear of being seen and chased by an angry public.

Five days after the attack and believing Jim to be dead, Sergeant Maddox went to Calder's residence. At 2:45 p.m., the time Maddox remembered seeing Jim be carried out of the refinery, the Grainger City Police Department received a telephone call requesting they respond to Calder's address.

The police found the former security superintendent in the garage with his neck snapped and dangling from a rope. His body swayed in a gentle motion and nearby was an overturned chair on the garage's concrete floor. The investigating officers ruled the death a suicide after interviewing Maddox, a former Grainger City police officer prior to being employed at the refinery.

"He was pretty depressed over losing his wife and job on the same day," Maddox said, lightly scratching his right cheek as he slowly shook his head. "I came by and when no one answered the door, I looked through the garage door window and saw his body swinging hard. Maybe if I'd arrived a minute or two sooner I could have stopped him." Maddox inhaled deeply. "I broke through the front door and ran into the garage. It was too late. That's when I called the police department and asked dispatch to send an officer."

After completing the interview, Maddox lit a cigarette and impassively watched as the body was cut down and wheeled away on a wobbly gurney. When released by the police, Maddox thanked them and drove home.

He met his wife, softly kissed her cheek and apologized for having run an errand that delayed their departure. They talked about their retirement plans as they stood in the front yard of their former home and watched the men close the rear doors of the large moving van. When the truck drove away, his wife turned to him.

"Are you ready to go?"

"Now I am," he replied with a smile.

They left for the mountains of Tennessee, never to return to Texas.

• • •

In the month following the attack on Titan Oil's flagship refinery, no news held greater interest for the world than Murdock's failed raid. Experts paid by the media seemingly fell from the sky and came to rest on spotlighted thrones of news broadcasts. With chests authoritatively swollen, they dissected the motives of the terrorists, the tactics of the unknown heroes, and the upset of the world's oil market as if their every word was the gospel.

Against backdrops of smoldering cars and pillars of smoke, newscasters and talk-show hosts pointed fingers in all directions. Film footage of bloody corpses sprawled across the landscape, and three men being shot before plummeting six stories to their deaths, became the lifeline of every broadcast. Always, though, came the gratitude for the unknown team who dared to take up arms against the fanatics when so much had been at stake. The cost of saving the flagship and lives of countless citizens had required a high price tag of sacrifice.

• • •

The team's hide-a-way was a well-guarded estate north of Houston in the piney woods of East Texas. As recuperation progressed and liberty was given to walk about the grounds, the men realized they were not the first to ever use the secluded location's facade. The surroundings silently spoke of covert operations. Offices, meeting rooms, medical facilities, helicopter pads, and other guest accommodations were established under the guise of being a private resort.

Jeff McCall flew to Houston. Under his personal direction the survivors were hidden for weeks until their futures could be decided and their injuries healed sufficiently to allow them to return. Because of their prolonged disappearance the corporation believed the recovering men were dead and had listed them as killed in the fiery inferno.

By nightfall of the attack though, McCall had secretly brought the wives and children of Allen, Fischer, Braun, and McLawchlin to the private estate to be with their loved ones. Sam Garrett's widow and son were escorted to the premises and remained with the team for several days. Herschel Cannish's parents were brought to the estate as well. Tommy McLawchlin and Joshua Allen asked to be the ones to tell them of their son's valor. There was no one to contact for Jake Pierson.

When Thurman's health returned enough to speak, Jim asked Jeff McCall to use his resources to locate Jake Pierson's daughter. He wanted to personally tell her about the brave father she never knew.

It wasn't until an evening in the third week of their stay, after Jim's condition improved, that the team gathered about his bed with their families to discuss returning to the refinery. With Jim's permission, Jeff McCall and Alex sat in on the solemn meeting.

To avoid retaliation by other terrorist organizations, Jeff suggested the intelligence community conceal everyone's names and courageous efforts in order to protect their families. Jim asked to meet only with his teammates and waited until the room emptied before talking. In the somber hour that followed, the team chose to disband under a vow of secrecy and never reveal their identities, or the actions they had taken.

Jim's face and name were too well known to allow him to quietly return. On behalf of his trusted men and against their protests, he chose to take whatever punishment resulted from their actions. Having made the decision, he refused to do otherwise.

The day the team left the estate, Sam Garrett and Jake Pierson's bodies were transported to the same Grainger City funeral home where Herschel Cannish had been taken. After the bodies were formally turned over to the funeral home by McCalls' agents, the remainder of the team reported in to the refinery's Human Resources department.

Titan Oil welcomed them back into the mainstream of activity with few questions. In the mass confusion created by the attack, the corporation accepted the excuse that they had fled in panic with other employees. It was a believable enough story because people were still trickling back and reporting in each day stating the same.

• • •

Grasping for favorable press, Titan Oil heralded the security officers killed on the day of the attack at the Gate House as heroes. Their funerals, as well as all employees and contractors who died from the acts of terrorism, were resplendent with accolades and flowery speeches. But there were families of the dead that resented Titan Oil and forbid them to be present.

The team's dead were quietly buried, honored only in the hearts of their families and the surviving members. Jake Pierson's daughter was present at her father's funeral. At the end of the service she brushed her fingertips over his casket, patted it softly, then left with her husband and daughter.

Sam Garrett's widow requested that no one from the corporation speak as they had at other employee funerals. Instead, she asked Jim to, and through choking emotions he did.

Respecting her wishes for privacy, the Chairman of the Board and Dave Simmons, the refinery manager, quietly stood twenty yards back from the gathered families. They watched the heart-wrenching scene and earnestly listened to the eulogy.

At the edge of the cemetery, a bugler blew 'Taps.' Mrs. Garrett clutched her son's shoulder and cried in Jim's arms as Sam was laid to rest. Joshua Allen openly wept.

A sentence Jim had spoken in the eulogy kept repeating itself in the Chairman's mind.

"No greater valor and no greater love can a man have than to lay down his life so that others may live."

In that moment, after having observed Jim and four men gently lay their hands on the caskets of Garrett, Pierson, and Cannish, the Chairman realized he was looking at the true members of the warrior band. With the ghostly sound of *Taps* echoing in his ears, though, he vowed to keep his belief to himself.

· · ·

After Jim's recovery, his meeting with the Chairman of the Board came behind closed doors. All that is known of the three-hour talk is that he steadfastly declined to reveal names, and the Chairman did not press the issue. Assistants to the Chairman publicly announced that Jim Thurman was offered the vacant job of security superintendent of the flagship, but had declined the offer.

Investigative teams from federal agencies continually descended upon the refinery like starving vultures, filled with questions and anxious for answers. Throughout the inquisitions that followed, under constant threats of criminal charges and imprisonment, Jim refused to identify anyone who helped him. Aside from the names, he answered all questions as best he could. Nationwide press coverage of his bravery provided such commendatory news that the federal government and Titan Oil hesitated to condemn any actions he had taken. No charges were ever filed against him.

Jim Thurman became known as the man who spearheaded the unknown counterterrorism unit. He declined all media interviews, speaking engagements, and awards offered to him. His repeated statement to the press was that his 'team' deserved the true praise, and until the War Dogs could publicly stand by his side without retribution, he would not accept any token of appreciation nor speak of them individually. His modesty and the mystery behind the warriors endeared them to the heart of America, especially when it became known that Jim had intended to resign that day and move away due to the grief of his family having been killed in a car accident.

Two months after the attack, Jim received an unsigned, typed letter with no return address and postmarked from Tennessee. Reading the one page letter, he smiled inwardly then burned it. He hoped to one day take a vacation in the mountains and visit an old friend.

• • •

A special congressional committee was assigned by the President to investigate the CIA's cover-up of the attack. He wanted no doubts in America's mind that his office was innocent of any wrongdoing. In time, Duncan Stewart, the Deputy Director of the CIA, was charged as being Bill Haverty's accomplice and indicted on numerous counts of conspiracy. Stewart pled guilty and due to his clandestine operational knowledge was sentenced to life imprisonment in the high-security United States Penitentiary at Lewisburg, Pennsylvania. Later, in 1994, he was transferred to *the Alcatraz of the Rockies*, the United States Penitentiary, ADX, in Fremont County, Colorado.

After the attack Ben Dawson and Alexandra McCall left the Central Intelligence Agency. Their resignations went unnoticed in the turmoil the agency was undergoing from the President's congressional committee. Bill Haverty's suicide and Duncan Stewart's trial had cast a dark cloud over the secretive institution that stifled all curiosity about the two agents departure.

Alex stayed at her parents' estate in Virginia for a week after her resignation, wandering aimlessly about its grounds, spending hours by their lake, staring out across the water. At dusk of the fifth day, her mother walked out to sit with her on the pier. Realizing the emotional turmoil her daughter was undergoing about Jim Thurman, Beverly McCall embraced Alex.

"Follow your heart or live a lifetime of regret," she told her daughter.

The next day, Alexandra McCall left for Houston.

• • •

Jim's former in-laws would not allow him to return to his desolate home. At their insistence he stayed at their ranch south of Houston to further recuperate from his injuries and deal with the government investigations.

He sold his house and its furnishings, stored several boxes of Susan and James' mementoes and formerly submitted his resignation to the Chairman of Titan Oil. Truck packed, ready to leave, he went to the cemetery and laid fresh flowers on their graves. He knelt between their head stones and read the inscriptions as his hand squeezed the gold cross at his throat. When he left the gravesites, he vanished from public eye. Only Tommy knew his destination.

Rumors surfaced of his whereabouts at dozens of locations yet the media was never able to find him. Each morning, though, as the sun rose over the majestic landscape of the Texas Hill Country, a solitary figure stood atop a tall hill.

The local ranchers never spoke a word of it to the press.

AFTERWORD

hen and *now*, the difference in corporate thinking is as contrasting as night is to day.

Like in the book, was there ever a Security Superintendent who stated terrorism only happens overseas? Unfortunately, yes. I remember the day years ago when it was said with haughty laughter to me. In defense of that shallow minded belief, though, there were many managers and industry leaders in 1990 that denied or ignored the rising tide of extremism and violence our nation was destined to face. Today, such absurd words are no longer spoken.

The majority of America's refineries were built in the 1930s and 1940s when there were few, if any, restrictions and regulations as exist today. Through the years refineries have been reworked, patched, and in many cases struggled to maintain a semblance of high operation. Our nation's thirst for oil and its byproducts seeped into our veins long ago and became an addiction that only magnified. Federal environmental regulations continually increased and changed, making it difficult and far too expensive to build new refineries in America. Construction overseas then became inviting.

There are no arguments against the need to protect people and the environment from the dangers of oil and chemical aerial releases, or leaks into waterways and onto land. But as has occurred, many of the mandated, costly, physical environmental modifications could never be fully completed before newer and higher-priced requirements and regulations came. It became a vicious circle in trying to comply with a confused regulatory agency.

Oil truly is 'Black Gold.' From it come lubricants and fuels for vehicles, tractors, machinery, jets, rockets, lighter fluids, and more. Chemicals derived from oil make plastics and an astonishingly long list of products society uses daily without the realization of where the materials come from, or the technology to make them.

Through history men have grown rich from oil, craved and killed for it, used oil as a powerful leverage over nations such as OPEC has done, and wars have been fought under many guises to control its flow. Can we replace the usage of 'Black Gold' with something different? Quite possibly, yes. Time will tell, but until the day arrives, society will forever be its addict.

Wherever money flows like a flooded river, greed will eventually be born and interfere with its raging current. Historically, industries such as steel, oil, chemicals, pharmaceuticals and railroads are known examples of greed rearing its ugly head because of the phenomenal profits they derived.

CEOs and ranking leaders across the spectrum of businesses raced to achieve mega-salaries. Their desire for emperor-like authority through greater industry profits regrettably became an obsession. The tail wagged the dog in all too many cases. Pay scales remained imbalanced with men at the tops of ladders always wanting and receiving more while those on the bottom rungs fought for better wages. The gambles that leaders took with timeworn machinery, aged pumps and powerful reactors were equally disturbing.

Orders were issued at high levels to run equipment around the clock at maximum capacity, risking explosive failures and workers' harm rather than halt for needed maintenance. Money was saved, and if one more day of profit could be achieved before a critical failure occurred, then the gamble had proved worthwhile.

If a department within a refinery didn't turn some form of profit, it was an expense, kept only if mandatory for public display, or as required for insurance ratings. The state of physical security was in this void until the tragic events of "9-11" shook the foundations of America and corporate thinking.

In those earlier years the majority of industries primarily employed contract security guards to sit at gates, smile, wave to employees, and do nothing more. There were corporations that employed their own in-house staff of security personnel, yet they were few and far between because of the financial drain without any return. Not all, but many of these in-house officers came from local police departments because the pay scales of cities and law enforcement were so low. Unfortunately, the professional performance of these former police officers was nearly ruined. They were allowed to do little in terms of true security and were often supervised by refinery engineers or others with no security knowledge. These non-security leaders often resented being over a security department because it was management's punishment for their previous poor refinery performance. A caste system seemingly existed where salaried personnel looked down upon hourly, and everyone unwittingly looked down upon the next beneath them. Security officers were at the bottom, quietly viewed as incapable of performing 'a real job.'

It was from such a setting that "Steel Jungle" was born…

…For years Texas ranchers along Mexico's border have been plagued with burglaries of ranch homes as well as cattle thefts and robberies by marauding bands of Mexican thieves, drug caravans crossing the land and a steady flow of unknown illegal aliens. When the federal government ignored their growing problems, ranchers called upon groups of former military men for protection and assistance. It was these requests that the

'War Dogs' answered which allowed them to retain a sense of pride, maintain unity, and display their expertise to grateful people.

Fifteen years after Vietnam, returning military veterans had quietly taken labor jobs at all levels, wanting nothing more from their nation than to earn a decent salary for their families and pay their bills. America still held a silent distaste for the war and those that had served. It seemed the only respect veterans received was when they were with other veterans or their families.

In the refinery, engineers that had never known a day in a branch of military service were placed over them as supervisors, and often treated the blooded veterans as being subservient in knowledge and skills.

The former police officers employed in the refinery's in-house security department were being ruined by a lack of leadership and direction, left to their own demise by a corporation that viewed security as a necessary evil, an expenditure without a return.

And OPEC was always in arguments with its members such as Venezuela who often violated oil production quotas and always wanted more than their share of money.

· · ·

You may relax, though. There are no security secrets given away in this novel about refineries and chemical plant operations as many may fear. This novel is set in 1990.

That was *then*, a time when the physical security of most industries was of vague importance.

In those years, oil corporations didn't consider the security aspect of the information they disseminated publicly. Aerial photographs of entire refinery complexes were often proudly published in magazines along with in-depth stories about their operations. The Internet was a treasure trove of data about refineries and chemical plants. Site maps detailing the descriptions and locations of every process unit were handed to entering visitors as if they were tourist brochures for an amusement park. Town Hall meetings were held due to citizen fears and anger over the types of chemical releases, devastating refinery fires, explosions—and even the fatal consequences of a catastrophic release of HF, hydrofluoric acid. In the greatest display of a disregard for personal safety, aluminum-walled, full-sized, mobile home trailers were shoved into every cubbyhole and vacant space on operating units to be used as contractors' offices during construction repairs. These death traps were often positioned between a live process unit and the unit shutdown for repairs.

But *now*, the face of physical security and safety has changed.

"9-11" was the turning point whereby industry, society, and our nation awoke that morning to the harsh reality that America's security was vulnerable, and could never be the same again. Today security in refineries, for example, have improved compared to the 1990s. Not to the best level it can be yet certainly a far cry from what it was.

Visitors and employees are access controlled and volumes of sensitive refinery information have been removed from the Internet. *(Yes, there is still much to be found on the Internet today.)*

The U.S. Coast Guard mandates security procedures in the Code of Federal Regulations for refineries, chemical plants, and the ports connected to them. In accordance with these federal mandates, devices are required to physically halt the dramatic penetration of unauthorized vehicles. Of course many corporations were brought to the table kicking and screaming, forced to make improvements because security doesn't produce a return on funds spent. But, at least physical security improvements and changes in mindsets to some degree have been made.

As for the aluminum mobile home and double-wide trailers that were commonly used as contractors' temporary offices on process units, after the BP Texas City refinery explosion on March 23, 2005 where fifteen people were killed and one-hundred eighty were wounded, these flimsy trailers were ordered to be replaced with steel '*Conex*' shipping containers converted into offices—and could no longer be placed on process units within defined blast zones.

Complacency will always remain the greatest threat to America. After "9-11" the public's anxieties were high, and for several years America accepted the need to properly protect citizens and industries. As time moves further away from "9-11" without another devastating act of terrorism occurring, memories will grow lax, complacency will spread like a cancer, and one day someone may again say, "Terrorism only happens overseas."

ABOUT THE AUTHOR

G lenn Starkey is a former USMC Sergeant, Vietnam veteran, Texas law enforcement, retired from a global oil corporation as security manager of a refinery, chemical plant, and its marine facilities. He's been a lecturer, consultant, and Interim Director of Security for a Gulf Coast port. For the past eight years Glenn has volunteered to mentor and assist elementary grade children with their reading skills in his local school district. He lives in Texas.